THE PLAYMAKER

CATHRYN FOX

COPYRIGHT

Discover other titles by Cathryn Fox at www.cathrynfox.com.
Please sign up for Cathryn's Newsletter for freebies, ebooks, news and contests:
https://app.mailerlite.com/webforms/landing/c1f8n1
ISBN Print 978-1-928056-84-3
ISBN ebook 978-1-928056-83-6

1

NINA

F at drops of spring rain pummel my head, wilting my curls as I dart through Seattle's busy traffic to the café on the other side of the street. My best friend, Jess, is inside waiting for me, undoubtedly hyped up on her third latté by now.

I step over a pothole and search for an opening in the traffic. I hate being late, I really do. I totally value other people's time, but when the email came through from my editor, asking me to write a hot hockey series, my priorities took a curve. I've worked with Tara for a couple years now, and I know her like—pardon the pun—a well-worn book. To her, hesitation equals disinterest. She's a mover, a tree-shaker, and it wouldn't have taken long for her to offer the opportunity to another author. She wanted a quick reply and I had to give it to her.

I got this!

Yeah, that was my response, but what did I have to lose? I've been in such a rut lately, thanks to my fickle muse, deserting me when I needed her most. I swear to God, sometimes she acts like a hormonal teenager. I need to whip her into shape so I don't lose this gig. The royalties from a series will help make a sizeable dent in the bills that are piling up high and deep.

High and deep.

I laugh. One of those self-derisive snorts that crawls out when you'd really rather cry. Yeah, that pretty much sums up the *I got this* response I emailed back. High and deep, like a big steaming pile of—

A car horn blares, jolting me from my pity party. With my heart pounding in my chest, I step in front of the Tesla and flip the guy off. I safely reach the sidewalk and once again my mind is back on my job, and off the impatient jerk in the overpriced car.

I step up on the sidewalk and lift my face to the rain, the cool water a pleasant break from this unusual spring heat wave we're having. Pressure fills my throat. The hum of traffic behind me dulls, leaving only the sound of my pulse pounding in my ears. Panic.

Why the hell did my editor think I, former figure skater turned romance novelist, would want to write a series about hot hockey players? Yeah, sure my brother is an NHL player, but that doesn't mean I'm into the game. I hate hockey. No, hate is too mild a word for what I feel. I loathe it entirely. But you know what I don't loathe? Eating. Yeah, I like eating. Oh, and a roof over my head. I really like that, too.

I draw in a semi self-satisfied breath at having rationalized my fast response.

Except my reply was total and utter bullshit. I don't *got this*. In fact, I...wait, what's the antonym of *got this*? All that comes to mind is, *you're screwed*. Yep, that pretty much describes my predicament.

Why didn't I just stick to figure skating?

Because you took a bad spill that ended your career.

Oh right. But seriously, a hockey series... Ugh. Kill me. Freaking. Now.

I reach the café, pull the glass door open and slick my rain-soaked hair from my face. I quickly catalogue the place to find Jess hitting on the barista. Ahh, now I get why she picked a place so far from home. I take in the guy behind the counter. Damn, he's hotter than the steaming latté in Jess's hand, and from the way she's flirting, it's clear he'll be in her bed later today.

I sigh inwardly. It's always so easy for her. Me? Not so much. Men rarely pay me attention. Unlike Jess, I'm plain, have the body of a twelve-year-old boy, and most times I blend into the woodwork.

I pick up a napkin from the side counter and mop the rain off my face. Doesn't matter. I'm not interested anyway. From my puck-bunny-chasing brother to all his cocky friends, I know what guys are really like, and when it comes to women, they're only after one thing, and it isn't scoring the slot. I roll my eyes. Then again, maybe it is.

And of course, I can't forget the last guy I was set up with. What he did to me was totally abusive, but I don't want to dredge up those painful memories right now.

I shake, and water beads fall right off my brand-new rain-resistance coat. At least something is going right for me today. Semi-dry, I cross the room and stand beside Jess.

"Hey, sorry I'm late."

Jess turns to me, smiles, and holds a finger up. "I'll forgive you only if you're late because you were knees deep into some nasty sex, 'cause girlfriend, it's been far too long since you've been laid."

Jesus, what ever happened to this girl's filters?

Thoroughly embarrassed, my gaze darts to the barista, who is grinning, his eyes still locked on my friend, looking at her like she's today's hot lunch special and ignoring me like I'm yesterday's cold, lumpy oatmeal.

Ugh, really?

"Non-fat latté," I say, and scowl at him until he puts his eyes back in his head. I might be an English major but I have a PhD in the death glare. Truthfully, I'm so sick of guys like him, one thing on their minds. Then again, Jess only wants one thing from him, so I really shouldn't have a problem with it. Why do I? Oh, maybe because Mr. Right, my battery-operated companion, isn't quite cutting it anymore, and it's left me a little jittery and a whole lot cranky.

Jess is right. I *do* need to get laid.

Jess's lips flatline when she takes me in, her gaze carefully accessing me. "What?" she asks, her mocha eyes narrowing.

God, sometimes I really hate how well she can read me. "Nothing."

She straightens to her full height, and I try to do the same, but she dwarfs me, even without her beloved two-inch heels. I square my shoulders, but it's always hard to pull off a high-power pose when you're only five foot two, and teased relentlessly about it.

"Come on," she says, and guides me to a corner table. I peel off my coat and plunk down. Jess sits across from me. "Spill."

I point to my forehead. "Do I have 'idiot' written here?"

She looks me over, and cautiously asks, "No, why?"

My phone chirps in my purse, and I reach for it. Great, it's my editor wanting to set turn-in dates. "How about never?" I say under my breath.

"Uh, Nina. You're talking to your phone. You better tell me what's going on."

"You're not going to believe what I just agreed to."

"Do tell," she says and leans forward, like I'm about to spill some dirty little sex secret. If only that were the case.

I grab my phone and hold it up, showing her Tara's message. "I just agreed to write a hockey series," I say, and toss my phone back into my purse, mic-drop style—without the bold confidence.

Jess pushes back in her chair, clearly disappointed. She lifts her cup, and over the rim, asks, "I don't see how that makes you an idiot."

My mouth drops open. Jess and I have been friends since childhood. She of all people knows how much I hate hockey. "Are you serious?"

She shrugs. "You're a writer."

Mr. Sexy Barista brings me my coffee and he shares a secret, let's-hook-up-later smile with Jess. "And...?" I ask when he leaves.

"Writer's write and make things up. I know you hate hockey, but what does that have to do with anything?"

"I can't come up with a plot, or write about the game, if I don't know anything about it."

She shakes her head. "And I can't believe your brother is a professional player and you never once paid attention to the game."

"I was busy pursuing a professional skating career, remember?"

She reaches across the table and gives my hand a little squeeze. "I know. I'm sorry."

My tailbone and neck take that moment to throb, a constant reminder of a career lost.

I didn't just lose my dream of skating professionally the day my feet went out from underneath me, I lost my confidence, too. A concussion will do that to you.

Good thing I majored in English in college. Once I hung up my skates, I began to blog about the sport and sold a few articles. I joined a local writers group, and after talking to a group of romance writers, I tried my hand at one. Much to my surprise, it actually sold. I went from non-fiction to fiction, in every sense of the word. Happily ever after might exist between the pages, but it certainly doesn't in real life. At least not for me.

I take a sip of my latté, and give an exaggerated huff as I set it down. Jess instantly goes into problem-solving mode when she sees that I'm really stressed about this. As a brand-new high school guidance counselor, she can't help but want to fix me.

"Okay, it's simple," she begins. "You have to learn the game."

"How am I supposed to do that?"

"Turn on the TV and watch."

"I can watch a bunch of guys chase a stupid puck around a rink all I want, I still won't be able to understand the rules."

"How dare you call my favorite sport stupid."

"Jessss..." I plead. "What am I going to do?"

She crinkles her nose. Then her eyes go wide. "I've got it. Shadow your brother."

I give a quick shake of my head. "No, he's on the road, and he won't want me hanging around."

Jess goes quiet again, and that hollowed-out spot inside me aches as I think about Luke. I miss my brother so much and wish we were closer. Luke and I grew up in a family where there were no hugs or words of affirmation. I know Mom and Dad loved us, but as busy investment bankers, work consumed their lives. Sure, they put me in figure skating, and Luke in hockey when we were young, but they never shared in our passions, or really supported our pursuits.

I guess I can't expect my brother to display love, when none was ever displayed to him.

"Why don't you teach me?"

"It might be my favorite sport to watch, but I don't really know all the rules. I think you'd be better off getting your brother or..." She straightens. "Wait. I got this," she says, and I cringe when she tosses my three-word email response back at me. A warning shiver skips along my spine, and I get the sense that whatever she's about suggest, is going to take me right down the rabbit hole.

"What about Cole Cannon?"

I groan, plant my elbows on the table, and cover my face with my hands. "Never," I mumble through my fingers. "Not in a million freaking years."

Jess removes my hands from my face. "Why not? He's your brother's best friend. I'm sure he'll help you."

"Cocky Cole Cannon, aka, The Playmaker. Do I need to say any more?" I reach for my latté and take a huge gulp, burning the roof of my mouth. Damn.

"I know you hate him, Nina, but—"

"Of course I hate him. You remember the nickname he used to use when we were kids—Pretty BallerNina. I was a figure skater, not a ballerina," I could only assume he was mocking me about being pretty too, but I keep that to myself.

"At least he worked your name into the moniker, and hey, it could have been worse. He could have called you Neaner Neaner, like Luke did."

I glare at her and she holds her hands up. "Okay, okay. I get it. But Cole's been home for a month, recovering from a concussion, and his team—the Seattle Shooters, in case you don't know the league's name," she adds with a wink, "are probably going to make it to the playoffs, so you know he's watching all the games. You don't have to like him to ask him to explain a few of the plays, right?"

"I suppose."

Wait! What? Am I really thinking about asking The Playmaker to help me? I reach for my latté and blow on it before I take another big gulp.

"And if you ask me, while he's helping you learn the plays, I think you two should hate fuck."

I choke on my drink, spitting most of it on my friend as the rest dribbles down my chin.

OMFG, how embarrassing. All eyes turn to me. Mortified, I grab a napkin and start wiping my face, but Jess is laughing so hard, I start laughing with her.

"Couldn't you have waited until I swallowed?" I ask.

"That's what she said."

"Ohmigod, Jess. How are we friends?"

She waves a dismissive hand. "You know you love me because I'm hellacioulsy funny."

"I do, just stop cracking jokes when I'm drinking."

She leans towards me conspiratorially, and I brace myself. "I wasn't joking. You and Cocky Cole Cannon should hate fuck. He's as sexy today as he was when he used to hang out with Luke at your house when we were teens." I give her a look that suggests she's insane. She ignores it and wags her brows. "He's explosive on the ice, but do you know why they really call him the Cannon?"

"Because it's his last name."

"Yeah, but that's not the only reason."

Don't ask. Don't ask.

"Okay, then why?" I ask.

"'Cause he's loaded between his legs."

Yeah, okay, I totally set myself up for that.

"You don't know that," I shoot back. My mind races to my brother's best friend, and I mentally go over his form. He's athletic, tall and—as much as I hate to admit it—hot as hell. The perfect trifecta. Could he be packing too? Working with some top-notch equipment?

Jesus, what am I doing? The last thing I should be thinking about is Cole's 'cannon'.

"Come on." Jess grabs her purse. "I'll drive you there."

I flatten my hands on the table. "I'm not going to his house, especially not unannounced."

"Give him a call then."

"No."

She sits back in her chair and folds her arms, a sign she's changing tactics. "And here I thought you liked your condo and food in your cupboards."

I groan at the direct hit.

Her voice softens and she touches my hand. "But you know you always have—"

"Fine." I stop her before she brings up my trust fund. Yeah, sure, Mom and Dad set money aside for me, but I don't want to use it. I want to live by my own means, make it on my own merit. Besides it wasn't their money I wanted, then or now, it was their attention, their love. I moved out years ago and only ever hear from them on my birthday or at Christmas.

I pull my phone from my purse. "I'll text him. If he doesn't answer, we don't talk about this again." I go through my contacts and find his number, having stored it years ago when he called to check on me after my injury. The call had taken me by surprise; so did his concern. Maybe my brother put him up to it. I don't know. Nor do I know why I kept his number.

My fingers fly across the screen, but in no way do I expect him to respond. At least I hope he doesn't. I read over the text. *Sorry to hear about your concussion. I was wondering if you could help me with something.* Then hit send.

I set my phone down and look at Jess. "Happy?"

"Hey, I'm not the one who's going to be homeless."

Point taken. Maybe I should be hoping he *does* text back.

My phone pings, and we both reach for it. Jess gets it first, and from her smirk, I guess my wish just came true—Colin responded.

Careful what you wish for.

"What does it say?" I ask, afraid of the answer.

"It says, sure what's up?" Jess's fingers dance over the screen as she responds for me.

"What are you saying?" I ask, panic welling up inside me. "So help me, if you're telling him I need to get laid..."

The phone pings again and she holds it out for me to read.

"I asked—I mean *you* asked if you could stop by his place, and he said sure."

"I don't know whether to kiss you or choke you," I say.

Jess laughs. "I think you'll be thanking me." She stands. "Come on."

We make our way outside, and the rain has slowed to a light mist as I follow her down the street to her parked car. I hop in and question my sanity. Am I really going to ask Cocky Cannon to teach me the game?

Jess starts the car and the locks click as she pulls into traffic. Guess so.

"You remember where he lives?" I ask. I think back to when he bought the house. He had a big party to celebrate. I was invited but didn't go. Why would I? Watching the hockey players with their bunnies was not my idea of a good time.

"Of course." She jacks the tunes and sings along off-key as she drives. Twenty minutes later, she pulls up in front of his mansion. It's a ridiculously big house for one person. I stare at it, and once again question my sanity.

"Go," Jess says.

"I'm going," I shoot back. I open the door, and smooth my hand over my mess of curls. Why the hell did I do that? It's not like I'm trying to make myself presentable or impress him. We don't even like each other.

I force my legs to carry me to his door, and I'm about to knock when it opens. My breath catches as I take in Cole, standing before me shirtless and barefoot, dressed only in a pair of faded jeans that hug him so nicely.

God, he is so freaking hot—and I never, ever should have come here.

As we stare at each other, like we're in some goddamn Mexican standoff, I can't stop thinking about his 'cannon'. My gaze drops to the lovely bulge between his legs, and a moan I have no control over catches in my throat as Jess's words come back to haunt me.

You two should hate fuck.

Thank you, Jess, for planting that idea in my brain. Christ, I should have choked her when I had the chance.

COLE

I can't believe sweet little Nina Callaghan is standing on my doorstep staring at my package. *She's fucking checking me out—like it's her job.* Should I call her on that?

Nah that would probably just scare her off, then I'd never find out what she wanted from me. I have to say, I *am* curious. She hasn't talked to me in a long time, and I'm a little surprised she even knew my number. We don't like each other much, but I'm man enough to admit that I like having her eyes on me. Still, she can't think for one minute that she's going to get an eyeful and I'm not.

My gaze races over her, and I take in her long damp hair, a raincoat that hides her sensual body—I'd never forget her barely there curves—and a pair of jeans that are rolled up at the ankle. Her slim frame might be well hidden, but her sandals showcase sexy toes and pink-painted nails that tease and torment my thickening cock.

Hate each other or not, she's as hot today as she was all those years ago. But she's still my best friend's kid sister, and that makes her completely hands-off.

"What's up?" I ask, and her big blue eyes dart to mine. I

can't help but grin, a telltale way of letting her know she's busted, and that I don't mind at all. Hell, she can stare all she likes, as long as I get to do the same.

"I...uh..." She swallows and glances over her shoulder. I follow her gaze to see her friend Jess in the car, waving at us from the driver's seat. I remember Jess. She was always hanging around Luke's place when we were kids. I wave back to her, and Nina refocuses on me. She angles her head and clears her throat. "How are you feeling?"

"Is that why you're here?" I ask. "Worried about me?"

"No," she blurts out quickly. "I mean yes...I mean...I just..."

She's definitely uncomfortable, and I'm not sure why. I practically lived at her house growing up. People used to think I was her brother, although my thoughts toward her were anything but brotherly, especially when I teased her and she got so spitting mad in response her cheeks would turn pink. My favorite color.

"What can I do for you, Nina?"

She bites on her bottom lip, and damn it, I like that, too. "I was going to ask..." Her breath comes out with a hint of frustration. She gives her head a little shake and takes a step back. "Maybe this was a mistake."

Nina leaving is not an option, at least not before she's said what she'd come to say. The fact that she'd come to me in the first place, considering how she doesn't particularly like me, well... "You can ask me anything," I say, more curious than ever, and wanting to help her out.

"It's just...I could use your help with a little problem."

And I could use hers with a big one.

I angle my body and lean against the doorjamb, anything to hide my thickening boner. "Yeah, how can I help you?"

"You see, my editor asked me to write about hot hockey players, and I thought maybe you—"

"You think I'm a hot hockey player?" I ask, purposely teasing her.

She opens her mouth and closes it again, clearly flustered. I'm not sure why I keep provoking her. Then again, maybe I am. Back in the day, I called her Pretty BallerNina. She was pretty, still is, and I meant it as a compliment. She never took it that way though, and always gave me the death glare. I could have stopped calling her that, just like I could stop teasing her now, but the only time she ever paid me any attention was when I was playing around, and yeah, I kind of like her attention.

"No, it's not that."

"So, you're not here because you need me to teach you some hot moves for the sex scenes?"

Her eyes go round and her cheeks turn a bright shade of pink. "No," she blurts out. "That's not it at all."

I lean toward her, catch her sweet scent, and she visibly quivers as I crowd her. "Then what is it?"

"I'm here to see if you'll help me learn the game, teach me the rules."

I grin at her. "Hard to believe you don't know the rules, considering your brother is an NHL player."

She shrugs. "I was busy figure skating."

"I know." I remember watching her. She was fucking amazing on the ice, had so much talent. Goddamn crime that a spill took her out. Broke my fucking heart, really. A concussion laid her up for six month—I know all about *that*, but unlike her, I plan to get back on the ice. Hockey is my life, the breath that fills my lungs.

Jess starts her car, and Nina quickly looks in that direction. Her phone pings and she grabs it from her purse.

"Shit," she says. "I'm going to kill her."

"Problem?"

She jerks her thumb over her shoulder. "Jess says she has

some errands to run and she'll come back for me."

I push off the doorframe and we watch as Jess drives away. "I guess you should come in then."

I step to the side and wave my hand for her to enter. She hesitates for a second, then breezes past me. I close the door and turn to see her glancing around the big entranceway.

"You have a beautiful home."

"Thanks." I look around, too. See what she sees, but from my perspective. This house is my sanctuary—no one other than my sister and a few select friends allowed. It's the one place I can hide out, be myself, and let go of the fucking act. "Something to drink?"

"Water, please."

My bare feet slap the tile as I walk past her, and she follows me into the kitchen. I grab the old pizza boxes from the counter and stuff them in the garbage.

"Wow, I love your kitchen. My whole condo would fit in here."

"I don't really cook."

"Then why do you have such great equipment?" As soon as the words leave her mouth, her gaze drops to my crotch again, and then she quickly turns away, but not before I catch her blush. "I mean, this stove. It's a chef's dream come true."

"My decorator insisted I buy it." Five thousand bucks for a stove seemed steep to me, but she assured me someday my wife would love it.

I scoff at that. Wife? Nope, not going to happen. My whole life, I was forced to live by the 'nothing but hockey' rule, thanks to my hard-ass prick of a father who told me I was nothing but garbage, soft like my mother.

He might be right, which is why I don't let anyone know the real me, a guy who wasn't even good enough for his own mother to stick around. It's Cocky Cannon, The Playmaker, who women want to bed and the crowd goes crazy for.

Nina runs her hand over the stainless-steel appliance. "I would kill to have a stove like this," she says.

I have a sudden flash of her standing at the stove, cooking for us, and before I can think better of it, I say, "You can cook on it anytime you like."

Shit, what did I say that for? I turn from her and busy my hands getting two tumblers from the cupboard.

"Really?"

"I know you love to cook," I say, making light of it. "I know you like to watch TV while doing it, too." I gesture to the television built into the wall. I pretty much have one in every room. Another suggestion from my decorator, and one I actually liked. I can go from room to room, and never miss a play if a game is on.

"How do you know that?"

"I practically lived at your house, remember? You always made the meals."

She frowns, and that's when it hits me. She made the meals because her parents were always preoccupied with something else.

Hating that I brought back a hard memory for her, I open the fridge and change the subject. "Would you prefer lemonade?"

"Sure."

I take the jug out and pour us each a glass. Her lips part as she takes a drink. Jesus those lips, soft, lush, so fucking kissable. How would they feel on my body, wrapped around my cock? I stifle a groan as that appendage begins to appreciate the thought as well.

Fuck. Three boners within minutes of opening the door to her might not be the best way to starts things off after all this time, even for me. I open the patio door leading to the pool.

"Let's sit out. The rain stopped." I walk outside. "Only in

Seattle can you go from a downpour to hot and sunny in five minutes, right?"

"It's this damn heat wave," she says, and follows me out. As the sun beats down on us, her eyes drop. "You, ah, you should probably put on a shirt."

Her gaze roams over my bare chest, lingering on the scars marring my body. Most think the wounds are from hockey. They're not. I can't remember a day when I hadn't felt the sting of the jump rope my father forced me to train with. *You need to toughen up if you want to play in the NHL.*

The NHL was my father's dream, not mine. Not that I don't love the game. I do. It's my entire life now. But as a pro player who never made it to the big leagues, my father was determined his son was going to play in the NHL.

Bastard got what he wanted, and I learned early on to shut down my emotions and present cocky to the world. It was the only way to get through the day. If I don't feel, I can't get hurt, right? That motto carries me through life, and into each game, and it's that guy the crowd loves.

I rub my hand over one ugly scar and ask, "Why should I put a shirt on? It's hot out."

"You might...ah, burn."

"I'm good." I grab a bottle of sunscreen off my patio table and hold it up. "Want me to lotion you?"

"No," she responds quickly as she peels her coat off. I grin as my gaze rakes over her thin T-shirt, Aerosmith emblazed across the front.

"What's so funny?" she asks.

"Aerosmith," I say. "That was a fun night, and I remember you buying that. You were fourteen. I can't believe it still fits you."

"You remember that?"

"Yeah." I open the lotion and pour a generous amount on

my chest, keeping to myself just how much I remember about her.

Nina drops into a chair, her eyes darting around the patio, looking everywhere but at me. What is going on with her? Is my near nakedness bothering her? Doing hot things to her? Damned if I don't hope it's the latter.

She's hands-off, dude.

"So how exactly can I help you?" I ask.

She finally turns to me, and her gaze latches onto my hands as I finish rubbing the lotion in. She clears her throat and says, "I know you're out with a concussion, and I don't want to take up too much of your time, but if I could watch a couple games with you, and you could explain the plays and calls, some of the slang, it would really help."

I shrug. "Sounds easy enough."

Her eyes light up, and I don't even want to think about how good that makes me feel. "Yeah?"

"Sure." I reach for the button on my jeans. "Damn, it's hot out here."

Panic flashes across her pretty face as she points to my pants. "What...what are you doing?"

I gesture with a nod toward the pool. "Going for a swim. Why don't you join me? Cool off a bit."

"I don't have a bathing suit."

I do a mental search of the dresser drawers in the spare room. "I have one that might fit you."

She folds her arms across her chest. "I am *not* wearing some puck bunny's bathing suit."

I grin, and she gives me the death glare. "Naked it is then."

I unzip my pants and kick them off. A gasp catches in her throat.

"Don't worry, I'm not going to get completely naked. I'll keep my boxers on."

"How is that any better?" she asks.

"You've seen me in my boxers many times, Nina."

"Yeah, well, I never said I liked it."

"If you don't like it, then why are staring so hard?" I might be teasing her, but the truth is, her eyes *are* latched onto my package, and the hard part...yeah, that's my current condition. What this girl can do to me without even trying is fucking crazy.

"I'm not staring." She pushes to her feet and looks away. "This was a bad idea. I should go. Is there a bus route around here?"

"It's not a bad idea," I say softly, seriously, anything to stop her from leaving, and if she does, no way is she taking a bus home. She can borrow one of my cars. "Anything you need, Nina."

She looks at me, her eyes cautious. "Anything?"

"Sure, but what's in it for me?" I ask, calling on my alter ego, Cocky Cole Cannon, before things get too fucking serious. Nothing good can come from her seeing the real me.

She rolls her eyes. "I should have known you'd want *quid pro quo.*"

"I call it tit for tat."

"Of course you do."

"I like the sound of it better." I turn and dive into the cool water because I *really* like the 'tit' part, and boner number four is about to make it obvious. Staying under, I swim to the shallow end of the pool and surface when I reach the wall. I brush my wet hair back and blink the water from my eyes. Nina is standing at the deep end, watching me. "Come on in, it's beautiful. Just wear your underwear."

"I'm not undressing in front of you."

"I'll turn around," I offer.

"What do you want, Cole?" she huffs out.

"I want you to come in."

"That's not what I mean. What do you want for helping me? What are your conditions?"

I dive under and swim back to her. I surface and put my hands on her ankles. I give them a little teasing tug, threatening to pull her in clothes and all as I bounce in the water.

"Don't you dare," she says, and tries to back away, but I've got a good hold on her and she's not going anywhere soon.

"You, on the ice with me," I say.

She stops struggling, and her eyes go wide. For the briefest of seconds, I see fear backlighting her baby blues, but then she quickly blinks it away. "You have a concussion. You can't skate."

"When I get the all clear, I'm going to need a skating partner to help me out."

She goes quiet for a minute, and I can almost hear the wheels turning in her pretty head. I know her well enough to understand she's figuring she can get the game information she needs, then bail before I ever get back on the ice.

"Like someone to spot you?" she asks.

"Yeah, something like that."

"Okay," she agrees.

"But until that time, there is something else I'm going to want." I let go of her legs, brace my hands on the edge of the pool and lift myself out. I stand over her, invade her personal space. Water from my hair drips onto her thin shirt, wetting it enough that I can see a hint of her lacey bra. Fuck, she's hot —and if her brother knew what was going through my head, a concussion would be the last thing I needed to worry about. He'd rip my left nut right out of the sac. He's not called Crazy Callaghan for nothing.

She lifts her chin an inch. "What?"

I cup her face, and I swipe my thumb over her plump bottom lip. Are having two balls really that important? "I get to kiss you whenever I want."

3

NINA

I get to kiss you whenever I want.

Even though it's been a full day since Cole dropped that ridiculous bombshell on me, I'm still fuming mad. I clench and unclench my fingers, wanting to hit something— mainly that devil-may-care smirk that crossed his too-handsome face when he laid out his terms.

"Cocky son of a bitch," I mumble and pace around my small living room. From the sofa, Jess examines her fingernails, only half listening to me. Not that I blame her at this point. I've been ranting ever since she arrived over an hour ago.

"How dare he think I'm some puck bunny dying to climb all over his...stick?" Jess snickers and my gaze flies to hers. "What?"

"Nothing," she says and waves her hand for me to continue.

I pace some more, and a tortured growl catches in my throat. Kiss me whenever he wants. As if. I am not kissing him. Even if I wanted to—which I don't—I *wouldn't* kiss him. Not only is he a cocky bastard, he's my brother's best friend and I've known him since forever. He might as well be my brother, too, or a really close cousin.

Ah, but you don't think of him that way at all.

I shut down that line of thinking and say, "By rights, I should have just introduced my knee to his crotch."

"But you didn't, did you." Jess says.

I cut Jess a look. I could almost swear there was laughter in her tone, but she's still looking at her nails. "No, I didn't."

"And why do you think that is?"

I draw in a long breath and slowly blow it back out. "Oh, I don't know. Maybe it's that thing about eating and having a roof over my head."

Jess pulls her phone from her purse and slides her finger over the screen. With her attention half on her latest text and half on me, she says, "Is that the only reason?"

"Yes," I shoot back quickly.

She drops her phone, and her lips quirk as dubious brown eyes gaze at me like I'm telling half-truths, which I very well could be, but I'm not about to admit that.

"Are those the only reasons, Nina?"

"Of course they are."

"If you ask me——"

"I didn't ask you."

"Come on, admit it. You want a rage ride and you know it."

I stop and turn to face Jess, planting one hand on my hip. "Save the therapy for the classroom, Jess. I'm not one of your seniors in need of sex advice."

"Okay then, don't anger-bang him." She shrugs. "But what's a little kiss between friends? He gets what he wants, you get what you want."

What do I want?

The sudden vision of his mouth on mine flashes through

me, and a big ball of fiery heat follows. I gulp, and work to refocus.

"Okay, counselor. In your opinion, what do you think he wants, exactly? Why would he make kissing a condition? He doesn't like me. I don't like him."

"Ah, so now you want my advice, do you?"

"Seriously, I just don't get it." I start pacing again.

Her jaw drops open and she looks at me like I'm a bit dense. "Did you ever stop to think that he might like you?"

"Like me? Ha! I think it's more about teasing me, like he used to do when we were kids. He's on a power trip, always has been. God, what an ass." I walk to the window and pull my curtain back in time to see Mr. Johnson circle the black Mustang parked on the street in front of my building. What a ridiculous muscle car. With that ridiculous muffler that the neighbors can hear long before they see me coming.

Overcompensating much?

"If he's such an ass, he wouldn't have lent you his car to drive, for as long as you need it, instead of you bussing out to his place all the time."

"Yeah, so, that doesn't mean anything. It's probably so I can get there faster so he can toy with me longer. This is all your fault, you know."

"Hey, I didn't twist your arm."

"But you did put the idea of sex in my brain," I whisper under my breath, but not quietly enough, because Jess, with her Vulcan hearing, jumps from the sofa with a huge-ass grin on her face.

"I knew it."

Giving up the act, I sink down onto the coffee table and bury my face in my hands. "Jesus, Jess, you should have seen him. He's a cocky ass, yes, but that doesn't change the fact that he's freaking hot. He walked around in nothing but his jeans, and then he took them off to get in the pool. He actually went swimming in his boxers. In front of me. He even invited me in."

I spread my fingers and glance at my friend. Her eyes go wide, and she plops onto the sofa across from me and rubs her hands together, waiting for all the juicy details. "Ohmigod, I can't believe you've been holding out on me. Tell me everything."

"He took his pants off. Like it was nothing. Like we undress in front of each other all the time." I groan and shake my head.

"So, is it true then? Do they call him the Cannon because he's loaded?"

I nod, unable to form the words as my mind races back to the sexy image of him standing by his pool...to the big bulge in his shorts, specifically.

Excited by my confirmation, Jess throws her hands up in the air. "I knew it! Now you *have* to sleep with him."

"I don't have to do anything." I glance at my clock. "Other than go to his house and watch tonight's game with him." I stand and smooth my hair back. "But first I'm going to eat a Caesar salad with extra garlic."

Jess laughs. "I think it might take a lot more than garlic to deter him from kissing you." She gives me the once over, her face thoughtful as she taps her chin, her eyes narrowing in concentration as she takes in my clothes. "Is that what you're wearing?"

I look at my frayed jean shorts and tank top. "It's too hot for anything else. Do you think I should change?"

She points at my legs. "No, you're sexy as hell in those shorts, and that tank really shows off your tits."

Tit for tat.

"Then I'll change." I make a move to go to my room and she captures my arm to stop me.

"No, keep this on. I'm kidding. You look like hell. But when was the last time you trimmed the triangle?"

I blink once, then twice. How are we friends? "Excuse me."

"You know, trimmed the triangle, beat down the beaver, Georged the bush."

"Georged the bush?" A laugh bursts out of me. "Ohmigod, girl. Who are you?" I ask. Georged the bush. Only Jess would come up with something like that. She really does crack me up, and when it comes down to it, she's right about so many things. Like me needing to get laid...wanting to hate fuck.

"Something tells me Cannon is a *vagatarian*, and you want be all neat and tidy when he kisses you down there, don't you? I mean, it's not like he specified *where* he wanted to put his mouth, right?"

I point to the door. "On that note..."

She jumps up from the sofa, and blows me a kiss and she saunters away. "Have fun, and don't do anything I wouldn't do."

"There isn't *anything* you wouldn't do." I shake my head and laugh in spite of her absurdity. I mean, it is absurd, right? He's not really going to want to kiss me...down there. "I'll call you later."

"Will this be before or after you do the nasty with Cannon?"

"Jess..." I warn as the heat in my body spikes at the visual. *Cut it out, Nina. You don't want that.*

"Love you," she says.

"Love you, too."

She slips out the door, and I glance out the window to see her checking out the Mustang. She gives me two thumbs-up and slides into her car and takes off. I laugh again, despite myself. I do love Jess, but I think she's all wrong where Cole is concerned. Not the part about him having a cannon between his legs, but the part about him wanting to kiss me because he likes me. No way can she be right about that. Then again, it's illogical to kiss someone he truly hates. Is it possible that he likes me, at least enough to kiss me?

As I contemplate that, I grab a handful of strawberries from my near-empty fridge, and pop them into my mouth. I snag my purse and notepad from the kitchen counter and take a deep breath. *Here goes nothing.* I head outdoors, lock up behind myself, and stare at the Mustang.

"Here goes nothing," I whisper.

I jump into the car and cringe as the rumbling muffler gains the attention of my neighbors. I smile politely and wave, then pull into traffic. Cole said the game started at seven, but I want to get there early in case he wants to go over anything with me first.

Like kissing.

No. No. No. Not like kissing. Like slang and things like that, so I can understand the plays better.

I jack the tunes and look around the clean vehicle. It still has that new-car smell and hardly any miles on it. With Cole being on the road, and then the concussion, he probably hasn't even had a chance to break it in yet, see what it can do. I press the gas pedal and speed up to find out for myself. Nice.

Truthfully, though, it was very kind of Cole to lend me a vehicle, since it was just sitting there unused. What a nice *brotherly* thing for him to do. Luke would be pleased by his friend's generosity.

As the sun begins its descent over the horizon, I pull into his driveway and power down the car. I stare at his big house and suck in a breath as I rationalize our deal. I can understand the skating part, but the kissing...

He had to be kidding about that, right? I mean, he's always teased me about everything, so he has to be teasing about this too. Yeah, he has to be, because the guy doesn't even like me. There was really no reason for me to fixate on that and get so worked up today. This was just Cole being Cocky Cannon. When it comes right down to it, he doesn't want to kiss me any more than I want him to.

I let loose a relieved breath—and try not to examine the tiny twinge of disappointment fluttering in my gut.

Damn you, Jess.

I climb from the car and the front door opens, and I once again find Cole waiting for me as I make my way up the long walkway. Funny how that makes me feel so strange. Growing up, there was never anyone home to greet Luke or me after school, after practice, after...anything. I kind of like the normalcy of it, of having someone waiting for you, looking forward to seeing you. Not that I think Cole is looking forward to seeing me.

He removes the shirt hooked over his shoulder and tugs it on as I approach, his big frame filling up the doorway. Thank God he's dressing. I don't know how I'd make it through the night if he were half naked again.

"Do you just stand at your door and wait for people to come by?" I ask.

His smile is slow, cocky as hell. "No, I heard you coming."

"Hard not to." I jerk my thumb over my shoulder. "I think your muffler is broke."

"That's just how it sounds."

"You know what they say about guys with noisy mufflers." What the hell am I doing? *Shut up, Nina. Shut up right now before you back yourself into a corner and have to use the word penis in front of Cole.*

"You mean about overcompensating?" he asks, and turns to the side to allow me to pass. "That a man with a small cock compensates by getting a noisy muffler?"

Heat burns my face, and I keep my back to Cole, dying of

embarrassment. But he steps around me, and a sexy grin splits his lips when he sees the color on my cheeks.

"Hey, you're the one who brought it up."

I tug my notepad from my purse. "We should get to work."

"What's the hurry? The game doesn't start for another hour." He rubs his stomach. "I was about to order pizza. Are you hungry?"

"I could eat," I say, the strawberries I had for dinner doing little to fill my stomach.

"What do you like on your pizza?"

"Vagatarian." Shit. Shit. Shit. I'm really going to kill my bestie. "I mean vegetarian. Vegetarian," I say again.

"You don't eat meat?"

"No, I eat meat," I say quickly. "I love meat." His grin widens, and I know exactly what's going through his little pea brain. Why oh why does everything sound sexual when I'm around him. "I just don't like all the processed meats on pizza," I add. "They're full of nitrates, and not very good for you."

"So you only like to put things that are good for you in your mouth."

I stare at him, pretty sure he's making this about sex. With every ounce of me fighting the urge to punch that playful grin off his face, I choose my words carefully, so he can't twist them into something dirty. "Yes. I like to eat healthy," I say.

He nods in agreement and runs his fingers through his dark hair, messing it up. Damn, that makes him look sexier— and here I thought that was impossible.

"I normally do too, but the pizza joint is just around the corner and it's quick and easy."

That gives me pause. The last time I was here, there was a

pizza box on his kitchen counter. "Wait, have you been eating takeout for the last a month?"

"Yeah. I can't drive to get groceries because of the concussion, and I don't really do a lot of cooking anyway."

"What about your dad? Couldn't he help you out?"

He stiffens at the mention of his dad. "No," is all he says, but I don't miss the defensiveness in his tone.

"Friends?"

"I live on the ice, my friends are all hockey players, and they're on the road right now."

"Girlfriend?"

"Single."

I hate the little thrill that goes through me with that admission. I don't care if he's single. It means nothing to me, other than he has no girl to help him out when he's down, and that just plain sucks.

"Sister?"

He frowns, and looks down, like he's remembering something painful. "She's away, working on the East Coast."

"Oh, wow, I didn't realize. She sure moved far away from home."

"Yup," is all he says.

"Well, you shouldn't be living on takeout. I can take you to the grocery store. You should at least have fresh fruit and vegetables. I can even pick us up some steaks and cook them for us instead of ordering in." I gesture with a nod to the deck area. "When I was here yesterday, I saw a barbeque out by the pool."

"Yeah?" He cocks his head to the side. "You'll take me shopping?"

Why does that surprise him so much? Okay, yeah, sure, we don't like each other, but I'm not a monster. I'd help anyone out in this kind of situation. Enemy or not. "Of course."

"And you'll cook?"

"Yeah, it's not a problem." I throw my purse back over my shoulder.

He frowns, and waves his hands to stop me. "Wait, wait, you did enough cooking growing up. You shouldn't have to do it for me."

"I really don't mind. I like being in the kitchen, and your equipment...I can't wait to try it out."

"Oh. Yeah."

Oh, shit. I really need to stop saying things about his equipment, even if I *am* referring to his appliances...at least I'm pretty sure I am.

Gawd...

I steal a glance at the clock and clear my throat before saying, "I think I'll have time to prepare a healthy meal before the game starts."

"You will if I help."

"You?" I poke my finger into his chest—and wish I hadn't touched him. It does the craziest things to the needy little spot between my legs. Working diligently to pull myself together and pretend his hard muscles and strong heartbeat hadn't affected me, I continue with, "The self-proclaimed bachelor who can't cook is offering to help me?"

His cocky grin is back. "Sure, tit for tat, remember?"

I roll my eyes. "Come on. You can talk to me about hockey in the car."

"Okay, but is that the tit or tat part?" he asks.

"Just so we're clear, there will be no tit part," I say, but then embarrassment floods me when I realize what I said. Sure, I write hot sex in my books, but in real life, I don't talk dirty or say things like...tit, or penis, or worst of all...cock. Ugh.

"So all tat, huh?" He grabs his house keys from the table near the door and locks up behind us. "I can work with that."

"Good." We hop into the Mustang and I back out of his driveway, but being in such an enclosed space with him, and him smelling so damn good and clean and soapy, is messing with my brain. "Where is the closest grocery store?" I ask.

"You're asking *me*?"

"Right, what was I thinking?" I gesture to the bulge in his jeans. Not the one I can't seem to stop checking out, but the one in his pocket. "Check your phone."

From the corner of my eye, I steal a glimpse of him as he stretches out those long hard legs of his and tugs his phone from his pants pocket. He pulls up a map. "Turn right at the stop sign." I follow his directions and make quick, efficient turns, appreciating how the Mustang handles. A few minutes later, we pull up in front of the grocery store. I kill the engine and reach for the door handle, but beside me Cole hesitates.

He shuts his eyes and takes a deep breath.

Knowing exactly what's he's going though, I put my hand on his arm, and his lids flicker open. I shouldn't have dragged him along in his current condition. What was I thinking? "Why don't you take a minute?"

"I seriously appreciate your skilled driving, but I think the motion caused a bit of vertigo."

He thinks I'm a skilled driver?

No one has ever complimented me on my driving before.

I give a quick shake of my head. What does that even matter? What's really important here is his health. I look him over, take in the pallor of his skin, the sweat beading on his upper lip. My heart squeezes. It can't be easy for him to be down and out with a concussion, missing out on playing a game he obviously loves, and having no one to help him.

Something inside of me softens. I squeeze his arm. "Why don't you wait here? I can run in and grab a few things."

"No, I'll come." He pulls a pair of sunglasses from the

glove box and slides them on. I study him for a moment, and he says, "Sometimes fluorescent lights bother me."

"I know. It was the same for me."

"What a pair we are, huh?" I'm about to pull my hand away when he slides his big warm palm over it, his rough calluses scoring my flesh as he holds me in place. "Nina, I'm sorry I wasn't here to help you when you had your concussion." He frowns, and behind his lenses I'm almost certain I see sorrow in his eyes.

What the hell? Who is *this* Cole?

"Luke and I," his voice catches, like his words are stuck in his throat, "were on the road and—"

"It's okay, Cole. I'm not your responsibility."

He goes quiet for a moment and looks down at his lap, his brow knitted tightly. "Yeah, well, I just wanted to say I was sorry, about that and your injuries. You were one hell of a skater."

My stupid heart jumps at his second compliment of the night. He'd been at the rink a few times when I was practicing or competing, but I never thought he paid me much attention. I figured he was there to check out the girls in their skimpy performance outfits.

"Thanks," is all I say, not wanting to talk about it. Think about it. Remember it. The past is the past, and I need to focus on the writing now, and paying the bills. "We'd better hurry. We don't want to miss the start of the game."

He looks at me for a moment and then nods, and we both exit the vehicle. He meets me at the front of the car, and we walk into the brightly lit store together. He leans into me and nudges me with his shoulder. His scent reaches my nostrils, and as I breathe in his clean, soapy smell, every goddamn nerve in my traitorous body comes alive.

Shit. Shit. Shit. I do not want this. Becoming attracted to Cocky Cole is the last thing I need.

"So, this is a grocery store?" he says.

I laugh, anything to hide the storm going on inside my body. "Yes, Cole. This is a grocery store." I grab a cart. "Want a ride?" I tease.

"If I didn't have a concussion, I'd be all over that idea."

"I somehow don't doubt that." I guide him to the fresh vegetables section, and as I reach for the lettuce to make us a salad, a hush comes over the crowd.

I glance around, take in the quiet mass gathering around the produce.

"What's going on?" I ask Cole, but then I see the way people are pointing, staring, whispering to each other. A little boy of around seven is gawking at Cole, his eyes the size of the apples in his mother's cart.

Ah, I get it. Cole is the infamous Playmaker, and everyone is star struck. I don't know why I never stopped to think about that before. I look at him, see him through the eyes of the crowd. Truthfully, he's charismatic, larger than life. It's no wonder he has women handing over their panties.

A child in a cast makes a move toward him, and at first Cole stiffens. The mother grabs her son to stop him from approaching without permission, and as Cole takes in the family, a fast change comes over him. He takes his glasses off and drops to one knee. "Hey kid," he says, his Playmaker grin in place. "What happened?"

"I broke my arm. I just got this." He holds his cast up, like it's a badge of honor.

"Want me to sign it, then we can get a picture together?" Cole hands me his phone. "Would you mind?"

I take the phone, and the wallpaper is that of Luke and Cole. I pull up the camera app and try not to think about how much I miss my brother.

"Mommy, can I?" the boy asks this time, his voice bursting with excitement.

"Of course," his mom says, but from the way she's eyeing Cole, I get the sense that she's as infatuated as her son. I can see why, but there's a part of me that doesn't like the way she's looking at him, like he's nothing more than a piece of meat.

Feeling a little protective of my brother's best friend, I step closer, under the guise of getting set up to take a picture, and partially block the woman's view.

The boy comes bouncing over, his body practically vibrating with excitement. Cole tosses his arm around him and nudges his chin. "You play hockey?" he asks.

"Yeah, but I'm not as good as my brother."

"Do you want to be?" The kid nods fast. "So you love it?"

"I do."

"Good. Work hard and stay focused. But only do it if you really love it, okay? Do it for yourself."

The kid nods, and when Cole stops talking, I say, "Say cheese."

They both smile, and I snap a few pictures while the kid's mom does the same with her phone. After Cole signs his cast, the boy runs back to his mom.

"I'll put that up on Facebook," Cole says, and the boy is totally losing his mind over that, talking about how Caleb is going to be so jealous. I can only assume Caleb is his hockey-playing older brother.

A few more people make their way over, and even though we're in a hurry, Cole makes time for them. His smile is wide and his stories are animated as they ask him questions. I shake my head. He's in total Playmaker mode, enjoying the interaction with his fans.

"So that winning play you made in Pittsburgh. That was awesome," a man in his mid-forties says. "When you got that breakaway and put the biscuit in the basket, it was a beautiful thing, man."

"Thanks. It was a great play, and I couldn't have done it without Luke. He's my wingman. The whole team actually made that play happen."

The commotion gains the attention of men, women and kids alike, and they all make their way to the produce section. They all want to ask questions, touch him, and get their pictures taken. I step back a bit, a little overwhelmed, and I'm not even the one in the spotlight. I'm not sure I could handle that kind of attention.

Cole, however, handles it like the pro he is, taking credit when it's due, then praising the plays made by his teammates. I have to say, I kind of admire him for it.

When the crowd dies down, and he's alone for a second— unaware of my eyes still on him—he takes in a deep, shaky breath, and his Adam's apple bobs as if going down for the third count. He swallows uneasily and briefly pinches his eyes shut.

What the hell? My heart trips up at the deep sadness on his face, and a heaviness fills my chest. The orange in my hand slips and falls into the cart.

The sound does something to him—makes him aware I'm still there. He turns and, when he sees me watching him, quickly snaps out of it. With his big, contagious smile back in place, not a trace of that discomfort to be found, he walks over to me.

"Sorry about that."

"You okay?" I ask.

His hand brushes mine, sending shivers down my spine. He shrugs easily. "Yeah, great, why?"

"I...uh...well, you know, concussion and all. I've been there, remember?" I say, although I don't think what I just saw had anything to do with his concussion at all. "That must have taken a lot out of you."

"I'm fine." He snags an orange, examines it, and drops it into the cart with the other one.

He seems fine now, but what the hell was that? Could it have been his concussion or something else? If something else, what?

"You really made that kid's day."

He nods. "I'm glad. Hey, can we get some Captain Crispies? I haven't had them since forever."

I laugh at his childlike enthusiasm. "You can get whatever you want, Cole. These are your groceries. Although Captain Crispies aren't very good for you."

"I'll eat a banana to make up for it." He grabs a bunch of bananas and adds them to the cart. He nudges me with his shoulder again—a gesture I'm growing accustomed to—and my body reacts to his closeness. "Actually, I put the banana in the cereal. A real time-saver," he teases.

Needing a measure of distance, I turn toward the grapes. "How old are you, anyway?" I mock.

He reaches around me and chooses a bag of plump grapes. "Old enough."

His breath is warm against my ear. Goose bumps prickle my neck. To hide my traitorous body's reaction, I roll my eyes at him. "Come on, let's get those steaks and your cereal."

As we go down the aisles, Cole pulls food from the shelves and tosses everything in the cart, his attention solely on shopping. No more subtle touches, no veiled sexual innuendos. I'm both relieved and confused. Had I read too much into his actions?

By the time we reach the cash register, the cart is overflowing with groceries.

Nighttime falls over the city as we head back to his car and load the bags into the trunk. "You won't have to order takeout for weeks," I say.

"Yeah, but I'm going to have to hire someone to cook for me."

"Well, since you're helping me out, I can teach you how to cook. It's not that hard."

"Okay, but don't think for a minute that crosses out any of my other conditions." As soon as the words leave his lips, his gaze drops to my mouth.

My throat dries, and without thinking, I swipe my tongue over my bottom lip. His eyes darken, and my pulse jumps in my throat. Uh, maybe he was serious about the kissing after all, and maybe I kind of like that idea.

Oh, Nina, this is so bad.

"We, ah, should get back before the game starts," I say.

"Okay," he says, but doesn't make a move to go. I grasp the trunk lid to close it, and he reaches over me, his big body pressing against mine as he slams it shut.

We both get back into the car and my damn body is on hyperdrive, my mind racing a million miles an hour as I retrace the route back to his place. From my peripheral vision, I catch the way he's looking at me, the way his breathing has changed slightly. Fidgety under his scrutiny, the heat I see in his eyes, I try to think of something to say, but can't seem to formulate a coherent sentence. I pull into his driveway and we're both silent as we unload the bags, dropping them on his kitchen counter.

"There's only one left. I'll get it," I say, and dash out the door, needing a reprieve from the hot looks he's casting my way.

When I come back in, he's in the living room, the remote in his hand. "Come on, the game is about to start."

"Can we watch it on the TV in the kitchen? I want to get the steaks on the grill and make our salad."

"Sure."

I head to the kitchen and glance around for the remote.

When I can't find it, I turn, about to ask where he keeps it, but shut my mouth when I run smack dab into a hard wall of muscle, aka, Cole Cannon.

"Whoa," he says, and slides his arm around me. He splays his big hands over the small of my back, the heat from his fingers dancing over my skin.

"I...uh, didn't realize you were there. Sorry about that." I try to extricate myself from his arms but he keeps me pressed up against him. His strong heart beats against my palm as I put my hand on his chest.

"Don't be." He dips his head, and his hair falls forward, shading his eyes as they move over my face. "I was thinking."

"About what?" I ask, my voice coming out a little higher than I would have liked it to. But how the hell can I talk normal when I'm meshed up against his body like this— thinking about hate fucking?

"About kissing."

4

COLE

I want to kiss her. I want to kiss her so fucking bad, but her eyes are wide, her lids flashing rapidly, panic jumping all over her face. She's practically shivering with anxiety, every muscle twitching.

Jesus, if she still hates me and doesn't want me to kiss her, no fucking way am I going to force her—no matter how desperate I am for a taste.

For the last twenty-four hours, since she first stepped foot on my doorstep, all I've been able to think about are her lips, how they'd taste and feel on my mouth, my body.

She's so goddamn beautiful, and when she showed up here tonight, in her Daisy Duke jean shorts and tank top that gave me a glimpse of her gorgeous breasts, it was all I could do not to rip her clothes from her body and have my way with her. But while I'm an expert asshole, on and off the ice, this is sweet little Nina Callaghan—my Pretty BallerNina—and I'd never, ever do anything she didn't want me to.

I remove my hand from her back and inch away. "Hey, if you don't want—"

"I never said that," she responds quickly, and flicks her tongue over her bottom lip like she's moistening it for me.

Motherfucker.

I run my hand through my hair, messing it up as my heart rate doubles. I've lusted for women before, many of them, but with Nina it's different. It's a longing, many years in the building, but I don't want to do anything to taint her sweetness.

"Yeah?" I say.

She gives a casual shrug of her shoulder. "I mean, it's one of your conditions and I agreed, right?"

"Right," I say, and step back into her, until my thickening cock is pressing against her stomach. No sense in hiding what she does to me. Her breath changes, and her eyes widen when she feels me, but she doesn't back away. I take that as a good sign and press on. "But do you *want* to kiss me, Nina?"

I need to know it. I need to hear her say it. I'm not sure why. She's agreed to the kiss and that should be enough, but there's a part of me—the real me that no one knows—that needs to be *wanted* by her. Since I've always shut down my feelings, this foreign emotion scares the living fuck out of me. I should walk away, end this right now. I don't want to feel. Nothing good can come from it, on or off the ice.

She exhales, and her warm, minty breath washes over my face. "We don't even like each—"

"We don't need to like each other to kiss." I cup her face to stop her. "But that's not what I'm asking."

A moment of hesitation, then she answers me with an upturned face, her lips parting slightly, her actions letting me know she wants this too. I brush my thumb along her cheek, and suck in a fast, fueling breath.

If I do this, if I kiss my best friend's kid sister, there's no going back—and if Luke finds out, I'm a fucking goner. Stupid bro code.

But I'm already a goner.

As Nina stands before me, her cheeks a pretty shade of pink, her mouth opened slightly, welcoming me to kiss her, not even the toughest defensemen on the Seattle Shooters could keep me away.

I lower my head slowly, wanting to draw the moment out, fearing I'll never get the opportunity again, and press my lips to hers.

As soon as I do, she makes a soft, sexy bedroom noise, and it takes every ounce of restraint I have to stop myself from picking her up and carrying her to my bedroom. I angle my head, deepen the kiss as I touch her body and shape her curves. I place my hands on her hips, pull her against me, and rock into her softness. My tongue slips between parted lips and tangles with hers, and she slides her hands around my back, her breasts pressing against my chest.

The kiss deepens and expands, and when her eyes shut, my dick whispers at me to do wicked things to her.

But this is little Nina, which means this is so fucked up.

I break the kiss, and inch back. She remains in front of me, her mouth still poised, waiting for mine. I breathe fast, push down the things building inside me. The heat that could destroy my world.

Her eyes fly open, equal measures of disappointment and shock staring at me. "I...we're done?" she asks, her innocence totally fucking me over. Man, she's really too sweet and pure for a guy like me. Then again, the thought of her in another man's bed burns in my gut like acid.

"Game's on," I say, switching back to Cocky Cannon mode. "Can't let anything interfere with the game."

"Right," she says, and turns from me, but not before I see the way she's swallowing hard. "That's why I'm here."

Fuck man, had I hurt her feelings? It wasn't my intent but what the fuck can I do? No one gets into my head, my heart, or my home, and I've already broken one of those sacred rules with her.

I grab the remote and flick the TV on. Nina half listens to me as she unpacks the groceries and starts putting them away.

I glance at her moving around my kitchen like it's where she belongs. "Leave them there, I'll put them away."

"No, I don't mind," she says, her voice infused with a lightness that seems fake. "And I want to get the steaks marinating." She glances at the TV. "So there are five players on the ice at a time?" she asks, bringing the conversation back to the real reason she's here, and I'm glad, because I'm much more comfortable with that.

"Six actually, if you include the goalie. We have two defensemen, a left winger, right winger and center."

"What do you play?" she asks as she moves about the kitchen, and I suddenly find my eyes on her ass, and not on the game.

"Center. I quarterback the team at both ends of the ice."

"Is that why they call you The Playmaker?"

"One of the reasons," I say, and when she turns to me, I offer her my signature Cocky grin.

She has a soft, thoughtful expression on her face. "Your team must be missing you."

"Yeah," I say, and turn from her. It's fucking killing me to be off the ice. I live for the game.

"Maybe you'll be better for the playoffs."

"I hope so. I'm doing everything the doctor told me to." The first play of the game is on and the commentators are listing stats. Burns, a motherfucker who plays for the Illinois Icemen, takes off with the puck. I hate that guy. He's the one responsible for my concussion. I scoff. All he got was a five-minute penalty and I'm out indefinitely. I hope they make it to the playoffs so I can make him pay. I've been obsessing over it.

"Cole?"

"Yeah."

Her eyes are narrowed, tentative. "If having me here is too much, I—"

"No, Nina," I say quickly. Her leaving is not an option. I want to help her. But it's more than that. The truth is, she's the one bright thing in all of this. "It's fine. You're actually cooking for me so that's even one up on my road to recovery."

She sprinkles salt and pepper on the steak. "Maybe you should hire someone to help you out around here while you're recovering."

"No," I say, my tone harsher than I meant. I wince when she flinches. "Sorry. I didn't mean to jump down your throat." I don't let just anyone into my house. This place is my sanctuary and strangers aren't welcome. "I don't let people in here."

"Oh, because you're famous. I get it."

"Yeah," I agree, even though that's not the real reason.

She goes quiet for a moment, then says, "Well, I could help you."

"I never thought of that."

Her T-shirt shifts over her cleavage as she gives a casual shrug. "I mean, if you wanted me too."

Nina in my house. All day. Cooking and helping out. Moving around and bending over. I swallow the groan rising in my throat. Like my cock isn't tortured enough already.

"If you don't, I won't be offended."

"It's not that at all. If I hired you, wouldn't that take away from your writing time?"

She chokes out a laugh, but there's no humor in it. "You

wouldn't have to pay me, and as far as writing time, I haven't been doing too much of that lately."

"I'm not going to ask you to cook and clean for me for free."

She points a knife at me. "Hey, I didn't say anything about cleaning."

I flash her a smile. "Damn, I was hoping you wouldn't pick up on that."

She laughs. "Nice try though."

I look her over as her laugh dissolves. What's going on with little Nina Callaghan? "Why haven't you been doing too much writing? Writer's block?" I ask, even though I know as much about that as she does about hockey. Maybe it's not even real, maybe it's a term tossed around when you can't get the words down right.

"Something like that, but I'm hoping to knock out a killer hockey romance."

A commercial comes on, and when she stretches out her back like it hurts, I stand. "I'll go light the barbecue."

She squares her shoulders and stands up to me. "I'm capable."

"I know. So am I."

Ignoring her power pose, I step out into the night and flick the lights on in the pool. A soft blue glow lights up the deck as I start the BBQ.

Nina follows me out with the steaks. She slides them onto the grill and bastes them with sauce. I wonder if she even knows she's humming softly. Maybe she really does like cooking, maybe it takes her to another place.

"How come you hate hockey?"

She closes the lid on the grill. "I never said I did."

"You didn't have to. You never came to any home games, that says enough."

"I didn't want to bother Luke," she says, and walks back inside, abruptly putting an end to the conversation.

Why would it bother Luke? I follow her, and I'm about to ask, when she drops down into a chair at the table and picks up her pad and paper. "Tell me what's going on?"

I sit next to her, and for the next few minutes, I lean into her and explain the game, even drawing a few plays on her pad. Then I talk about the icing call after the ref blows his whistle.

"Interesting," she says, but seems a bit distracted. She's not the only one; her closeness is fucking me over, big time. "I'll be right back." She slips outside to flip the steaks, and I sort of feel useless.

"Is there anything I can help you with?" I ask when she comes back in.

"You *are* helping me. Okay, what did I miss?"

"Not much, really." Her eyes narrow when Burns shoves a guy hard into the boards.

"Ouch. That can't be allowed."

"Oh, it's allowed. It's called checking, and that guy is a pro at it." I point to my head. "That's how I got this."

Her mouth drops open, her indignant gaze going from me to Burns, back to me. "He did that to you?" Anger flares in her eyes, and I'm a little touched by her concern, actually.

"Yup."

"Then why is he still playing? Shouldn't he be benched?"

"Hey, you know more about hockey than you think."

She beams at me, and I like that so much more than her death glare. "I know the term from figure skating."

"Good. Write down that he had to sit in the penalty box, that's what it's called. Oh, and he spent all of five minutes in there."

"Well that's just wrong."

"It is what it is."

"I'd better not run into him in a dark alleyway."

I laugh at her boldness and nudge her chin with my fist. "Are all five feet of you going to take him out for me?"

She straightens. "I'm five-two, thank you very much." I'm about to laugh again, until she winces and puts her hand on her back.

"What's wrong?"

"Fractured tailbone. Still causes me pain." She rolls her neck and stretches it out. "Also a damaged C-5 in my neck."

"Then you shouldn't be doing all this cooking, and you shouldn't have been lifting the grocery bags," I say, as a surge of guilt rolls over me. I shouldn't have let her drive me to the store, then cook. Why the hell didn't she tell me she still has pain?

She rolls her eyes at me. "I'm not an invalid. I can take care of myself, Cole. I have for a very long time now."

My gut twists. Yeah, she has, and it couldn't have been easy on her with her parents so absent and Luke on the road all the time. Could that be why she hates hockey? It took her brother away? They really only had each other growing up, and she must miss him. But even though he's not here, it doesn't mean he doesn't care about her. He sure as fuck does.

Until he's back, I'm going to make it my own personal mission to help her, the same way she's helping me.

"Okay, explain that play to me," she says, and taps her pen on her chin. I turn back to the TV, and as I talk, she makes notes. When another commercial comes on, she darts outside to check on the food.

"Medium well," she says and comes back in with the steaks. "I hope that's how you like them."

"I like them any way I can get them," I say, and rub my stomach. She fixes two plates with steak and salad, then roots around inside the fridge for dressing.

"Poppy seed, my favorite."

"I have no idea how that got there," I say. Maybe my twin sister left it here the last time she visited me.

She stares at the dressing for a minute, like she's debating on whether to use it or not.

"I think it's still good," I say. "Even if it's not, that stuff never goes bad." I stand and grab us forks and knives from the drawer, then open the fridge. "I have beer...oh, wait, I think I have a bottle of wine around here somewhere." Tabatha likes wine, so I always try to keep a few bottles on hand for her. She doesn't visit much, being on the East Coast, but when she does come, I try to have everything for her. I miss her like fuck, but she's better off on the other side of the country, away from our bastard of a father.

I know she's grown up, but I don't want the old man to have any kind of influence or hold anything over her. He pissed his money away on the bottle, and I don't want him going to Tabby for money. What she has is hers, and no way will I let him guilt her into giving him a dime.

That doesn't mean he's on the streets starving. He's got a pension coming in, and I take care of medical bills when they come up. Yeah, he was a fucking bastard, and I should have walked away, never to look back, but I guess I just don't have that in me.

Maybe Nina and I are more alike than I realized. She says she doesn't like me, but she stayed to help.

Then again, she does want something from me. Story of my fucking life, right?

"Beer is fine, actually."

I grab two bottles, crack them and pour hers into a glass. "A girl after my own heart."

"I like something cold when it's hot out. I can't believe this crazy heat wave we're having. But it's not hot in here."

"Air conditioning. If it's too cold, I can turn it down."

"No, I'm okay," she says, and sits down. I slide into the seat beside her and shift closer.

"Here, steal some of my body heat," I say, as I press my outer thigh against hers. She visibly shivers, but I don't think it's from the cold.

What the fuck is going on between us? Well, I know what's wrong with *me*. I've always crushed on my best friend's sister, but up until yesterday, she'd always treated me like I was something that needed to be scraped off the bottom of her boot.

I cut into my steak and she does the same. "Damn, this is good. Best steak I ever had."

"I doubt that."

I turn to her, only to see her sliding her fork into her mouth. Oh, fuck. My dick flinches. *Down boy*. I curse under my breath and wait for my erection to shrink, but the damn thing has a mind of its own. And Jesus Christ, does she have to moan like that? She's eating steak, not having sex.

"Good, huh?" I manage to get out.

"Really good." She takes a sip of beer and turns her attention back to the television.

If hockey is the most important thing in my life, then why am I watching sweet little Nina, and the way her lips pucker when she drinks, instead of the game that could very well determine if our team makes it to the playoffs?

5

NINA

When the game finishes and Illinois wins, I put my notepad down and glance at Cole, who is snarling at the TV. His hair is a mess from running his fingers through it, and the overhead light glistens in his green eyes as they narrow. I can almost hear the wheels in his brain turning as he considers the playoffs, and going up against his nemesis. But he shouldn't be thinking so hard in his conditions.

I touch his arm and drag his attention to me. "You okay?"

His face softens, making him look younger, boyish, the tough kid from my youth. "Yeah, I'm good."

"So that's your happy face?"

His grin is slow. "Yeah, fingers crossed we make it to the playoffs, and I get to go one on one with Burns."

I have an instant tightening in my gut at that. "What if he hurts you again?" Too many concussions can be detrimental in the long run, and I'd hate to see Cole have any kind of permanent damage.

He links his fingers and cracks them. I cringe at the sound, and he gives me an apologetic look. When we were young, I always glared at him when he did that, but he never apologized or even pretended to be sorry.

"That's a chance I'm willing to take."

"It's kind of a barbaric sport, don't you think?"

"Nah, far from it."

My gaze roams over his face. "Judging from your scars, I'd beg to differ."

Something comes over him, fast, and he stands, his chair nearly toppling backward as he glances around the kitchen.

Heavy silence fills the air, takes up space, seeps under my skin. Uncomfortable in its wake, I follow his gaze, note his deadly stillness, along with the tightening of my throat as I wait for him to speak. I've clearly hit a soft spot. His scars are something he doesn't want to talk about.

"I better clean up," he finally says as he scrubs his chin. The rustling of the hairs reaches my ears, and I fight the urge to run my fingers along the hard angle of his jaw, tug him to me and hug him.

Happy for the change in subject, I jump up and say, "I'll help you load the dishwasher, and then I'll get going."

"You don't have to do that. You cooked and I didn't really help."

"There was nothing for you to help with." I look at the few dirty plates, salad bowl, glasses, and silverware. "Actually there's not much, and there's no need to put the dishwasher on with so few dishes." At home I'm always conservative when it comes to things like this. "How about we just wash and dry the quickly. Working together we'll be done in half the time? Then the next time I cook, I'll do it when there's no game on and you can get more involved."

"Okay, I'll wash, you dry," he suggests.

"How about the other way around, since I don't know where anything goes?"

"Sounds good."

Cole clears the plates as I fill the sink with soapy water. From the window, I can see the pool all lit up and the hot tub tucked into the corner. It looks so nice and relaxing. What I'd do to top off a long night with a hot soak. But I don't have a suit, and even if I did, I'm not stripping down in front of Cole.

"Just drop them in here," I say, and splash my hands in the bubbles, flustered at the directions of my thoughts. Cole steps in beside me, and his body brushes against mine as he sets the dishes into the water. The clean, fresh sent of him takes over my senses, and my pulse flutters in my throat. Electricity snaps between us, hot, volatile, impossible to ignore. I try not to show a reaction, a difficult task, considering his closeness, the way his body is pressed against mine and lighting me up like I'm one of the July 4th fireworks.

"Do you like living in this big place all by yourself?" I ask, a tactic to get my mind on something else other than his hard body and how every touch makes my sex flutter. I soap the dishes, and water splashes over my shirt. Dammit.

"Yeah, I do. I spend a lot of time on the road with the guys, sharing rooms, meals, and sometimes beds. Here, well, I can just kind of relax, you know?"

I turn to face him, and his gaze rakes over me, lingering on my T-shirt.

I glance down and, thanks to the water I splashed on to myself, see that my bra is visible. Damn, how many times am I going to embarrass myself in front of this guy? I turn from him, hide my chest and say, "If I didn't know better, I'd say you were an introvert."

"What makes you say that?"

"You like to unwind, relax and rejuvenate alone. Nothing wrong with that. I'm an introvert," I say. "I prefer libraries and quiet spaces over parties."

He frowns at me. "Is that why you didn't come to mine?"

He noticed that I hadn't come?

Jeez, I never thought I'd be missed by him, or any other guy. Like I said, men rarely pay me attention.

But Cole was paying attention.

As my gaze trails to Cole, I go on to explain, "Partly. It's not that introverts don't like parties, they just need quiet time to refill the well. I think almost all writers are introverts. Maybe that's why I gravitated toward it after the accident."

Cole tosses the dishcloth over his shoulder and gestures with his head. Something mischievous sparkles in his eyes. "Come on, I want to show you something."

My body instantly goes on high alert. Yes, I've been checking him out like, a lot, but if he thinks I'm going to follow him to his bedroom so he can show me *something*, no matter how much I want to see that *something*, it's not going to happen.

I put my soapy hand on my hip, wetting my T-shirt even more. "What exactly is it you want to show me?"

"Come on, it's a surprise."

I lift my chin. "Forget it. I don't like surprises."

"You'll like this. It's a big one."

Oh, I just bet it is.

His soft chuckle curls around me as I give him the death glare, and when that sexy grin materializes, my nipples harden. "Don't you trust me?"

"No," I shoot back quickly.

He laughs. "Come on, what did I ever do to you?"

"You called me names, Cole. Mean names."

He angles his head, his eyes softening. "I'm sorry. I never meant to be mean...not to you, Nina."

My heart flips at the softness in his voice, the sincerity, the... What the hell? That can't be real. This is Cocky Cole, and he must be playing with me somehow.

I clear my tightening throat. "A little too late, don't you think?"

"Can you please just come with me?"

"No."

"Why not?"

"Because you won't tell me where you're taking me. Lord knows what you have in mind."

That slow-ass sexy grin of his is making me insane, making it harder and harder to keep from just throwing myself at him and letting him take me wherever he wants.

"If you're worried it's my bedroom, it's not," he says.

"I never thought that," I blurt out, but his brow arches, like he's begging to differ. God, am I that obvious? A blush comes over me at my presumptuousness. Just because we kissed doesn't mean he wants me in his bed. A little embarrassed, I say, "Then show me here."

"I can't."

"Well—"

"Nina, are you always so stubborn?"

"That's name calling again, Cole."

"Jesus, woman."

Before I even realize what he's doing, he scoops me up and leaves the kitchen.

"Put me down!" I say and squirm against him.

"You're going to want to stop that."

"I will not stop."

"Nina, I'm getting a hard-on again, so if you're okay with that, go ahead and keep wiggling."

OMFG.

"Oh."

Maybe I wasn't so wrong in thinking he wanted to take me to his bedroom. I mean this is the second time I've felt his hard on tonight. Then again, he's been out of commission for so long, a grilled cheese sandwich would probably turn him on. The steak sure seemed to, and he was pretty excited about his sugary cereal.

"Yeah. Oh."

He carries me down the hall and turns left. Then sets me back on my feet. My eyes go wide as I glance around.

"Cole, this is...amazing!" I walk around the gorgeous dark-wood circular library, a few reclining reading chairs near the window.

"My decorator thought I'd like this."

"Don't you?"

"I don't read much." He jerks his head toward the cabinets. "The shelves are still pretty empty. My decorator put a few books up there on hockey, and a few autobiographies. To give it a bit of a lived-in look. All for show, you know?"

"Oh, man, I could help you fill these shelves." I run my hands over the bare bookcases.

"With *your* books?"

"Oh, hell no. Don't read my books."

"Why not?"

"Just...don't."

He steps up behind me, his body close enough that I feel his heat. "Because of the sex? Are you worried that I'd be peeking inside your brain, learning all about little Nina's wants and desires?"

"No, it's not like that. That's all made up."

"All of it?"

"Of course." I turn to see him. "It's fiction, Cole. No sex is *that* good, and no man is that good."

He opens his mouth like he's about to respond, then his lips curves downward. He bends forward a bit, as he releases a long, slow breath.

Next thing I know, he squares his shoulders and Cocky Cole is suddenly standing before me, a smile on his face, but it's fake, grim, and reminds me more of young Cole, when he'd show up at our house unexpectedly, a little shaken up but trying to hide it.

To all the world, Cole had it all...but now that I think about it, maybe there was more going on in his life than he let on. Perhaps he was suffering from the absence of his mother. What kind of woman just up and left her two kids, right?

"Yeah, you're right. Let's go finish up in the kitchen," he says.

I follow him out and wonder what I said to flip the switch on his mood. To be honest, he's all kinds of contradictions. Wild and alive, and thriving off the crowd at the grocery store, but mellow and...kind, when he's here at home. Most of the time. While I liked seeing him in his element, giving autographs to the crowd and giving credit to his team, I sort of like this side of him a little better. When he allows me small glimpses.

I walk back to the sink as he's putting a glass away, and grab the removable nozzle from the tap. I turn it on, but the damn things shoots out of my hand and soaks me with water. I catch Cole trying to stifle a laugh.

Oh, he thinks this is funny, does he? I wrestle the hose into submission and turn it on him. It's freezing cold, and he yelps and jumps.

"Jesus, Nina!"

"That's what you get for laughing."

He tugs his wet shirt away from his skin, pulls it off, then I'm suddenly not laughing anymore. Nope, not laughing at all. Drooling would probably be a more appropriate word.

But I have no time to think about his hotness when he spins the dishcloth and snaps my ass with it. I yelp, and reach for the hose again, ready to give him another good soaking, when my stupid back twinges.

"Oww," I whimper, and Cole goes perfectly still, every muscle in his body tight.

"Shit, I'm sorry Nina." When I meet his gaze, there is deep-seated concern on his face. "I never thought."

"It's okay, it happens a lot."

His brow pulls together, and he puts his big hands on my shoulders. He dips his head. "What helps?"

"Just rest and heat. I'll have a hot bath when I get home."

He looks past me, out through the kitchen window. "Why don't you get in the hot tub? You can turn on the jets, massage the area."

"I don't have a bathing suit."

"Hang on."

"Cole..." I begin, but my words die when he disappears from the kitchen. If he's digging out some bathing suit left by a former girlfriend, he's wasting his time.

I glance out the window again, take in the warm glow of the pool and the hot tub tucked into the corner at one end of it. It really would be nice to soak in that thing, but that's not going to happen.

I quickly finish washing the dishes, then turn to find Cole coming back, a bathing suit in his hand.

"I think this will fit."

A little white tag is still attached to the one-piece suit. To be honest, I'm surprised it's not a skimpy bikini.

"I bought this for—"

I hold my hand up to stop him. "I don't need the details," I say, and he lifts it for my examination.

"Do you think it will fit?"

I take the suit from him and check the size. It's one size up from what I normally wear, but that's okay with me. I'd rather bigger than smaller. "I think it will."

"You can change in the bathroom if you want. There are towels in the closet. I'll just finish putting the dishes away."

"Thanks," I say. I'm about to head to the bathroom, but turn back to Cole, who is now focused on the dishes.

"Thanks, Cole, for..." I glance at the TV, the dishes from the delicious meal we shared, and the hot tub he's offering me. "All this."

He shrugs. "It's the least I can do for my best friend's kid sister."

"Right," I say at the reminder of who I really am to him. God, I have no right to feel so weirded out. I *am* his best friend's kid sister, and don't want to be anything more than that to him anyway.

I dash to the lavish bathroom, hurry into the suit, and wrap a big, fluffy towel around me.

When I exit, I find the door to the back patio open for me, and I slip out into the warm night. The lights are dim, and I follow the path to the hot tub and climb in. The warm heat wraps around me, and a small moan slips from my lips. Good God, I could totally get used to this kind of luxury.

I fiddle around with the buttons until I figure out how to put the jets on low, and the water sprays against my body, a gentle massage that can only be described as heavenly.

I let my lids fall shut, and try to shut my mind down. Now is not the time to let my piling bills, my hockey series or... Cole invade my thoughts. No, now is the time to clear the mind and just relax.

Seriously though, what would Jess say if she knew I was in Cole's hot tub? I'm going to have to shoot her a text when I get home. She'll want all the juicy details, even if they're rated PG.

"Hey."

I open my eyes to find Cole standing on the edge of the hot tub, a glass of wine in his hand. "I found the wine, thought you might like a glass to help you relax."

I sit up and accept the glass. "Thanks," I say, but my mind isn't on the white wine. No, it's on Cole, dressed only in his board shorts. At least they cover more than his underwear. Not much, but I'll take it.

"I thought I'd go for a swim, stretch out the muscles, but I won't if you just want quiet time out here."

"That's thoughtful, Cole, but this is your place. You can do what you want."

The second those words leave my mouth, he scrubs his hand over his chin—a familiar gesture. His gaze roams over me, and heat creeps up my neck and into my face. I set the wine in the cup holder and sink deeper into the water, as I get pulled into a storm of want and desire. It's dark out here, but I'm not about to take a chance on him seeing the hardening of my nipples.

He walks to the other end of the pool and eases himself in. I reach for my wine and take a sip as he slowly does a few laps. Although I'm not sure he should be exerting the effort when trying to recover from a concussion. I sit up straighter and watch his long, lean body glide through the water. I grip my stemware tighter, and agonize over the riot of need taking up residency in my stomach.

I shouldn't want him as much as I do. This is Cocky Cole, who's reached out and touched more women than Hallmark. But seriously, the last time I was properly laid was...never. I mean, I've had sex, just not good sex, and if his reputation is right, well...he can deliver—big time.

He surfaces in front of the hot tub, and I scramble back into my seat, but my reaction is too slow. He gives me that grin again, the one that says he knows I've been watching, and he doesn't mind.

"I'm not sure you should be exercising," I say.

"I know, but don't worry, I took it easy." He cocks his head, his eyes teasing. "Wait, you *were* worried, right?"

"Of course I was," I say quickly. "You're my brother's best

friend, and even if you were a jerk to me growing up, I don't want anything bad to happen to you."

"I wasn't always a jerk. If I was, you wouldn't have called me that night, remember?"

I cringe at the reminder. "Yeah, I remember."

I'll never forget the night I snuck out and went on a date with Kenny Foster. He was older and had a car. Luke didn't like him, and Mom and Dad would never have allowed me in a car with a guy at fifteen. But he paid me attention when other guys didn't. He was a fighter, a troublemaker, with a bad-ass reputation. No one messed with him, so when the bad boy paid me attention, I fell for it. That night, he drove to the lookout point, and told me to either put out or get out.

I got out—and ran.

"Yeah, thanks for that. I couldn't tell Mom or Dad, and I didn't want Luke to know. He would have gone after him, and I didn't want my brother to get hurt."

"I never told him. I promised you I wouldn't, and I didn't."

I nod, really appreciating that he'd kept my secret. "Kenny ended up with a broken nose somehow, anyway."

"Yeah, I know."

My head jerks back and I catch the small grin on his face. "Wait...*you?*"

"Yeah."

My heart stutters. "That was crazy, Cole! He could have killed you."

"I'm still here, aren't I?"

I shake my head. "I had no idea you did that to him."

"You didn't need to, but *he* needed to know if he ever put his hands on you or put you in that kind of situation again, he was a dead man."

"Thank you," I say quietly, my insides on a roller coaster ride. *Cole went after Kenny for me?*

He goes quiet and glances past my shoulders, his eyes are narrowed, like he's remembering something from long ago. "I'm kind of going insane here, Nina," he says, his honest admission and the stress in his voice taking me by surprise. "I'm not even supposed to be watching TV, but how can I sit around all day and stare at a wall?"

My heart squeezes at his loneliness. "I know exactly what you mean. Cabin fever is real, even in a mansion like this. At least I had Jess to keep me occupied though."

"I'm worried that if I don't swim and keep my muscles warm and active, I'm going to fuck up when I get back."

This vulnerable side of him is messing with me head. I spread my arms over the surface of the hot tub, plucking at the bubbles. "The best place to warm your muscles is in here," I say without thinking.

"Don't mind sharing?"

Oh, shit. A half-naked Cole is going to slide in beside me. *Well done, Nina. Well done.* But how could I *not* invite him in, especially after seeing that little-boy-lost look on his face? This is harder for him than he's letting on, and it breaks my damn heart that he has no one to help him. Where the heck is his father when he needs him most?

"Like I said, this is your place."

He lifts himself from the water, and I take another big gulp of wine as he opens a plastic box beside the hot tub and pulls out a bottle of something.

"What's that?

"Tiger balm. Good for sore muscles."

He uncaps it and adds it to the water, and the scent of aloe vera and wintergreen fill the air. I breathe it in as he climbs in and sits across from me. Our feet touch, and I quickly pull my legs back.

"How's the back?" he asks.

I take a deep breath and let it out slowly. I can do this. It's not like we're in the bath together. People get in hot tubs in groups, for God's sake. No one's having an orgy. Nothing intimate about it.

Then why does being in here with Cole, alone, feel so cozy?

"Good." I spread my arms and brace them on the top of the hot tub. "This is so much better than a hot bath."

"You can use it anytime." A dog barks in the distance, and we both go quiet for a bit. "So, after watching the game tonight, any ideas for a story come to you?"

"No, not yet. I've been in kind of a creative rut lately."

"How come?"

"I don't know," I say. "Sometimes it happens. I have to do other creative things and it helps the muse."

"What do you like to do?"

"Watch movies, cook, just go for walks. Meet Jess for coffee."

He nods and rakes his hair back. "That's pretty much been my life for the last few weeks. Except for the cooking, and coffee with Jess," he adds with a grin. "Maybe we can do those things together. The company would be nice."

I take another sip of wine, and when I start to feel the effects, I set it down. "I better not finish this if I'm going to drive home."

"I was thinking. Why don't you stay here—"

"I can't stay here," I say quickly.

"Why not? I have tons of spare bedrooms, and if you're going to help me cook, and *not* clean," he says with a laugh, "we can start with something simple like breakfast. You might as well stay and avoid the commute. I have a laptop you can use if you want to get some writing done."

"I..." I let my words fall off as I look at him. That little-boy-lost look is there again, giving me the sense that he doesn't just want me to stay, but needs me to stay. He might have been a jerk most of the time, but he was there for me that night when I had no one else to turn to.

"It's not a big deal, Nina. You'd have your own space. But if you don't want—"

"I want."

Oh, how I want...

COLE

Darkness falls over the house, the light from the street filtering in through the crack in the curtains and creating shadows on the walls as I quietly make my way downstairs. Nina had gone to bed long ago, and all my restless tossing and turning, my lust-drunk mind preoccupied with the girl in the room next to me, is doing fuck all to help me sleep.

The fifth step creaks under my bare feet, and I go still for a moment, partly so I don't wake Nina and partly because there's a tug at the base of my neck, a headache brewing. I stand for a moment, until the ache subsides, and glance over my shoulder, listening for sound. It's a pretty rare occasion when I have to worry about waking someone. Other than my sister and Luke, and the party I threw with friends when I first moved in, no one enters my safe zone.

I listen for a few seconds longer and scratch my bare chest. When I'm sure I hadn't woken my guest, aka my newly hired cook—one I want to taste in the worst fucking way—I take the rest of the steps and pad quietly across the wood floor to the kitchen. I slide my finger over the dimmer light, keeping the room shadowy so the bright light doesn't bring back that headache.

I grab the milk from the fridge and my box of Captain Crispies. After pouring a generous amount into the bowl, I dip a spoon in and take a big bite. Fucking delicious. I'd forgotten how much I like this crap.

Instead of sitting, I stand at the big patio door and look out over the pool, lost in thoughts, until footsteps sound behind me. I turn, startled to see a figure in the archway.

Except my alarm turns to lust when Nina comes into the kitchen dressed in the big T-shirt I'd given her for bed. Jesus, talk about hot. Sexy as fuck.

An ache of need twists inside me as my gaze drops, takes in the length of her. The light is dim, but I can still make out her barely there curves that drive me fucking wild, those sleek legs I'd give my nut sac to feel wrapped around me. Fuck, is she wearing any panties under that shirt? Is her sex brushing up against the fabric, no barriers? Is her scent weaving its way through the cotton? Damned if I don't want to find out.

"Oh," she says, startled. "I didn't know you were up."

Oh, yeah, I'm up, in so many fucking ways.

She stares at me though sleepy eyes, then points toward the sink, and it's all I can do not to cross the room and kiss her again. "I was thirsty. I was going to get a glass of water. I hope you don't mind."

"I don't mind. You're welcome to anything, Nina. You don't have to ask permission. While you're staying here, what's mine is yours." Including my bed and body, but I think it's best to leave that unsaid.

"Thanks." She strolls to the cupboard, and I watch her hips sway beneath the too-long T-shirt. My cock stands at attention as she reaches into the cupboard for a glass, and I set my bowl of cereal on the counter, my hunger shifting.

"I hope I didn't wake you."

"No, I was just restless." She shrugs. "Strange place, different bed, you know."

No one has ever slept in the room I put her in—the one directly beside mine. It's one of the smaller rooms, but I wanted to give her the best view of the pool and, well, maybe I wanted her close. Which is all kinds of fucked up. I want her in my bed, yes—and that's all kinds of fucked up, too—but I shouldn't want her close. Sex and intimacy are two very different things, and I don't do the second.

"Too cramped? Bed uncomfortable?"

"The opposite, actually. The room is bigger than my condo, and it's the most comfortable bed I've ever slept in."

"My—"

She holds her hand up to stop me. "Let me guess, your decorator suggested you spare no expense and buy a top-quality mattress." Her voice is full of teasing laughter as she smiles at me, and goddammit, her sweetness is like a sucker punch to the gut.

As air leave my lungs, I try to laugh with her and say, "Yeah."

She leans against the counter and folds her arms across her chest. The innocent movement tugs the T-shirt higher on her legs. "Why did she insist on the best of everything?"

I scrub my hand through my hair, messing it up. "Cause someday my wife would like that? She said something about quality things attracting a quality girl." I laugh. "Stupid."

Nina cocks her head, a challenge in her gaze. "If it was so stupid, why did you agree?"

Good question. "No clue. Maybe because I didn't care one way or another."

"Or maybe in the back of your mind, that's what you want. To settle down with a nice girl."

A half laugh, half snort rumbles in my throat, and Nina

stands still and stares at me like I'm an escaped mental patient. Jesus, she couldn't be more wrong. "I'm an expert asshole, Nina. Assholes don't attract nice girls. Besides, I'm not marriage material." I know nothing about being a good man or father, considering the role model I had. Not to mention I wasn't even enough to keep my mother around. She didn't care enough about me to stay. Yeah, I have the funds and means to search her down now, but why would I bother. Why would I ever go after a woman who didn't want me in her life?

Nope, wasn't going down that path. Don't feel. Don't get hurt. A motto to live by.

"Me neither," she says matter-of-factly.

What the hell? Why would she think that?

Taken aback by her nonchalant statement, I'm about to ask when she redirects with, "Did you have a say in any of the rooms, add any of your own personal touches?"

Right now, there's something I'd like to give my own personal touch.

"Things from your childhood?"

"I'm not much of a decorator, and I don't have a lot of stuff from my childhood."

She angles her head and her eyes narrow, like she's remembering something from our youth. "Why not?"

"I just don't," I say, not wanting to tell her the real reason. My father was a bastard, and I wasn't allowed personal things. I don't want her pity. I don't want anyone's pity.

"So you—" she begins, but I cut her off.

"There was one room I made mine."

She puts her hand on her hip, her look somewhat disgusted. "Let me guess, your boudoir, or rather, dude-oir. Turned it into something that resembles the Playboy Mansion."

"Dude-oir?"

"You know, boudoir but man style."

"Actually no," I say, for reasons I don't understand. I want people to think I'm that guy, to see me as The Playmaker, but for some fucking reason I don't want *her* to. Shit man, she's really getting under my skin, and nothing good can come from that.

"Really?"

"Yeah, really," I say. I never take a woman in my bed. It's either her place or an impersonal hotel. Completely detached, no insight into me. No girl has complained yet. Why would they? As long as they're showered with nice gifts and bragging rights for nailing The Playmaker, they're happy.

Surprise comes over her. "Oh, man cave then? Big-screen TV, big lounge chairs, fridge full of beer?"

"Something like that. I'll show you tomorrow in the daylight. I don't want to turn the lights on tonight. It can set off the headaches."

She mellows, and gives a slow nod of understanding. "Is there anything I can do to help?"

My heart twists up at the sincerity in her voice, the genuine concern. "No, I'm good."

"It was the same for me. Loud sounds, too. That's probably why you were dizzy in the car yesterday. You really should get that muffler fixed." She turns on the tap and lets it run.

"I told you, that's how it sounds, and in case you're still wondering, no, I'm not overcompensating."

As things shift between us, I put my hand over hers to turn the tap off and listen to her throat work as she swallows. With my bare chest pressed against her back, I keep my hand on hers for a moment, let it linger, revel in her softness, the scent of aloe vera and wintergreen in her hair. I put my mouth close to her ear and say, "I have cold water in the fridge." As tension fires between us, and my blood pumps fast, I reluctantly let her hand go, and pad barefoot across the room to pull the jug of cold water out of the fridge.

"I can get it," she says, and hastily crosses the room and reaches for it.

Why does she hate anyone doing things for her? I know she's always been independent, but come on.

She misjudges the distance in the dimly lit room, and her hand hits the jug. Water sloshes over the sides, landing on my bare chest and her nightshirt. She yelps and jumps back.

"Damn that's cold!" she shrieks.

It might be cold, freezing even, but my skin is so fucking hot from pressing against her body, the water practically sizzles on my chest. But I can't think about that. No, I can't think about that at all, not when the prettiest girl I know is standing before me, looking like she's about to take center stage at a wet T-shirt contest. Her breasts are small, like her, but so goddamn perfect, she'd win hands down.

"You, ah, you're all...wet." Christ, way to state the obvious, but my brain isn't quite up to speed right now. I gulp, swallow down the lust building inside me, but it refuses to be leashed in front of Nina. No, as the water spreads across the fabric, exposing her pert nipples, my lust expands, deepens, and demands attention.

"I seem to be wet around you a lot." As the words spill out, her eyes go wide and her sweet mouth forms an O, like what she said held all kinds of sexual connotations, too much, and she wants them back. She stays immobilized like that for a second—long enough for me to visualize my cock sliding between those lush lips—then she rushes on with, "I mean... first the rain, then the sink nozzle and the hot tub...now the water jug." Jesus, she's cute when she's rambling. But I don't want her flustered. Not around me. "I sort of have a wet theme going on around you. I mean..."

I set the jug down, and even though every instinct is

warning me to back off, pack a fucking bag and leave the country, before I get myself into something that can only lead to trouble, I grip the hem of the shirt and pull the cold dampness away from her body.

"You should probably get out of this," I say, and lift it slightly. I run my knuckles over her skin, creating warmth with friction. She's so fucking soft, my cock is clamoring for attention, tenting my boxers in ways that Nina can't seem to ignore, judging by the way she keeps sneaking peeks downward.

Her breathing changes, becomes faster, erratic as I touch her. "It's soaked," she says. "I won't be able to sleep in it now."

"I have more." I nod toward the archway. "You want to come to my room and I'll get you one?" I say, but we both know what I'm really alluding to. Her, in my bed. Me over her. Under her. Inside her.

"I...ah..."

Please say yes. Fuck man, fifty hand jobs aren't going to cut it if she says no.

"I..." she says, and even though she's hesitant, there's no denying the want in her eyes, the need in her body. But I have to hear her say it. I'm a motherfucking prick with a cocky reputation that I do my best to uphold—a detached guy who sleeps with nearly every woman who has ever thrown herself at me, and walks away come morning. But this is Nina, and it has to be her call, and I'm not so sure walking away is going to be that fucking easy.

"Remember our deal?" I ask.

"Deal?"

"You know, tit for tat."

She takes in a quick breath, like she's trying to suck all the air out of the room, then she nods quickly and says, "Yeah."

Testing her, and not sure if what I'm about to do or say is

going to get me a kick in the nuts, I slide my hands up her body, lightly brush my thumbs over her nipples. Fuck, she feels good. When she doesn't pull away, I apply more pressure to her lovely tits that my mouth is watering to taste.

"You said there would only be the tat part," I remind her. "You were pretty adamant about that."

"Yeah, I remember," she whispers on a moan, and arches into me, her needy body betraying her completely, and I fucking love it. But I'm not about to take her until I'm one hundred percent certain it's something she wants too.

I lightly cup her breasts, massage gently, and her moan of want seeps under my skin and strokes my thickening cock. Her small hands go to my shoulders, her fingers burn my flesh as she explores my muscles.

She wets her lips, a familiar habit when she's needy. "Cole," she murmurs, her head falling back, her long hair splaying over her shoulders. Goddammit, lust looks so good on her, and my fucking cock is done for.

"Yeah?"

"I...I might want the other part, too."

"Say it, Nina." I reach up and give a slight tug on her hair, simply because I like the way it forces her mouth to open for me. "Tell me what you want."

Her eyes meet mine, her pupils dilating. "You know what I want. Don't make me say it."

I run my hands over her curves, pull her against me, let her feel my hard cock through my boxers. "If you can write dirty words in a book, why can't you say them?"

"It's...I can't. Wait, how do you know what I write in my books?"

Ignoring her question, and wanting her to shed every and any insecurity with me, I say, "You can say whatever you want in front of me, Nina. We don't even like each other, remember? No sense in worrying about getting embarrassed or offended. I'm a prick, you know that, and you know I'm only out for a good time, so it's safe to say things to me that might not go over well with someone else."

"I'm only out for a good time, too," she says.

"You do this kind of thing all the time, then?"

"Yeah."

Liar.

I slide my hand back up her body, coming perilously close to her nipples but never touching. "Then tell me. Tell me what you want."

She's quiet for second, like she's tossing something around in her mind, then a change comes over her. "You're right. We don't like each other much, and I guess if you want me to speak frankly, Jess put the idea in my head that we should hate fuck."

Holy Fuck. Her bold words catch me by surprise. I know I'm not good enough for her, and I know she's an innocent, but if she's asking me for this, I have to give it to her. I'd give sweet Nina anything she ever wanted—other than my heart, that is. But it's not my heart she wants, it's my body, and I'm *more* than willing to give her that.

"Hate fuck, huh?" I wrap her hair around my hand three times, and rub my cock harder against her. "When anger and desire mix."

"Yeah, something like that."

"And you think this is a good idea."

"I think we're past the point of good ideas, Cole" she says, and moves her body, grinds against my rock-hard cock, the sexy move prompting me into action.

Desperate to taste her again, I dip my head and capture her mouth with mine. She goes up on her toes, and I let go of her hair, slide my hands around her body and lift her. I back her up, until she's sitting on the kitchen island, and I widen her legs to position my body in between.

I put my hands on her legs and slowly slide them up. Her eyes are wide, filled with desire, and it rocks my fucking world.

"How much did you hate me growing up?"

"A lot," she whispers. "You were always there, everywhere I turned. In my space, in my head, driving me crazy."

"Did you want to hit me, throw things at me, scratch my eyes out?"

"All of the above," she says, and wiggles restlessly beneath my invading fingers.

I touch her lacy panties. "You always had such a smart mouth on you, Nina, and that fucking death glare." I chuckle. "It made me want to hit something—or better yet, rip something." I grip the thin lace on her panties and give them a good hard tug. The stitching tears, and she gasps.

"Yeah, like that." I ease the material away and toss it aside, giving myself full access to her sweet sex.

She runs her nails over my back and scores my skin, deep enough to leave her mark on me, but that's okay because I want it. "That's all you got? I thought you said you hated me," I taunt.

"Still do," she says, and drags more skin. I fucking love it.

"When you would shoot your mouth off to me, this is how I wanted to shut you up." I press my lips to hers for a hard, punishing kiss. She kisses me back, and I thrust my tongue into her mouth, taste her deeply. Jesus, there is so much volatile heat between us, it's sparking something inside me, igniting things I'd never felt before—shouldn't be feeling now.

Shit. Why do I find it so hard to keep my shields up with her? If I knew what was good for me, I'd end this now. But when was the last time I did something that was good for me?

I pull her closer, kiss her harder, and when she gives a low, needy moan, I inch back, and we're both breathless as we stare at each other. I take in the anger mixed with desire dancing in her eyes, and I damn near shoot off in my shorts. I suck air, take deep, serrated breaths as I think about fucking her senseless, until I'm the only man she's ever able to think about.

"When you called me names, I wanted to grab you by the balls, show you exactly who you were messing with." She puts her hand on my stomach and slides it down until she's cupping my sac through my shorts. I suck in a fast breath, prepared to be punished, but she explores me gently. Thank fuck.

"You know what else I wanted to do to shut you up when you shot your goddamn mouth off?" I say.

"No, what?" she asks, her eyes alive, full of excitement as she slides her hand inside my boxers and takes my cock into her palm. Jesus, I love seeing her like this.

"I wanted to push you to your knees and put my cock in here." I shove my thumb into her mouth and she sucks on it. Hard. I feel the pull all the way to my dick.

Motherfucker.

I pull my thumb out and she says, "When you used to walk around like the cock of the walk, like I was just a little girl you could so easily overlook, know what I wanted to do to *you*?"

"Throw something at me?" I gently bite her bottom lip, and she runs her hand over my cock, like she's checking the length and girth, weighing it in her palm. Damn, I love the way she's blatantly examining me, not bothering to hide her curiosity or excitement at what she's discovering.

"Yeah. I wanted to throw something at you," she agrees.

I push against her hand and groan. "Like what, one of those books you were always reading? Or maybe it was your fist. Did you want to throw your fist at me, Nina?" I take in the heat in her eyes, all her creamy skin and sexy curves, and that's when it hits me. "Did you want to throw *yourself* at me, prove you weren't a little girl to be overlooked?"

"Yeah, I did, Cole. You were a real bastard."

"Still am," I say, then brush my finger along her slit. A hard quiver moves through her and her eyes roll backward. I groan at her responsiveness and her chest heaves.

She grips my hair and tugs. "I wanted to show you exactly what you were missing out on."

I dip my finger inside her tight pussy, and she's so wet and wanting, I nearly fucking sob with pleasure. "Do it, Nina. Make me pay for overlooking you. Show me what I was missing out on," I say, even though I'd never in a million years discount someone like her. She was just off limits. Still is.

I can't even count the amount of black eyes Luke handed out back in high school. If a guy so much as looked at his sister the wrong way, or the right way, he was done for. But she was so goddamn pretty, how could we *not* look? I guess I was just better at hiding it through the hateful teasing.

I couldn't risk losing Luke. He was the best friend I ever had, still is, and the one thing he never knew was that by always keeping his door open for me, he saved me more times than imaginable.

Then why are you seducing his sister?

"You first," she says, and when she wets her bottom lips, I lose track of my thoughts. Truthfully, my mind is so fucking blown at this wild, sexy side of her, it's all I can do to keep my shit together. "Show me," she says. "Push me to my knees and show me how you wanted to shut me up."

My cock throbs, my whole body on fire, eager to do just that.

"I need this off you. Now," I say and tug on her wet shirt.

She lifts her arms for me, and I peel the wet material over her head. My heart beats triple time when I glimpse her gorgeous body. I stand back for a second, and if she didn't need me to do things to her, I'd spend the rest of the night just looking at her.

"Cole," she pleads, and reaches for me. Her warm fingers touch my jaw, trail to my shoulders, to pull me to her.

I lift her from the counter, put my hands on her shoulders, and push until she's on her knees before me. Jesus Christ, this is my every fantasy come true. My cock throbs against my boxers, and she runs her fingers over it.

"I heard a rumor," she says, her voice hot and thick with lust, but also with a hint of teasing.

"What did you hear?"

"That you're as fast as a cannon on the ice, but the real reason they call you Cannon is because you're packing."

"Is that why you've been checking me out these last couple day?"

"Maybe."

"They call me Cannon because it's my last name, but if you think there's another reason, feel free to find out for yourself and see firsthand what I'm working with."

I grip the counter, and hold on as she fingers the elastic band on my boxers and slowly drags them down. Her breath catches on a gasp when my cock pops free and hits her mouth.

"So it's true," she says, those desirous blue eyes of hers meeting mine. She turns her attention back to my cock and stares at it, like it's a toy she's too afraid to play with.

My dick pulses under her examination, grows harder, and the room sways around me, but it has nothing to do with my concussion.

"Jesus fuck, Nina, please," I moan. "Touch me. Take me into your mouth."

She takes me into her hands, slides them along the length of me, then parts her lips as she leans forward. Her wet, hot mouth wraps around me, and she takes me to the back of her throat. Perfect, so goddamn perfect, I have to clench my jaw to stop from shooting off.

"Mmm," she moans, and the vibration goes right through me. She inches back, sweeps her tongue out and licks the pre-cum dripping from my slit. Jesus, that's sexy as hell. She runs her tongue along my length, teasing me with her warm heat, and my cock pulses hard.

She gives me a coy look. "Is this how you envisioned it, Cole? Me on my knees, your cock in my mouth, anything to shut me up?"

"Yeah, this is it exactly," I say, and grab the back of her head as she opens her mouth wide, waiting for me to feed her my cock. I move my hips, slowly inch into her waiting mouth, and blood pounds hard in my ears as I hit the back of her throat. My fuck, I've never felt anything better. She works me with her mouth, and her small hand cups my sac for a soft massage. But I'm so damn close, my balls tighten, and she gives a little whimper when I growl.

"Keep it up and I'm going to come in your mouth."

That only seems to drive her wilder, but I'm not ready to come, and when I do, I want to be inside her. "Nina," I murmur, and pull her off me. She goes back on her legs and wipes her mouth with the back of her hand. Sexy as fuck.

"Yeah?"

"Come here. There are things I need to do to you." Her eyes go wide as I reach for her and pull her to her feet. "Leg's around me," I say as I grip her ass and lift her onto my hips.

Without too much thought, I carry her to my bedroom and kick the door shut behind us. We're the only ones in the house, so it's not like we need the privacy, but for some reason I want the door closed, want to lock the rest of the world out while I have Nina in my bed.

She steals a quick glance around, and I look at the room

from her eyes. Pretty masculine, sparsely decorated with dark wood furnishing, and a light grey paint on the walls. The blinds are pulled, draping us in darkness.

"I want to see you," I say, and reach for the dimmer lights, giving a silent prayer of thanks that my decorator suggested them for every room. She did a few things right, that's for sure.

"I want to see you too," she whispers against my throat, her breath hot on my neck.

The dimmer makes a humming sound as I turn it up a notch, just enough so that I can see her eyes, her expression, her beautiful body. I carry her to the bed, gently set her down, and give her shoulders a little nudge. She falls back onto my mussed sheets, and her hair splays. Jesus, she looks so good, so right, invading my personal space like that.

"Show me what I was missing, Nina. Make me regret being such a bastard to you."

She pushes the blankets away and repositions herself on the bed until she's sprawled out on *my* side of the mattress. I'd have taken offense, felt violated, if it were any other girl infringing upon my space. Then again, I've never brought a girl to this room before.

"If you were nicer, you might have had some of this." She bends her knees and lets them fall open.

My heart crashes, and blood pulses behind my eyes as need surges inside me. I glimpse her pretty pussy, her wet desire glistening in the dim light. Her hand goes to her mouth. She wets her finger then rubs it over her hard nipple.

"Yeah, but then we'd never get to hate fuck, and this is kind of fun, don't you think?"

She crooks her finger. "What I think is that you should come here and show me some of your plays."

Her teasing words hit like a hard body check—a reminder that she's just another girl who wants something from me.

But that's a good reminder, and I'm actually grateful for it. I strengthen the shield around my heart and climb between her legs, and spread them wider.

"I think you'll like this play," I say, and flatten myself over her. I lower my mouth to her throat and run my tongue along her flesh, until I find a sensitive spot that has her squirming. Her hands race over my back, touching every inch of flesh, like she can't get enough. Her hard nipples press against my chest, abrade me as I begin a slow path downward,

I find those hard buds with my mouth and suck them in, one by one, giving them a tongue bath, followed by a gentle nibble. Her soft bedroom moans and hard breaths urge me on, and I kiss a path to the hot spot between her legs. Her sex is wide open, completely on display for me, and I take a moment to look at her. She has the most beautiful pussy I've ever set eyes on.

"Please," she begs, the need in her voice—need for *me*—fucking me up just a little.

"You ready for my next play?" I ask, working overtime to keep my shit together when all I want to do is go at her, to keep the need—far too many years in the making—at bay so I can make this good for her.

"Yes," she cries out and lifts her hips, until her sex bumps against my face.

"Such a needy girl," I say, and flick my tongue out to taste her. The world spins around me, as her flavor dances on my tongue. Desperate for a deeper taste, I lick her from bottom to top, and circle her inflamed clit until she's writing beneath me.

"Cole," she murmurs, and bucks against my mouth. I center in on her hot core of nerves as I push one finger insider her. She's so fucking snug, I'm not sure my cock will fit without hurting her.

Her muscles tremble around my finger, and I move it in

and out, taking note of her every movement, her every moan and shudder.

"Yes," she rasps as I work her with my tongue and finger, wanting to stay between her legs for the rest of the night, wanting to make her come over and over and over again for me so I can still taste her on my tongue a week from now. "Fuck me, please."

Well, look at that. The shy romance writer has a dirty mouth after all. It thrills me that she's shedding her inhibitions.

"I will," I say, "but first I want you to come in my mouth. Think you could do that for me, Nina?"

I insert another finger, for a snug fit, and she moves against me. "That's it. Fuck my fingers," I say as my cock aches to get inside. I slide my tongue over her clit, changing the pressure as I penetrate her deeper. Her hands grip the sheet beneath her and a little whimpering sound catches in her throat.

I grin to myself. Pretty BallerNina is coming undone for me, and I don't even want to examine how that's making me lose my damn mind.

Her muscles clench, and I continue to push into her, but she's coming so hard I think I might break a finger. I keep fingering her, despite the tightness, wanting to draw out her release until she's wrung out and strung out. We're both breathing like mad when her tremors subside, and the glassy look in her eyes does the craziest things to me.

"Cole," she says, and blinks rapidly. "I can't believe...that was...I...wow."

What, has no man ever taken care of her like that before? Brought her to orgasm? I feel equal measures of disgust and rage. I hate that no man has ever done right by her, but then again, I hate the thoughts of another man's hands touching her.

I rub her pussy, pet it gently, and then climb up her body, peppering her with soft kisses as I go. I settle over her, pin her with my weight, locking her beneath me. Tonight, I want to take her like this so I can see her face when she comes for me again, but tomorrow...well, tomorrow, I might just flip her over and tie her to my bedposts.

Wait, there isn't going to be a tomorrow.

Her legs go around my back, her feet pushing against my ass, her body telling me what she needs without words. I reach into my nightstand and grab a condom.

Nina goes quiet—too quiet—as I pull it on.

I slide back over her, hold the sides of her head and examine the unease in her eyes. "You okay?" I ask. Jesus, is she having second thoughts? If so, now is the time to say it.

She blinks, and when her eyes open again, lust replaces the discomfort. "I'm good," she whispers, and inches up to kiss me. My lips meet hers and all thoughts, except getting inside her, fade away.

I move my hips, position my cock at her entrance. Her body opens for me, and in one quick thrust, I seat myself high inside.

Motherfucker, she's as tight as a goddamn glove, but I somehow knew we'd be the perfect fit.

"Fuck," I whisper into her mouth as her moans of joy wraps around me. "You feel so good."

She moves her hips, and I move with her, a little thrown off at just how right this feels.

"I never thought we'd fit," she whispers. "I was a bit worried."

Ah, was that the apprehension I felt in her when I reached for the condom?

"I would never hurt you," I whisper against her damp forehead.

We move together, and she arches up, like she needs me

deeper. For some reason, I need that too. I power into her, and her moans ignite everything inside me. We create a rhythm of longtime lovers, lost in this all-consuming need between us. I inch back to see her face, take in the flush on her cheeks as her body sucks me in harder. Her fingers curl in my hair as I ride her with long, deep strokes. Her hot, wet sheath rubs my cock as I slide in and out, and I slip a hand between our bodies to stroke her clit.

"So good," she whimpers.

I angle my body for deeper thrusts, and press my thumb to her clit, applying more pressure.

"Cole," she says, and then continues to call out my name, over and over again. Fuck, I love hearing it on her lips.

"You like that?" I ask, as every ounce of blood in my body rushes to the swollen shaft buried deep inside my sweet Nina.

"Yes, please..." she says, and I pump faster, maddening little thrusts that send us both to the edge and leave us hovering. Knowing it's time to fall over, I pour everything into fucking her, and I'm rewarded when her muscles squeeze around my cock,

Her mouth opens but no words form, and when I see her desire, it's all I can do to hang on. Her hot cum sears my cock, but it's the gentle kiss she presses to my lips that sends me freefalling without a net.

"Nina," I murmur, and bury my face in her neck. She rocks with me, her sexy moans stroking my dick harder as I let go. She gasps slightly as my cock pulses with each hard release.

"I feel you." She runs her hands over me, the connection unlike anything I've ever felt before. "You feel so good."

I still high inside her and breathe hard against her throat. Her hands move over me, her touch and exploration a little slower, a little softer. "Mmm," she moans as she palms my muscles.

In no hurry to move, I remain inside her. The frightening thing is, I normally pull out and get out. Tonight though, I'm far too content to stay right where I am.

Needing to lighten things, I say, "Like what you feel?"

"Cole," she says breathlessly, as I reluctantly slide out of her. Settling beside her, I look at her face, see no humor. No, what I see is warmth, a woman sated, my best friend's sister, who has gotten under my skin for a long-ass time now.

"Nina." I pull her to me, and our lips meet. We kiss deeply, the exchange sweet and intense—mind-blowing.

When we finally break apart, I push her hair from her forehead and look her over. As a million thoughts attack me at once, something inside me comes unhinged, the latch released from a gate, and I draw in a quick breath. Truthfully, I don't remember kissing, or hate fucking, ever feeling so intimate before.

Jesus Christ, I was living a perfectly content life, one where I could keep my shit shut down, on lockdown behind a barricade where it belonged. But being with Nina is different, goddamn perfect, and that's a big fucking problem for me.

NINA

Call it hate fucking, or call it desire mixed with rage. Heck, call it whatever you want. But never, not once in my life, have I felt so desired or wanted by anyone. The way Cole fought for his restraint so he could see to my needs first, well, that seriously told me how much he wanted me, hungered for me. Most guys barely spare me a glance, are always overlooking me, but last night, I had all of Cole's attention, and I liked it, a lot. Too much, probably.

As a ridiculous thrill goes through me, I reach across the bed—and when I find it empty, I knife up, a chill going up my spine as every insecurity I've ever had comes crashing over me.

Why would he just up and leave in the middle of the night? Had he gotten what he wanted and walked away? Cripes just seconds ago I was living in bliss, now I'm second-guessing everything. And that's crazy, because this is Cole, and even though he'd just given me the best sex of my life, I can't forget that this is *still* just sex. Heck, he had a stack of condoms in his drawer. He's good at this sex stuff, has a harem of women falling all over him, probably because he's a master at pleasure and is working with some top-notch equipment.

So even though he'd put my needs first, it doesn't really mean anything. And truthfully, I don't want more. This is just about scratching an itch, and if he wants to sneak out under the cover of darkness, leaving me in his bed alone, then I shouldn't have a problem with that.

Then why do I?

Goddammit, Nina, get it together. It'll be a cold day in hell before you fall for this guy.

I think about calling Jess to come pick me up before I get myself into trouble here, but a noise in the adjoining bathroom gains my attention. I slip from the bed, grab the shirt Cole had been wearing earlier and tug it on. I breathe in his scent as I tiptoe across the floor. The sound comes again, and this time I recognize it. Cole is sick.

My heart races, panic welling up inside me.

"Cole," I say as I try the door and find it open, guilt niggling at me for thinking the worst of him. But he'd teased and tormented me for so many years, it was a logical jump.

"Don't come in. I'm sick," he says on a groan.

I don't normally like anyone around me when I'm sick either, but he has a concussion and needs my help. I slowly open the door, and when I see him on the floor, completely bereft and alone, my throat tightens. He's dressed only in his boxers, and has a thin sheen of sweat on his body as he rests his head on the toilet bowl, looking spent and completely worn out. How long had he been in here?

"You should have woken me," I say, and scramble to his side.

"Why? I'm not your responsibility," he says, shooting my earlier words back at me. I wince slightly, realizing how cold they must have sounded to Cole after he'd just finished telling me he was sorry he wasn't there for me after my fall.

Well dammit, he has no one else and I plan to be here for him whether he likes it or not.

I grab a cloth from the closet, run it under the cold water, and sit cross-legged beside him. I put my hand on his forehead to check for fever. His skin is clammy, his eyes sunken into the sockets, and it physically hurts me to see him like this.

"I don't want you to see me like this," he says, like he'd just read my mind.

"Too bad."

"I want you to leave, Nina," he says, putting more force in his voice, but he's so weak it comes out strained. "I can take care of myself."

"I know you can, but now I'm taking care of you. So shut up and get over yourself already."

"That mouth of yours," he murmurs, and despite the situation, we both grin at the reminder of what we'd done only hours earlier. I pat his forehead with the cool cloth and he moans. "Fuck, that feels good. But you need to get some rest."

"I'm fine, now just relax and let me take care of you." I dab his head some more, then run the cloth over his neck and shoulders. "This is my fault, anyway. So I deserve to be awake with you."

Eyes glassy and dazed seek out mine. "How is it your fault?"

Really? Like he doesn't know. "I seduced you and I probably shouldn't have. You need rest and relaxation, not me 'throwing myself' at you." I do air quotes around the words we'd used in our sexy banter.

One corner of his mouth turns up, and he squints at me in the dim light. "And here I thought I was the one who'd seduced *you*."

"Nope, I was the one who said we should hate fuck."

He groans. "Yeah, but I'd been thinking about fucking you since...well, since you showed up at my door and asked me for help."

A giggle I have absolutely no control over rips from my lungs. I have no idea why I'm laughing. It's an odd reaction in the face of his admission, but I can't seem to help myself. Maybe it's knowing how much he wanted me, maybe it's relief that he hadn't run out under the cover of darkness. Either way, it's inappropriate; so is the closeness I feel with him as we sit here in the dark on the bathroom floor.

Careful, Nina, you're here for hockey lessons and a little sex. Nothing more.

He grins. "That's funny?"

"No, I just get giddy when I'm tired."

"I remember. I used to hear you and Jess laughing late at night when I stayed over. I always wondered what you guys were laughing at."

"Probably you."

"Oh, thanks."

"And how much of an ass you were," I add for good measure.

"You can leave anytime now," he says, but he's smirking at me, and he's resting one hand on mine, his thumb caressing my wrist. Does he even know he's doing that?

It's hard to believe the chemistry between us, the way we instantly wanted each other after not seeing each other for the last few years. Then again, I'd be telling a big-ass lie if I said I'd never noticed him before. God, how many times did he walk around our house half naked? I hated it.

Oh, how I hated it.

"Stop talking and just relax," I say.

He puts his hand to his stomach, and his fingers curl as his entire body tenses.

"Shit, Nina, I'm going to be sick again. You need to leave."

Like hell I'm leaving him like this. I hold the cloth to his head as he leans over the toilet and heaves.

When he stops, I flush the toilet, rinse the cloth again and press it to his forehead.

"Thanks," he whispers weakly.

"Don't talk, just rest."

"I'm just—"

"Shh..." I whisper, and brush his hair back with the cloth. I check his pulse, finding it beating double time. "You need to go to the doctor tomorrow," I say.

"I actually have a checkup at noon."

"Good, I'll take you."

He opens his mouth like he's about to protest, then heaves again. When he finishes, I urge his head away from the toilet and reposition myself beside him against the wall, so he can rest on my shoulder. We stay like that for a bit, then he heaves once more. I wait a long while, and once I'm sure he's cleared his stomach, I slowly stand.

Tired green eye full of something I'd never seen before, something that very much resembles vulnerability, blink up at me.

"Where are you going?" he asks, a strange edge of panic in his voice as it breaks.

"To get you a glass of water, I'll be right back." Guilt eats at me as I dash downstairs to the kitchen. Cole should have been resting, not having crazy monkey sex with me. I grab a glass, and take the water jug off the counter and fill it. I put it back into the fridge and hurry back to him.

His smile is weak as I enter, but the way he's so happy to see me gives me a weird title thrill.

"Rinse your mouth with this."

He takes the glass and does as I say, then lets his head roll back and moans.

"Headache?"

"It's subsiding."

"Stomach?"

"Much better," he whispers into the darkness.

I run the cloth under cold water again and dab his body with it.

"That feels so good, Nina."

I slide back in beside him and we rest against the wall. I take his hand and hold it, wanting him to know he's not alone. I brush my finger over his hard calluses, note the strength in his hand. He's a big tough guy, probably the toughest guy I know, yet the way he touched me last night... So sexy and gentle.

We're quiet for a long time, then I break it and whisper, "Want to hear something messed up?"

He nudges me with his shoulder, and I'm relieved to see him coming around. "Always."

"When I was a little girl, I liked getting sick. Jess had the flu once, and I was determined to go to her place to catch it."

He chuckles, and rests his head back on my shoulder. "Yeah, that's messed up."

"It was the only time Mom was nurturing. She would stay home from work, put cool cloths to my forehead, make me my favorite kind of soup, and even snuggle me on the sofa. Tomorrow, I'll make *your* favorite soup," I say, but he goes completely quiet.

"Will you snuggle me on the sofa, too?"

There is a new strain in his voice, and I fear he's going to be sick again. I angle my head to see him, and his eyes are squeezed shut, like he's working hard not to fall apart. Gone is the Cocky Cole Cannon the world goes crazy for. In his place is another version of him, one who, on a few occasions when he didn't think I was watching, I glimpsed in my youth.

I have no idea what's going on, so I simply link my fingers through his and give him a moment. Silence falls heavy, the only audible sounds in the bathroom our breathing, and I try to quiet mine even more, not wanting to disturb him as he takes a few deep breaths. Unease and apprehension weave their way through my blood, and I want to ask if he's okay, but his lips open and his gaze meets mine.

"I'm sorry you had to get sick for attention, Nina. That's...not right."

My throat tightens at the somber way he's looking at me. "It's okay. I know Mom and Dad loved Luke and me, they were just busy with their careers. If I ever had kids, I'd want to be more involved on a daily basis, not just when they were sick. Not that I plan to have kids. I don't, but still..."

There's a strange hardness in Cole's eyes as she stares at me, and I clamp my mouth shut, wishing I hadn't just said that. Cole doesn't need to know those kinds of details about me. Why is it I don't seem to have any filters around him?

"Did they take care of you after your injury?" he asks, his voice a little rough.

"Jess mostly did. Maybe because I was older and they thought I could take care of myself."

"I wish I could have been there," he says quietly, and spreads the rag over his whole face, so I can't see his expression.

I take deep breaths, fight against the way my heart is slamming in my chest. "When you were little, did your dad take care of you and your sister like this when you were sick?" I ask for lack of anything else.

"Yeah, something like that," he answers.

I don't miss the strain in his voice, and can't help but think all this talk about my mom has him thinking of his own, and how she walked out on them when they were young? From what I know about his dad, he was very doting. Luke said he was at every single hockey practice and game, which makes me wonder why his dad isn't helping him now when he really needs it. Cole might have a million fans, but in situations like this, he's truly alone, and that guts me.

Deciding to change the subject, I say, "Next time we have sex, we need to take it easy."

He slowly slides the cloth from his face, and his lips quirk at the corners. "There's going to be a next time?"

"I think we have a lot of childhood hate issues to work though, don't you?" I say.

"Yeah, tons."

I nod and snuggle against him. "Good, then it's settled. While you're recuperating and I'm getting hockey lessons, we'll keep doing this. But next time we need to set a slower pace."

"Not sure that's possible," he murmurs softly, quietly, exhaustion clearly overtaking him

We go silent again, just sit in the dimly lit room for the next ten minutes, both comfortable enough with each other that we don't need to fill the space with words. Odd, really. How did we get here so fast when it was just the other day I was telling Jess how much I hated him?

Every few minutes, I turn to check on him and when his body cools, I push to my feet and hold my hand out.

"Let's get you back to bed. Get a few more hours' rest before morning."

He stares at my hand. "If you try to lift me, we're both going to end up on our asses."

"I'm stronger than I look, you know."

"I know you are," he says quietly, sadly, and I suddenly get the sense that's he's no longer talking about my physical strength.

He pushes to his feet, and I slide my arm around him to help him to the sink so he can brush his teeth and rinse his mouth. Once done, I guide him to the bed and my mind goes back to our childhood. Cole was at the house a lot, but I guess I never realized how much he'd been observing, knowing I had to do the bulk of the cooking and cleaning, while Luke took care of other chores, like the lawn and garbage. I didn't even realize he could hear Jess and me in my bedroom. I never really thought the self-centered hockey player had paid that much attention to me. I always thought he was too much into himself to notice, but now I'm not so sure. Maybe he's a little more complex than I ever realized.

I help him to the bed and he slides in. As I fix the blankets around his body, he tugs my hand. "If you keep taking care of me like this, I might start faking sick, too."

I laugh. "I'm pathetic, aren't I?"

"No, Nina. You're actually all kinds of sweet."

"You're just saying that so I'll take you to the doctor's and make you your favorite soup tomorrow."

He snuggles in. "Yeah, you're probably right," he says, and falls asleep just like that. I stare at him for a few minutes, and his hands slips from mine as his soft snoring sounds fill the room. I consider leaving, and going back to my room next to his, but decide against it. If he wakes up sick again, I'd hate for him to think I'd abandoned him.

I slide in beside him, careful not to wake him, and snuggle close, offering him my body heat.

The next thing I know, the light slanting in through the curtain pulls me awake.

I blink, rub the sleep from my eyes...and turn to find Cole watching me. He looks wide awake and his hair is wet from a shower. The fresh scent of soap reaches my nose.

"How long have you been awake?" I ask.

"Maybe you should be asking how long I've been watching you sleep?"

"Creeper much?"

"I've been called worse."

"I'm sure." I look him over. "I'm glad to see you're feeling better." I steal a glance at the clock to see that it's nearing eight. "Why are you up so early though?" I prop up on my elbows and look him over.

"I was sleeping well, until I woke and heard you snoring." He puts his hand to his forehead. "All that loud noise was bringing on another headache."

"I do not snore," I say, and lift my pillow, threatening to hit him, but I won't. He was too sick last night, and I don't want to do anything to bring the nausea back.

"I thought someone started my Mustang and was backing it out of the driveway," he says, continuing to goad me. Clearly, now that he's well, Cocky Cole is back, ready to duel.

"Fine, you can make your own breakfast and drive yourself to your appointment." I roll over, and put the pillow over my head. "I guess you haven't changed at all," I mumble to myself.

"Ah, come on, Pretty BallerNina," he says.

"Cole..." I warn, a tightness in my gut. "I thought we were past the name-calling."

He takes the pillow from me and pulls my hair from my neck. The second he presses a soft kiss to my flesh, a shudder races through me.

"But you *are* pretty, Nina."

He thinks I'm pretty.

OMG, get over yourself, Nina. You're not twelve.

"I was never a ballerina," I counter.

"I know, you were just as graceful as one, though."

"I hated you calling me that."

"I know."

"Asshole."

He grins at me "How about tonight, when we're back in this bed, you can tell me all the names you secretly called me. Work out some of those hate issues."

I slide onto my back and he smiles down at me. "I like the idea of that," I say, wanting to do it right now.

As if reading my mind, a sexy, crooked grin that bring back some of the more pleasant memories from last night spreads across his handsome face. But then I remember the consequences—Cole over the toilet, sick.

"We need to get you ready for your appointment."

He looks me over. "But there are so many other things I want to do right now."

Yeah, me too.

"We're not doing anything until you see your doctor."

"Hey, you're the one who said we'd be doing it again."

"I didn't mean right now. You need a good breakfast, and rest."

"But these are the only things I want to put in my mouth right now, and I promise to pace myself." He pulls my blankets down and places the softest kiss on my nipple. A groan catches in my throat.

His chuckle curls around me. "Like that, do you?"

"Of course I like that." I sink into my pillow as he licks and nips at my nipple until it's rock hard. His hand finds my other breast and gently massages it. He pushes against me, and his arousal brushes my outer thigh. I slide my hand down and capture his long length, and his deep groan fills me with satisfaction.

I know better than to be doing this, and by rights I should put a stop to it right now. And I will, in just a minute.

He draws my nipple deeper into his mouth and runs his tongue around it.

"Cole," I groan as my entire body lights up. "We need to stop," I say, and move beneath him, my words contradicting my actions.

"I know," he says around my nipple, and the vibration of his voice goes straight to my sex. When he finally breaks the contact, he grins and says, "It's just that I never got to spend enough time with these last night."

"Boob man, are you?"

"Only when it comes to you, Nina," he says, and when I meet his gaze, I expect to see humor—but what I see instead surprises the hell right out of me.

How is it with one look he can make me feel so special? Believe me, I've seen the big-breasted women he goes out with. Mine certainly pale in comparison. Like I said, I have the body of a twelve-year-old boy.

"But mine are…"

"Are what?" he presses

"I'm just…small."

He makes a sound, a snort of sorts. "Jesus, girl. Do you have any idea how perfect these are?" He cups my breasts, brushes his thumbs over my puckered nubs. "The way they fit my hands and mouth…Christ." His lids fall slowly as he gives a slow shake of his head.

I stare at him. Is he messing with me or is he serious? I'm going with the former, considering he's The Playmaker. I've seen the way he acts around the bunnies. A guy like him knows all the right things to do and say to get the results he wants—a woman in his bed.

Doesn't matter. I'm in this for me, too. Some more excellent sex until hockey season is over and I have my plot.

He shifts beside me, and a flash of red on his nightstand catches my attention. I look past his broad shoulder, pitted and scarred from years of hockey, and what I see has my heart jumping into my throat.

My jaw drops open and heat crawls into my face as I sit up, moving a little away from Cole as I press my back against the headboard.

"What?" Cole asks.

My gaze goes from the nightstand to Cole back to the

nightstand again. I shake my head and my hair tickles my breasts as it falls forward and brushes over my flesh.

"You've got to be kidding me," I say, never more mortified in my life. I grab the sheet and cover myself, but the point is moot. Cole has been inside my body. And from what I see on his nightstand, he's also been in my...head.

He turns to see what I'm looking at, and then looks back at me. "Oh, yeah," he says, his expression neutral, like he reads romance books all the time.

"Oh yeah? That's it? That's all you have to say?" I question, my voice rising, getting far too close to hysteria. "You have every single book I've ever written on your nightstand, and all you have to say is, 'oh yeah'?"

He angles his head and looks me over, his eyes—which I wouldn't mind gouging out at the moment—full of confusion. "Why are you so upset?"

"Because...because..." I stumble as my mind races at what feels like a personal invasion. Did he buy them so he could make fun of me? I know how everyone laughs and makes fun of the romance industry. So help me God, if he says one derogatory word, or throws a sex scene in my face, I'm leaving and never coming back. Hockey series be damned. I don't need to eat that badly.

"You already said everything is fiction," he begins. "Sex isn't that good, and no guy is that good, right?"

I glare at him as past hurts come back to haunt me. "You shouldn't have bought them."

"Why not?"

"They're not for..." Oh, God, none of this is coming out right.

"Guys?"

"Right, they're not for guys. Especially guys like you."

He sits up straighter, clearly offended. "What's that supposed to mean?"

Desperate to escape before he does or says something that will cut deeply, I tug the sheet and stand, looking around the room for my clothes, and realizing we discarded my shirt on the kitchen floor when Cole pushed me to my knees.

Oh, my God. I search my mind, trying to remember if I ever wrote something like that in a book. Was he fucking with me? Having fun and wanting to recreate a scene, so he could mock me later? I could never go through that humiliation again.

I hurry to the bathroom and lock the door behind me. No way do I want him barging in. I need a moment to pull myself together and figure if writing a hockey series is worth it. I turn on the shower and climb in. Steam fills the room as I grab Cole's soap and rinse my body, washing away all traces of him on my skin.

I stay under the spray for a long time, hoping Cole is gone from the bedroom when I emerge. When the water turns cool, I wrap a big fluffy towel around me, and gingerly open the door.

When I do, I find Cole sitting on the bed, a coffee cup in his hand.

I lift my chin an inch, even though I don't feel an ounce of confidence. "If you'll excuse me, I need to get dressed."

I make my way to the door, but he holds the coffee cup out to me. "I thought you could use this."

I eye the coffee, and the need for caffeine overrules common sense, and I graciously accept it from him. He watches me as I blow on it, then take a much-needed sip.

"Thanks."

"Want to talk?"

"No, we need to get ready or you're going to miss your appointment."

"You're still taking me?"

"I'm not going to just abandon you, Cole."

He takes my elbow and leads me to the bed. "Sit," he says.

I lower myself and glance at his nightstand. The books are gone, and I'm grateful that he was considerate enough to remove them.

"I put them in the library." I nod, wishing he'd tossed them out. "I'm not sure I understand what the big deal is."

"It just is." With tears pricking my eyes, I turn from him. "I write under a pseudonym for a reason," I say. I pinch my eyes shut, hardly able to believe Cole went trough the trouble of finding out my pen name, so he could purchase my books. It had to be so he could tease me, mock me.

"I know you don't like me much, let alone trust me, but I didn't buy them for any other reason than to support you, and for what it's worth, I think you're an excellent writer. I used to read your skating blog, too."

"You...did?"

"Yeah. I didn't mean to embarrass you. I never even thought to put them away last night. To be honest, I never thought we'd end up in my room." I nod. He cups my chin and lifts it. "I'm smart enough to understand what you write isn't who you are, or what you do privately. Crime and horror writers don't go around killing people."

Something inside me softens, the knot in my belly uncoiling at his sincerity. "Maybe I overreacted. It just took me by surprise, and I didn't want you to tease me about it."

He lets loose a long, slow breath and shakes his head. "Jesus, I was such a prick to you."

I feel a laugh catch in my throat. "I wasn't all that nice to you either, Cole. And that's why we have to keep having sex. I have so much anger to work through. But this..." I glance at his empty nightstand. "It wasn't all on you," I admit.

"What do you mean?"

"There was this guy," I begin, and swallow down the lump gathering in my throat. "He...humiliated me."

His jaw tightens as he brushes my damp hair from my shoulder. "What did he do?" he asks between clenched teeth.

I don't look at him. I can't, and for God's sake, why the hell am I telling him this?

"I was set up on a date, and he really paid attention to me, you know? Most guys don't."

He frowns and looks down, like he knows something I don't.

"What?" I ask.

"Nothing, keep going."

"He was a bartender, but apparently his brother was a cop, so I guess he must have gotten him to do a search on me or something, and found out my pen name. He read my books, Cole, and he..." A hiccupping sob catches in my throat as my mind dredges up that painful memory. "I guess he thought it would be fun to recreate some of the scenes."

He scrubs his chin, a new look of understanding in his eyes. "Shit, I get it now."

"I didn't even realize it at the time, but he made a big joke out of it when it was over. I was mortified. It actually made me ashamed of what I write and made me feel dirty. Actually, I felt like a whore."

"This is on him, not you. What you write is romance and people falling in love. Sex come naturally from that, and you should be proud of yourself. I sure as fuck am proud of you." Anger backlights his eyes and his fingers curl into fists. "Fucking pig. Where can I find him?"

A laugh crawls out of my throat. "You have a concussion, you're not going after him."

"Well, you were going to go after Burns when I told you he was the one responsible for my concussion. Actually, you wanted to meet him in a dark alleyway, and you're all of one hundred pounds." He grins and gives my chin a nudge. "What a pair we are."

"Yeah, well, no need to go after him. I'm over it."

"You sure about that?" I nod, and he says, "I'm an expert asshole, Nina, but I'd never do something like that to you. I hope you know that."

I nod. He might have been a jerk growing up, but I guess deep down, I don't think he'd do something so cruel. "I don't share my pen name." I narrow my eyes and look at him. "How did you figure it out?"

"Your bro. He's proud as shit of you, girl."

"Luke told you my name?" I shake my head. "I'm going to kill him."

"Nah, he's just super happy that you found something you love doing after your injury, that's all." He leans in and nudges me with his shoulder. "We both are."

"God, I hope *he* hasn't read any."

"Me too," he says, and makes a face like he'd just sucked a lemon.

"It's not real," I blurt out. "It's not like I go out and do those things so I can write about them."

"I know that, and I'd never ask you to do any of those things."

My mind races to last night, and all the amazing thing he did with his hands and his tongue. My editor asked me to write hotter, and to be honest, there's a part of every writer that draws on personal experiences. Too bad I'm lacking in the sex department, and I fear my more intimate scenes are all staring to sound the same. Insert object A into slot B and repeat.

"Then again..." I say.

"What?"

"While we're working out our anger issues, maybe we can, you know, try some new things. You can teach me some new plays so I can add some spark to those scenes. Two birds with one stone and all." My gaze droops to his lap. One very big stone, indeed.

Confusion comes over his face. "I thought you just said—"

I place my hand on his chest, and his muscles ripple beneath my palm as I stop his protest. "You're not asking me to do things from my book behind my back. I'm a willing partner, fully aware of what's going on."

He thinks about it for a moment. "Do I get credit in the book? You know, like in the dedication?"

I whack his stomach and meet with a wall of muscle. The hit hurt *me* more than him. "Of course not. No one can know about us."

His smile momentarily drops, but then it's in place again so fast, I can't help but think I've imagined it. "No, don't worry. I won't tell anyone about us."

"So you'll do it then? Teach me some hot new moves for the sex scenes?"

His grin turns wicked. "That's what I was trying to do earlier when you stopped me."

8

COLE

After going over my latest MRI with me, I sit on the examination table as the doc pokes and prods me. As he takes my vitals, I think about Nina. Jesus Christ, I wasn't the only guy to do a number on her. No wonder she doesn't believe she's marriage material. But Christ, that girl is more marriage material than any woman I've ever met. She deserves the white picket fence, the kids, the minivan and whatever the hell else she might want.

When I'm fully recovered, I have every intention of finding the douche bag who humiliated her and giving him a good beating. I don't give two shits if his brother is a cop, or if I end up with another concussion. No one treats Nina like that and gets away with it.

Dr. Sanders flicks the penlight over my eyes and pulls my focus back to the present. "So, what do you think brought on the nausea last night? Were you doing anything strenuous?"

"I...uh, well, I had a girl over."

He tucks the flashlight into his pocket, folds his arms and stands back. He frowns at me, his bushy grey brows knitting together. "I thought you said you were going to take it easy. That hockey was more important than any woman."

"Yeah, I know. It just kind of happened." I'd sworn off women during recovery, but this is Nina we're talking about. "Believe me, I learned my lesson." Frenzied sex—years in the making—is not in the cards for me. But Nina asked me for bedroom lessons to help her writing. How can I possible say no to her?

Am I really going to let a girl come between me and my recovery?

But this isn't just any girl. It's Nina.

Careful, dude, she only wants sex and hockey lessons from The Playmaker. Nothing more, nothing less.

It's not the real Cole she or anyone else wants. That guy's unlikeable, and not worthy of a nice girl like her. Nope, that guy wasn't even enough for his mother to stick around. It's best to keep him under wraps.

"You're well on your way to a full recover, and I don't want to see anything keep you from your game." His white coat makes a swishing sound as he turns from me and grabs my file from his cluttered desk. "From here on out, rest and relaxation."

"No sex?"

He turns back to me, his eyes serious, but a small grin turns up his lips. "I'm not going to say that, if you're finding abstinence too difficult. You have to have a life, but just take it easy, okay? You need to keep your brain rested and your blood pressure level."

I climb down from the table. "When do you think I'll be able to get back on the ice?"

"The headaches are back, right?"

"They were gone for a long time, and it was just last night I had a severe one. I was hoping I could do some easy skating with a friend. Nothing strenuous, just like walking, but on skates."

"Let's give it a week before I give the okay on that. Come back then and we'll run some more tests, and then we'll have a better idea where you are. In the meantime, relaxing activities that don't take too much out of you."

He makes some notes on his chart and I thank him as I leave his office. My heart beats a little faster when I find Nina sitting there waiting for me, checking something on her phone. Keeping my blood pressure down in her presence is going to take a hell of a lot of work.

As if sensing me standing there, she lifts her head and gives me a smile that fucks me over a little bit. She stands, and after I make another appointment for a week from now, we leave together.

"What did he say?" she asks when we reach the car.

"I'm on the road to recovery but I can't do anything too strenuous." I give her a wink, and she shakes her head, and it's then I realize just how responsible she feels.

"I knew it. We shouldn't have had sex."

"Nina, none of this is your fault. I wanted you, and my team's entire defense couldn't have kept me away from you last night, concussion or not." When she gives me a soft smile, I say, "We can have sex as long as I take it easy. I believe he said something about you doing all the work."

She laughs. Hard. And I can't help but laugh with her.

"Nice try, Cole."

"I think he also said something about you cleaning the house for me, too."

She rolls her eyes. "Did you get a prescription for that?"

"Well, no, but I believe it was implied, and—"

"Get in the car, Playmaker, before I make you walk all the way home."

I climb in and she slides into the driver's seat. The engine roars to life and she gingerly backs up. I appreciate her keeping the movements slow. The last thing I want is for my vertigo to return, and to end up back on the bathroom floor.

"Is there a game on tonight?" she asks.

"Nope."

"So you don't have any plans."

"I thought *we* did." I wiggle my brows playfully and from the look she's casting my way, I know she gets the gist.

"Do you think about anything other than sex?"

"Hockey."

"Well, the Doc said you needed to do relaxing things, so I'm going to book us a Paint Nite. There's one at Freeman's Bar, not too far from your place. I was checking it out in the waiting room, and tonight they're painting a daisy."

"Paint Nite?"

"Yeah, it's fun. You don't have to have any skills for painting." She rounds the corner slowly, and when the car behind us honks at her unhurried pace, and she flips him off in the rearview mirror, I laugh. She grins and goes on to explain, "There's an instructor, and they go step by step, sort of like paint by numbers."

She turns her head to find me staring at her. "Me, paint?"

"Sure, why not?"

"Ah, because I don't paint daisies. I'm not a girl."

"Oh, stop." She whacks me, and I capture her hand. I bring it to my mouth for a kiss and her breathing changes slightly. "Lots of guys go. When I went with Jess, there were couples there on a date."

"So this is a date?"

"Noooo," she says, expanding that one word, to make sure I understand, I suppose. "This is about me finding ways to help you relax."

"Like I said—"

"Cole," she warns, and I laugh.

"I just like having sex with you, Nina. What's so wrong

with that?" Other than this is my best friend's kid sister, and I like her, a lot. Too much. Which is fucked, because it's not like we could have a future together. She's as messed up as I am about such things.

She casts me a quick glance, and I don't want to think too hard about the spike in my heart rate when she gives me a smile, like my words mean so much to her.

"I like having sex with you, too," she says.

"Now we have to have slow sex. Like lovemaking." Shit, why did I say that? I don't know, but if I keep it up, I'm going to have to hand in my man card.

My stomach takes that moment to grumble, and I'm glad for the distraction.

"I need to feed you," she says. "That sugary bowl of cereal hasn't taken you very far."

I feign disgust. "Cereal for breakfast. What am I paying you for again?"

"We ran out of time," she shoots back. "And don't pretend you didn't like those Captain Crispies. I heard your moans." Before I can come back with some smart comment about her moans, she says, "Besides, I don't want your money. I told you that. We're just both helping each other out." She takes a left instead of a right.

"Where are we going?"

"If I'm going to stay at your place, I need to get clothes. I can't live in your shirts."

"I'm okay with that."

"I'm not." She casts me an almost apologetic look. "I know you're starving, but do you think you can hold off on eating for a little bit longer?"

"We could always grab fast food at the drive-through."

"No, when we get back, I'm making us a proper lunch."

Us.

Damn, I like the sound of that.

"We could eat at your place."

"No, I haven't had a chance to go grocery shopping, since I was so busy with work and helping you and learning hockey."

"You could at least hook me up with a granola bar. Who doesn't have a box of granola bars stuffed in the cupboard, right?"

"I'm sure I can find you one."

Ten minutes later, she parks on the street in front of her place. "Wait here, okay," she says as I reach for the door handle. "I'll bring you out a granola bar."

"Nope." I open the door, and she frantically jumps out from her side and plants her hands on her hips. "You might have to carry something heavy."

"And you're supposed to be taking it easy," she shoots back, but from the near panicked look on her face, I get the sense there's something else going on.

"I'm helping, Nina," I say adamantly.

"Fine," she says and huffs off. "Hurry up then."

"Concussion, remember," I say as I race to catch up.

"Yeah, only when it's convenient," she says with a sardonic smile.

"You weren't complaining last night."

"Shh, I don't want my neighbors to hear that."

Okay, okay I get it. She doesn't want anyone to know about us. She fishes her key from her purse, and I follow her into her condo. "Nice place," I say, glancing around.

"Wait here," she says, and puts her hand to my chest to keep me in her front entranceway. "I don't want you touching any of my stuff."

"And here I let you touch *all* of my stuff," I say, my voice holding all kinds of sexual innuendoes.

"You're a funny guy, Cole," she says, and disappears down a short hallway.

"I'm here all week," I shoot back as she disappears into her bedroom. Unable to help myself, I step into her condo and glance around her living room. Nice, tidy, a buttery-yellow sofa with some throw pillows, a coffee table and small television. Across from the sofa there's a bookshelf filled with romance novels. It's all very Nina-like, and what I expected.

"Almost done," she calls out.

I make my way to her kitchen, and a stack of envelopes on her table catches my eyes—the red overdue notices, to be precise.

What the hell? How could Nina be hurting for money? Luke set up that trust fund for her ages ago.

Even though it's not in my nature to pry, I open one of her cupboards and find only a few boxes of crackers. Shit. Why didn't she tell me she was broke?

I hear movement in the bedroom and hurry back to the front hall. I don't want to embarrass her, but I have no idea why she has no food and bills piled up. Christ, her brother started a trust fund for her when he signed his first contract. Why isn't she using the money when times are tight?

I glance around the place, my mind racing. She never liked me much, so the fact that she came to me for help must have been hard on her—must have been a last resort. She needs to write these books, of *that* much I'm sure, and dammit, I need to help her more than I ever realized.

She comes back down the hall, her steps slowing when she sees me.

"What?" I ask.

"You have a funny look on your face."

"It's called starvation."

"Hang on." She hurries to her kitchen and comes back with a granola bar for me. I rip into it and take a big bite, then hold it out to her. "Share?"

"No, I'm good. Still not feeling well from that bowl of Captain Crispies."

"Hey, don't be dissing the Captain."

"Sometimes I swear you're still seventeen, Cole."

We step back out into the sunshine, and a few of her neighbors are admiring my car. "You remember a lot about me at seventeen?"

"Yeah, mostly how much of an ass you were."

"Still am," I remind her.

"Oh, I know," she says, then plasters on a smile. "Good afternoon, Mr. Johnson." She steps up to an elderly man with a cane. "Do you like it?" she asks as he examines the car. His eyes go wide when he sees me, and I instantly slip into Play-maker mode.

"You're Cole Cannon," he says.

I widen my arms. "The one and only."

"Can I get my wife, she's a huge fan too."

"Sure thing." I wink at Nina, who is watching me carefully —too carefully. I shift beneath her scrutiny, disliking that she might be the only person who can see through the veil. "I can't go anywhere," I say, cocky as ever. "Totally in demand."

The truth is, I like greeting fans, like making them happy. I just wish I could be myself, but it's Cocky Cannon they all want.

Mr. Johnson comes back with his wife, who is shrieking with joy, her hands on her cheeks, her mouth wide. I pose for a few pictures and give my autograph. Mrs. Johnson, all wide-eyed and excited, turns to Nina.

"Are you two a couple?" she asks, hope dancing on her face.

"Oh, God, no," Nina says quickly. "Cole is a friend of my brother's, and he's just helping me out with a few things."

"Ah, too bad. You make such a nice couple." Mrs. Johnson beams at Nina, then turns her focus to me.

"Nice meeting you," I say, sensing that Nina is uncomfortable with the direction of the conversation. "But we've got to run."

"Come around more often," Mr. Johnson says.

I hop into the car and Nina climbs into the driver's seat. "Thanks for that," she says. "They're big fans. That was nice of you, but I hope it didn't take too much out of you. I know smiling and interacting with fans can be exhausting."

"I'm okay," I say, just as my phone pings. I fish it from my pocket and read the message. Guilt niggles inside my gut as I text Luke back.

"Everything okay?" Nina asks.

"It's Luke. Checking to see how I'm doing."

"Oh, tell him I said hi," she says. "And that you're giving me hockey lessons."

I nod, and put the phone back in my pocket. No fucking way am I letting Luke know I'm with Nina.

"You didn't tell him."

"I will later, but you should tell him hi yourself. I'm sure he'd love to hear from you."

She frowns. "I don't know. He's always so busy and I don't want to bother him."

I reach across the seat and put my hand on her legs. She jumps slightly as my skin warms at the touch. "Nina, I can guarantee he'd like to hear from you."

She crinkles her nose and hesitates for a long moment. "You sure?"

"Yeah, give him a text and you'll see."

"Okay, maybe I will."

"Do you think maybe you don't like hockey because of Luke?"

"What is that supposed to mean?"

"I don't know. Just maybe you hate that he's gone all the time."

Instead of answering, she casts me a glance and changes the subject. "Do you hear from your sister much?"

I remove my hand and sink back into my seat. "Yeah, we're pretty tight."

"Even with her living on the East Coast."

As a shimmer of anxiety moves through me, I lean forward and pinch the bridge of my nose to chase away the dark images that race around my brain when I think of my sister, and her reason for living on the other side of the country. My goddamn demons are still as vicious and ruthless today as they were all those years ago.

"Shoot, sorry. I didn't mean to take that corner so fast."

"It's okay," I say, thankful she misinterpreted my reaction. "So, this Paint Nite," I say redirecting. "You're really going to make me paint a damn daisy?"

"Yes, and it will be nice to have something personal in your house, don't you think? Something of yours, your own personal touch."

Yeah, it would. Problem is, the only personal thing I currently want in my place is Nina—the only thing I want to personally touch—and she's not mine.

Never will be.

9

NINA

"I can't believe you're making me paint a damn daisy," Cole says as he leans into me, his warm scent and proximity overwhelming me, and making me feel insanely close to him, oddly content. Over the last couple days, we've developed an ease with each other. I'm not sure how it is for him, or if he's ever felt this way with anyone before, but for me, it's a completely foreign feel, and one I probably shouldn't like so much.

People all begin to file into the bar, and as drinks are served, the noise level rises. Guys and girls alike make their way to their seats, and many glances are cast our way. Whispers reach my ears as people shuffle by. From their hushed words, it's clear everyone is trying to figure out if they're looking at the real Cocky Cole Cannon—The Playmaker—or someone who just happens to looks like him. Although I can't imagine another man ever coming close to Cole's kind of good looks.

Cole is either oblivious or ignoring the stares as he shoots off a text and shoves his phone back into his pocket. Me, well, I just smile politely and try to give nothing away. Cole deserves his privacy, and honestly, I kind of like having him all to myself tonight.

"Stop complaining already. It could be worse," I say when he kicks his legs out and slides down in his chair.

"How?" He picks up his brushes to examine them, looking at them like they're foreign objects. I can only imagine they are. The only thing I've ever seen in his hands is a hockey stick for as far back as I can remember. There were times I'd take the shortcut home and secretly watch Cole practice his shots at the old skateboard park. He'd be there well into the night, unaware of his audience of one. I might have hated him, but I always admired his dedication to the sport.

I cock my head. "You could be sitting at home alone in the dark."

He nods in agreement. "Yeah, okay, you're right. That shit was getting old fast."

"So you're going to stop complaining and have some fun then? Or are you going to sit there and sulk like a baby?"

"You and that mouth," he grumbles under his breath, as his gaze races over my lips like he's considering all the ways to stop me from talking. "And I don't sulk."

"Actually, you should be thanking me. Your doc said to relax and I'm making that happen," I say. "Do you know the effort I went through to book this for us?" I add, feigning exasperation.

His slow, sexy grin materializes. "Oh, don't worry, I plan to thank you over and over again later tonight. Ropes and bedposts might even be involved."

Heat crawls up my neck at his dirty words, and my mind takes that moment to visualize me tied to his bed. Lust spears me and I gulp, and judging from his widening grin, my needy reaction doesn't go unnoticed. But anything involving bedposts and ropes will have to wait until he's better. Nothing strenuous during his concussion.

Then again, when he's better, he'll be back on the ice and our secret affair will be over.

I swallow down my disappointment and say, "You know we can't—"

My words fall off when I hear a gasp, and I glance up to see some cute, big-breasted blonde staring at me wide-eyed, like she can't believe Cocky Cole is with me and not her—and not so quietly talking about tying me to his bed.

"Excuse me," she says to me, then turns her attention to Cole. My insides tighten as she dismisses me, treating me like I'm not even important. But she's the kind of girl Cole normally goes for, and she likely knows it.

He angles his head her way, and I lean back in my seat, fully expecting him to charm the panties off her, literally. Maybe he'll even take her home, have sex with her in his bed, while I'm in the next room. Cole and I are not a couple, and truthfully, he can have sex with whoever he wants, and it really shouldn't bother me so damn much.

"Hey," he says to the girl, and with my throat tightening, I turn my attention to the front of the bar and pretend to examine the picture of the daisy on canvas, all the while working to ignore Cole as he does his Playmaker thing.

"Are you Cole Cannon?" the girl asks, her high-pitched voice reminding me of a yappy Chihuahua. Yap, yap, yap. Really, her voice is fine. I just don't appreciate her approaching when Cole is trying to have some relaxation time—among other reasons I probably shouldn't examine so hard.

"Yeah, I'm Cole," he says, and shifts backward so I'm in full view. "And this is Nina Callaghan." He puts his arm over the back of my chair—a possessive move that takes me by surprise—and shifts closer to me. "She thought it would be fun for me to paint a daisy on our date night."

Date night.

My heart leaps in my chest. We'd already established this wasn't a date, and if he was going to pick up this girl, no way would he allude to the fact that we were together—like *that*.

Deep green eyes meet mine, and I don't miss the spark as his gaze moves over my face. "Isn't that right, Nina?"

"Yeah," I say, my brain working to catch up. Cole isn't flirting with the blonde.

Cole isn't flirting with the blonde

Instead, he's pretending we're a couple and gazing at me like he can't wait to get me back in his bed. A flutter moves through me, settling deep between my legs.

He looks back at the girl as she leans into him, putting her cleavage right out there, inches from his face. Blatant much? Cripes, why doesn't she just offer him up a spoon?

"I'm Becca, by the way, and I'm sure there are other things you'd rather be doing tonight." She flashes him a come-hither smile, and I wait for him to take the bait. She laughs, a breathy little sound that grates on my last nerve. She waves her hand around the busy bar. "If I were on a date with you, we certainly wouldn't be here."

Bitch! Seriously, right in front of me, she's putting that out there. I'm not one for confrontation or sparring—unless it's with Cole, or flipping off impatient guys in their fancy cars—but no way am I going to let this girl treat me with such little respect.

I open my mouth, but Cole's hand closing over mine stops me.

"The thing is, Becca, I'm recovering from a concussion, so right here is exactly where I need to be. Thank God Nina knows exactly how to take care of me. I'd be a wreck without her."

The girl's gaze flickers to me for a second. "Ah, okay..."

"Good luck with your daisy," Cole says, and shifts his focus back to his canvas.

I stare at him, dumbfounded. He wasn't rude to the girl, but he certainly didn't turn on The Playmaker, either.

No, what he did, the way he pulled me to him, made me feel important, well, that was like...really sweet.

God, when did I start using Cole and sweet in the same sentence?

"You'd better close your mouth, Nina. Or you're going to eat that fly buzzing around your head."

I whack the fly away and shut my mouth. "We're not on a date," I say for lack of anything else.

"I know," he says, and I wait for him to say more, but instead he examines his brushes again.

"Cole," I say, wanting to ask what that was all about. Why did he say we were on a date and give up a night with a hot blonde?

Because he'd rather be with me?

I shake my head. Dammit, while I like the thought of that —and I wish I didn't—I probably shouldn't read too much into this. Maybe he's just following doctor's orders and trying to take it easy so he can get back on the ice. Everyone knows hockey is the most important thing in the world to him, and he'd let nothing and no one stand in the way of his career. I can't blame him for that. I'd never seen anyone put the work into the sport the way he had. He deserves to be on the ice for the playoffs, which is why I brought him here tonight to paint. It's always helped me clear my head, and I'm hoping it does the same for him.

"So you've done this before?" he redirects. "This Paint Nite?"

"Yeah, with Jess."

"What did you paint?"

"It was a sunset, actually." I exhale a slow breath, and think back to the times I climbed Mt. Rainier when I was younger. "I loved watching the sun set from the mountain," I say quietly, and the wistfulness in my voice takes me by surprise. I shake my head to snap out of it.

"I didn't know that."

When I lift my gaze and find him looking directly at me, those green eyes intense, not a hint of teasing or playfulness about him, something inside me melts. His mouth dips, and for a second I think he's going to kiss me.

I wait, and when the kiss doesn't come, I swallow against the tightness in my throat and say, "Remember when we'd all go to Mount Rainier? One of my favorite thing to do was watch the sun set."

Cole nods. "You know, for two people who didn't like each other, we used to do a lot of things together."

I grin and point to the canvas. "We still *are* doing things together."

"Yeah, lots of things," he says, a hint of humor in his eyes. But it disappears when he asks, "When was the last time you hiked?"

"Before the accident." I crinkle my nose. "I don't think I could make it very far now. I'd likely end up in traction."

A long pause, and then, "That's too bad, Nina."

"Yeah, it's okay. I've learned to live with my limitations."

He frowns like it's not okay. "Luke always wanted to take you with us."

I give a very unladylike snort. "And you hated that, didn't you?"

"I never said that."

I wave a dismissive hand. "Oh, please, you didn't have to. All the times you threatened to toss me over the cliff pretty much told me how you felt about your best friend's kid sister tagging along and getting in the way of you picking up girls."

"Jesus, I was a prick."

"Total nightmare."

"Seriously though, Luke loved when you came, and you

never slowed us down. You were always so fit and up for anything. You were different from other girls."

"I know that." That's me, different, overlooked, underestimated.

"Not in a bad way," he says, and I find him looking at me like he can read my thoughts. "Seriously, Nina, Luke liked it, and I kind of..."

His voice falls off, so I pick up the conversation. "Doubtful. I was the one who always asked to go along. Mom and Dad probably forced him to take me. I can't imagine he ever wanted me around. There isn't a teenage boy in all of the world who wants their sister on their heels."

"Luke did."

My head lifts at the seriousness in his voice. I stare at him for a moment, take in the narrowing of his eyes, the tenderness flickering there. It only makes me want him even more. My gaze rakes over his face, and I can't help but think he's lying, but everything about his expression, his body language, indicates he's telling the truth.

Luke wanted me around?

I take a deep breath, and it almost hurts to breathe. I miss my brother so freaking much. Miss the closeness we used to have. As loneliness invades my soul, tears pound behind my eyes. Maybe I should reach out to him.

Do not cry, Nina.

"Welcome to Paint Nite," our instructor says, and the speaker behind us gives a high-pitch squeal that nearly deafens us. We all cringe, and the instructor quickly makes an adjustment. "Better?" he asks as he twists the mouthpiece on his headset.

"Better," a few people call out.

"Okay, let's take a look at your brushes and I'll explain how we're going to use them, while Danni comes around and fills your paper plates with paint."

We all pick up our brushes, and the instructor goes over everything. Soon enough, we all fall into a rhythm and begin painting our flowers. It's cathartic, really. A daisy might not have been Cole's first—or even millionth—choice, but he's doing a fine job and seems quite happy and content beside me. If I'm not mistaken, he even has a hint of a smile on his place.

"Hey, Cannon, I thought that was you," a male voice says, pulling our focus.

We both glance up and I try to place the handsome blond who probably spends hours, and too much gel, to get his hair to fall into a hot messy look that the girls probably go crazy for. Still, no one comes close to Cole in the looks department, at least not to me.

"Scott," Cole says. "What the fuck are you doing here?"

"Blind date," Scott says, and cringes as he gestures with a nod to the girl behind him.

"Not working out?"

"Nope." Scott's gaze leaves Cole and slides to mine. He looks me over, and a smile tugs at the corner of his mouth.

"Well, well, if it isn't little Nina Callaghan," he says.

"You know me?" I ask, then narrow my eyes and search my memory bank. That's when it hits me. He used to play hockey with my brother and Cole in high school. From the snarl on Cole's face, I'm guessing they weren't really friends.

Scott scoffs. "Hell yeah. How could I ever forget Crazy Callaghan's sexy little sister?" I sit up straighter, sure I'd heard him wrong. "Fuck," he says as he scrubs his face and winces. "Bastard gave me a black eye just for looking at you."

"He what?" I ask, incredulous.

Luke gave Scott a black eye?

Scott's gaze goes from me, to Cole, back to me again. "Are you two—"

"We're friends," I say quickly, so quickly, Cole's head swings around and his eyes flash to mine.

What? Is he surprised that I actually called him my friend, considering all the 'issues' we're working through? But seriously, we're nothing more, and I don't want anyone thinking I'm a puck bunny who sleeps with anyone wielding a...stick. More importantly, I don't want *Cole* to think of me that way. I don't want to examine why. All I know is, I hate the idea of him thinking I'm one of those girls who stalks all the players—and sleeps with them.

Scott nods. "Cool, can I give you a call sometimes? Now that you're all grown up, and Callaghan isn't threatening every guy who looks at you, maybe we can hook up."

Hook up?

As in get together for sex. Damn, maybe he really does think I'm a bunny. My stomach clenches at that, but the truth is, isn't that what I'm doing with Cole? Hooking up for sex?

"I..." I begin, but I'm not really sure what to say. I'm used to guys overlooking me, not asking if I want to hook up, and truthfully, I don't like the way this guy is gawking at me. Sure, I'm hooking up with Cole, but he looks at me with appreciation, not like I'm some piece of skin, his for the scoring.

Hateful images of Kenny Foster, and the way he treated me like I was nothing but his plaything—not to mention my date with the bartender—come back to haunt me, and I shiver.

Cole moves closer to me, as if picking up on my unease. "She's already seeing someone," Cole says, the muscles along his jaw rippling as he clenches his teeth.

"Shit, missed my chance," Scott says. "If anything changes, you can get my number from Cole."

"Yeah," Cole says, and refocuses on his daisy. Scott saunters back to his table, and I look at my canvas, but from my peripheral vision, I can still see the scowl on Cole's face. "Did you want to date that guy?" he asks, his voice devoid of emotion, but his shoulders are pulled tight, his back poker straight.

"No."

He relaxes a bit, his steely expression softening. "Good, because he's a grade-A douche bag."

"I kind of got that."

"That's way worse than an expert asshole."

I laugh. "I guess that's why you told him I was seeing someone."

"I didn't like the way he was looking at you. You're a nice girl, Nina." A pause, a shrug of his shoulders, and then, "I mean, you can go out with whoever you want." He gives me a concerned look. "I just don't like him. But if you want—"

"I don't." He gives a tight nod, and I look at his canvas. "You're doing a good job," I say, wanting to lighten his mood.

His eyes go wide and when he pretends shock, I'm happy to see the old Cole back. "Was that a compliment?" he asks, disbelief in his tone as he looks down at his feet, like he's searching the ground for something.

"What are you doing?"

"Checking to see if hell froze over."

I cock my head and plant my brush-free hand on my hip. "I'm sure I must have complimented you before, at least once. Maybe even twice."

"Nope, don't think so, and there were so, so many times I think I deserved it."

I roll my eyes at him. "You're such a—"

"Dick."

"Yeah, that's one of the nicer words I've called you."

"Are you going to use that word tonight, Nina?" He wags playful brows at me, and my insides flutter, like a silly school-girl with a crush. "Are you going to tell me about all the nasty names you used to call me when I'm buried inside you."

I pucker my lips as warmth creeps through my skin at thoughts of being in his bed tonight. "It will take hours, and we don't have all night."

"No, but we do have another week or so." He points to his head. "Depending." He goes oddly quit for a second, and the playfulness is gone from his face, something I can't quite identify moving into its place when he says, "About that. Just us these next couple weeks, okay?"

"What do you mean?"

"I don't want you to be with anyone else."

Seriously? He's asking me for a commitment?

"And you?" I ask in return. "Do these rules apply to The Playmaker?"

"I don't want to be with anyone else either, Nina."

A thrill rushes through me, but I do my best to play it off as casual. "I don't have time for anyone else this week, Cole. Cooking for you and learning the game is going to eat away at the week fast."

"Okay," is all he says as he goes back to his flower.

We paint in silence for a little longer, and I lean back to take in our artwork.

"Not bad for your first attempt," I say. "I think that will look nice in your place."

He arches a brow and gives me a look that suggests I'm insane. "You think I'm hanging this in *my* place?"

"Of course you are."

"I just about lost my man card coming here to paint a damn flower, Nina. Do you want me to cash it in completely?"

I laugh. "No, I like your man card." That brings a smile to his face. "I just think something personal will be nice in your house. It's not like I'm asking you to hang it in the man cave you've yet to show me."

"We didn't have a chance today," he says as he makes a

long stroke for the stem, the green paint easily gliding across the canvas. He has a nice, even stroke with steady hands. Probably from hockey, or maybe even sex. "We won't have a chance tonight, either."

"Why not?"

He leans into me and puts his mouth near my ear. "Because I've been sitting here with a boner all night."

"Cole," I say, and whack him.

He laughs. "Come on, Nina. You can't dress like that in front of me and expect me not to get hard."

"What are you talking about?" I look at my T-shirt and jeans.

"Do you have any idea how your ass looks in those jeans?"

"They're just jeans, Cole," I say, but secretly like the way I get to him, the way he makes me feel special. "And I thought you were a boob man."

"I'm every kind of man when it comes to you, and as soon as we get home, all these clothes are coming off. Now hurry up and finish your damn daisy so we can go."

Feeling giddy and juvenile for reasons I can't even understand, I take my paintbrush from the water, dab it on my paper towel and flick it at him. Paint splatters his face and his mouth drops open.

Oops! I really didn't think there was any paint left on the brush.

"What do you think you're doing?" he says, his eyes darkening, but I think it's from lust and not anger.

"Red looks good on you," I say, and stifle a laugh as I look at the speckles.

"You know what looks good on you?" he asks, and loads his brush with blue.

"Don't you dare," I say, unable to hold my laugh back any longer.

He flicks paint at me, and it gets all over my face and in my hair. At least he spared my clothes.

"Cole!" I squeal, and all eyes turn to me. "You're going to pay for that," I say under my breath, but I love this side of him. He's not being The Playmaker. He's just being playful.

"You think you're not going to pay, too?" He grabs a piece of paper towel and wipes his face, but all he manages to do is smudge the paint. "You're the one who started it, like usual."

"Lies...all lies. You're the one who was always bothering me and picking fights. It was like it was your favorite pastime. Or your job."

His grin is cocky and arrogant. "It was. That's the job of the older brother's best friend, you know."

I huff out an exaggerated breath. "We really do have a lot of anger issues to work through."

"Can't wait."

"You're going to need a shower first," I say.

"You too." He captures my wrist, runs his thumb over my flesh and the room closes in on me. Heat flashes through me, crawls up my neck, and I have no doubt my cheeks are flaming pink.

"Since you got me dirty, you're going to be responsible for getting me clean."

"Oh, and what about me?" I shoot back.

"Don't worry, I plan to lather you up, too." He leans into me, puts his mouth to my ear. "Every single inch of you," he says, his hot breath sending ripples of delight down my spine. "Now finish up so we can get the hell out of here."

The hunger in his eyes prompts me into action, and I increase my brush strokes, because yeah, I want to get home and get in the shower with him.

Less than twenty minutes later, we stand and have our picture taken with our paintings so they can upload them to the website. I think about my brother seeing the two of us together, not that I think he checks out the Paint Nite website. Still, what would he think if he knew that Cole and I were secretly seeing each other—for sex only, of course? I never really dated in high school, and he didn't seem to care one way or another, so I can't imagine he'd think this was too much of a big deal. On the other hand, I'm his sister and this is his best friend, so he might not like the idea of us together at all.

Then again, Scott had said Luke decked him for looking at me the wrong way. Could that be true? Probably, considering Cole thinks the guy's a douche bag.

My hair is still a sticky mess as we walk to the car and drive back to Cole's place. I park and we make our way inside. Cole sets the locks and hurries me up the stairs to his big master bathroom.

"I can't believe you got paint in my hair," I say as he turns the water on and adjusts the spray.

He grins. "I was aiming for your shirt so you'd have to take it off. One way or another, I was getting you out of these clothes," he says and step up to me. His knuckles brush my sides and he tugs my T-shirt free.

Completely comfortable in my skin around him, despite my barely there curves and breasts, I lift my arms so he can remove my shirt with ease. He tosses it to the floor and steps back. Green eyes flash with raw hunger.

And right there—that look on his face is the reason I have no inhibitions around him. No man has ever looked at me like that before.

"Out of those jeans, now," he finally says.

I pop the button and turn from him, showcasing my ass as I slowly, teasingly slide my pants down my legs. Wow, when did I ever become so bold? Sure, I write about things like this, but never practiced the moves in real life—except for that time that jerk reenacted the scene from my story. But

Cole is not that jerk, and I like the way he looks at me, like a man who hasn't had a meal in a long time, and I'm an all-you-can-eat buffet.

I kick my pants away and turn, standing before him in my bra and panties.

"Jesus fuck, you are sexy," he mumbles, and brushes his hand over his chin. The scruff on his chin makes a soft chafing noise, and I shiver. How will that feel, abrading my skin? Damned if I can't wait to find out.

I point to him. "You're overdressed."

He makes quick work of his clothes, dropping a condom onto the counter before he steps into the huge shower. I look at all the jets and the rain-shower nozzle above us.

"We really do have a water theme going, don't we?" he says, his voice rough, raspy as he steps up behind me, his hard cock pressing into the small of my back. I gasp a little, and wiggle my ass.

"Stop poking the bear, Nina, or I'll never get this paint off you."

I secretly smile, and Cole grabs his shampoo. He pours a generous amount into his palm and starts washing my hair. I reach up to help, not used to anyone taking care of me, and he swats my hands away.

"I've got this," he says. "I'm the one who did this to you."

I relax under his touch and just enjoy the feel of his hands on me. He finishes washing my hair and positions me under the rain-shower nozzle. It falls gently over my body and washes away the shampoo. I'm about to do his hair when he lathers his hands and runs them over my body. He spends a few extra seconds on my nipples, and they grow hard from his ministrations.

"I don't remember you getting any paint there," I say.

"You never can be sure. I'm just exercising caution."

"It's good to exercise caution," I moan and arch into him,

blatantly letting him know how much I like what he's doing. His soft chuckle curls around me.

"I wonder where else I should check," he says, his deep voice rumbling through me as he turns me around, until my back is pressed against his chest.

I widen my legs, giving him full access to my body. "Everywhere."

His breathing becomes harsher against my neck, and his cock throbs against my back. I wiggle to make him crazy and he gives a breathy groan, his fingers trekking downward in a slow-ass seduction that's making me insane.

"Are you thinking here?" he asks as he parts my folds. He lightly runs his fingers around my clit, torturing me with things to come, and I moan.

I wiggle some more, desperate for him to touch me already. "Yes, definitely there."

He urges me forward with his knees, and when I reach the back of the shower stall, he takes both of my hands and presses them against the grey tile. "Keep your hands there," he growls.

"Cole..." With my ass to him, I'm spread wide open, his for the taking. Never in my life have I felt so exposed. I'm not sure I could do this with someone else but with him, and I love it.

He pushes my wet hair from my shoulders and runs calloused fingers down my back, until he reaches my ass.

"This ass," he says, and kneads my cheeks like dough. "I've wanted to squeeze it all night."

"Oh, God..."

"God? Is that one of the names you used to call me, Pretty BallerNina?" he asks, the horrible nickname pushing all my buttons. But I'm beginning to believe he likes teasing the hell out of me, because he likes it when I shoot my mouth off.

"Not even close."

"Then tell me. When I pissed you off, what did you call me?"

"Mainly an ass."

"I like ass," he says, and cups my cheeks harder. "Tell me what else you called me. When you and Jess stayed up late at night whispering, what were all the nasty things you said about me?"

"I said you were a cocky bastard."

"Cocky. Hmmm." He presses his lips to my neck and says, "Yeah, that sounds about right." His lips glide over my wet skin, and my stomach flutters. Jesus, he sure knows just how to touch me. "Did you ever call me a prick, Pretty Nina?"

He slides his hand around my waist and tugs, lifting my ass to him. His cock slips between my legs, and I cradle him with my thighs. Passion-drunk, I shift, move, anything to get him inside me, but he holds back, clearly wanting to play with me longer.

Bastard.

"Tell me," he says. "It's good to work out the anger."

"Of course I did. I hated you. You were a total prick."

"You weren't the nicest girl around, either, you know"

"I know," I say, and think about all the times I gave him the death glare. I'm pretty sure I flipped him off a few times, too. But I can't think about that right now.

Jesus, touch me already. Put your fingers inside me

"When you called me that, were you thinking about my prick?" He pauses, and when he inches back and breaks the contact, I nearly cry at the loss.

I glance at him over my shoulder, about to beg, but my mouth hangs open when he takes his big cock into his hands. He strokes it with long, swift caresses that burn through me, taking my temperature from simmer to inferno. As heat and desire bombard me, my knees wobble. Who knew I'd like that so much?

"Like what you see?" he asks, his lips quirking at the corner.

No sense in lying, so I whisper, "Yes."

Green eyes sweep over my body, linger on my spread legs. He slides a hand between my thighs, coming so close to my sex. "Yeah, me too. So, when you were calling me a prick, were you thinking about how good mine might feel sliding inside you?"

He strokes himself harder and I gulp, because yeah, I was thinking those things. But I can't admit that. I just can't.

"If you don't tell me, I'll know as soon as I put my finger inside you," he says, his voice full of determination and conviction. "I bet I'll find you all wet and clenching as you remember those days." When I go quiet, he says, "Don't forget, we don't like each other, so it's fair game to say whatever we want to each other."

At that quick reminder that this is some messed-up game we're playing, I suck in a fueling breath and say, "Yes. That's exactly what I was thinking."

"Would you touch yourself when you slid between the sheets, Pretty Nina? Play with this hot little pussy while you thought about me filling it?"

OMFG. His dirty mouth is doing the most delicious things to me, and I swear the second he touches me, I'm going to come all over him. I begin to pant. Seriously. I'm panting. Like a goddamn St. Bernard left in a hot car, in Death Valley.

"Yes," I manage to get out through gasps as my body quivers, aches to join with his.

"Yeah, thought so." A sound catches in his throat, a half laugh, half moan. "Do you have any idea how much abuse my cock suffered because of you? Fuck, girl. I can't even count up the amount of nights I fucked my palms until they were raw."

My heart nearly stops at that revelation.

I twist, trying to see him, to gauge his seriousness. Is this a part of the game, or did he really masturbate at night, thinking of me? That can't be right. It just can't be. We loathed each other. Right?

While my brain is functioning enough to know it's a lie, all part of this hate-fucking game, my goddamn heart isn't getting the message. It wants to believe Cole lusted after me.

I shift again, trying to face him, but he puts his hand on my neck and holds me in place.

"Now I get to do all the dirty thing I've always wanted to do to you," he says. "Stay put." The shower door slides open, and I listen to the foil crinkle as he rips into the condom and sheathes himself. A second later he positions his cock at my entrance. His hands slide to my hips, grip them for leverage, as he powers forward and slides all the way inside me, filling me up until I'm moaning and grasping at the wet tiled wall.

"I was wrong," he growls.

Wrong?

Oh, God, what was he wrong about? Having a secret affair with me?

He presses against me, caging me with his body. "Blue doesn't look good on you. I do."

He drives into me hard.

"Cole," I cry out. He inches out, only to slam back in again, a loan moan in his throat as he seats himself high inside me. I try to breathe, try to think, to move, but I can't do any of those things. No, all I can do is focus on the pleasure centered between my legs.

"You feel so fucking good," he says, and begins to slide in and out, creating a rhythm that shuts down my brain. I move with him, my body on autopilot, taking, giving, wanting...needing.

Friction builds between my legs, and my sensitive nipples pucker even more as he pounds into me. He bends over me, his chest pressed against my back, and his fingers slide between my legs. The roughness of his palms against my skin brings on a hard quiver, but then I begin to tremble with need as he applies the perfect amount of pressure to my clit.

"Yes, just like that," I cry out.

I angle my head and try to see him. I catch a glimpse of his face, his jaw clenched tight, a storm building inside him, and I must say, I love that look on him.

I push against him, wanting him deeper in my body, and the air leaves his lungs, spills over my neck and back. He flicks my clit, runs his fingers over it, and as much as I want this to continue, to make this last all night, I'm fighting a losing battle.

The pressure in my core amplifies, every nerve ending zapping, firing, sparking like I'd stuck my wet finger in a light socket, and I let out a whimpering cry as I let go, coming all over his cock. I close my eyes and focus on the points of pleasure as he stills high inside me. My sex grips him tight with each hard clench, and it brings on a round of hushed curses from behind me.

I try to suck in air as he lets go. "So good," I whisper.

"So fucking good," he says, and continues to fill me with his cum with each hard pulse. When he finishes, he puts his arms around me, and hugs me tight, his head resting against my shoulders, his heavy breaths on my neck.

Steam fills the shower, and once again I feel giddy. A sound catches in my throat, and there's nothing I can do to stifle it, seeing as my hands are still pressed against the wall, exactly where Cole told me to keep them, and my body is too boneless to move an inch.

"Something funny?" he asks, his voice vibrating against my body and sending heat through me again. God, what is it about this man? I just had sex with him, and I want him again.

"No," I say, and giggle some more. "Nothing funny."

"You kind of laugh at the weirdest moments," he says, but I hear the humor in his voice.

"I know." I move against him, take pleasure in his cock still buried deep inside me.

He puts his mouth near my ear. "I need more," he whispers, as he slides his cock out of me. "I'm not nearly done with you tonight." He inches back, and I can't see him, but I know he's giving me a long inspection. "Stay just like this, Nina. Seeing you wide open, with your sweet ass in the air, is making me hard again."

I glance at him over my shoulder, and his eyes are the darkest shade of green I'd ever seen. There is an intensity about him that kicks some small working brain cell into action.

I push off the wall, and my body collides with his.

"What do you think you're doing?" he asks, his deep voice filling me with a new kind of need. "I told you to stay put."

I turn to him, grab the soap and lather my hands. "Yes, I know, but you're supposed to be taking it easy, and because of that, you no longer get to call the shots tonight —I do."

"Call the shots, huh?"

"You like that," I say. "Getting some hockey terms in there."

He chuckles, but it turns to a heated groan when I run my soapy hands over his body and drag them lower, until I'm holding his cock.

"I believe your doctor said something about me doing all the work."

A grin tugs at the corner of his mouth and raw need shimmers through me. "He did, but you know me well enough to know that I don't take without giving."

"I do know that," I say. Cole might be a lot of things, but

he's definitely a considerate lover, always making sure to take care of me. But now it's my turn to take care of him.

"I was thinking you probably shouldn't be exerting so much energy."

"When I'm with you, I can't help it. Plus, I thought this shower scene would be a great one for your hockey romance."

"True, there is a lot I can pull from it once I figure out my plot, but I'm not going to be the girl to keep you from the ice. So there's only one way I can help you with this little problem," I rub his hard cock, which is anything but little, "and keep you from exerting too much energy, and winding up on the bathroom floor again."

"How?"

"By tying *you* to the bedposts."

10

COLE

I can't fucking believe my hands are tied to the goddamn bedposts. But more importantly, I can't believe that I'm giving Nina this kind of control. Keeping the reins tight, well, that's sort of my thing. But this is Nina, and that somehow has me going against everything that's protected me in the past. I know I'm not worthy of her, she deserves so much better, and I should end this right now, but when it comes to her, I'm so fucking weak. Not only that, how the fuck can I possibly walk away?

She asked for two things from me—hockey and sex lessons. She needs both for her books, and I can't forget her empty cupboards and overdue bills. I want to call her out on both. I really do. But it doesn't seem like something she wants to talk about, and I don't want to embarrass her or make her feel like a failure because she's not making a living with her writing.

"Look at you," she says as she clucks her tongue and walks around the bed, gazing at me likes she's a dominatrix about to make me pay for all the cruel things I've done to her. "All tied up and mine for the taking."

I squirm under her scrutiny, partly because I'm so fucking hard, and partly because she has a mischievous look in her eyes. "You're going to make me pay for being a bastard, aren't you?" I ask, and wince when she runs her teeth over her bottom lip and eyes my throbbing prick.

Dressed in one of my shirts, since I asked her too— because yeah, I like seeing her in my things—she grins at me. "Oh yes. I'm definitely going to make you pay, Cole."

She climbs onto the bed and settles herself between my legs. My cock is so goddamn hard, if she doesn't touch me soon, I'm going to blow my load.

"Is it going to hurt?" I ask.

She takes my throbbing dick into her hand and pouts. If I could only get my mouth on those lush lips of hers... "It looks like it already hurts."

"Fuck me," I groan as she leans forward to lick the pre-cum pooling on my crown. She moans, and it turns me on even more. Hard to believe, I know.

"If I was cruel, like you were, I'd take you into my mouth, bring you right to the edge and leave you hanging."

"Thank fuck you're not as cruel as me."

She grins. "No, I'm not. I wouldn't have stayed here to help you if I was a monster."

"I want to touch you," I say, and wiggle my tied hands.

"No, we can't risk too much exertion."

"But I want my mouth on your sweet little pussy."

Her cheeks flush at that, and I still get a kick out of her shyness. She uses all kinds of dirty words in her books, but hopefully after this affair is over, she'll be more comfortable saying them out loud, asking for what she wants. In the meantime, I'll use *my* words.

"Why don't you lift that shirt up and show me your hot cunt. Let me see if you're wet for me."

Her breathing changes, and I know I've got her right

where I want her, despite the fact that I'm the one tied up. That gives me a measure of comfort.

She grips the hem of my dress shirt and slowly lifts it, until I can see her sex.

"Yeah, that's it, Pretty Nina. Since I can't touch you, why don't you touch yourself for me, show my how you used to slide your fingers over your clit when you thought about me."

She gulps. "I've never..."

"But you want to, don't you? You want to get all kinds of dirty with me, so you can spice up those sex scenes."

"Yes, but—"

"No buts. Open those pretty pink lips and let me watch you finger yourself."

She has a brief moment of hesitation...then a change comes over her. She touches her hot cunt, widens her lips, and slides a finger inside.

Motherfucker.

Yeah, I was playing with her, unsure if she would follow my commands or not, but now that she is, I'm two seconds from losing my shit. I lick my dry lips, swallow against my parched throat, knowing there is only one way I'm going to be able to quench my thirst tonight.

"That's it, don't hold anything back, Pretty Nina. Push your finger in deep and rub your clit with your palm. Grind against it, baby. I want you to come for me, then I want you to climb onto my face and let me taste your sweetness."

My words seem to do something to her. She spreads her legs even more and tosses her hair back, her fingers moving inside her body at a faster speed. I swear to fuck the vision before me is the sexiest one I've ever seen. I wish like fuck I could free my hands to touch her, or myself. I supposed if I wanted to, I could, but Nina wants me tied up for her own reasons, so I won't break free.

Her keening cries grow louder, and I coax her. "Keep

doing that, keep making yourself feel good." Her eyes open, her gaze locked on mine as her sexy noises curl around me. "Jesus, you're beautiful when you come," I say.

Her body convulses, quakes, and she leans forward, gasping.

"Come here. Sit on my face and let me lick your hot juices." She shimmies up my body and lowers herself until her hot, wet cunt is on my mouth. I dip my tongue in and swirl it through her wet heat, lapping up every delicious drop and wanting more. She moves against me, presses harder to my mouth, and whimpers as I taste her. I find her clit, give it a long, slow lick, then flick it with the blade of my tongue.

"Cole," she cries out as arousal pulls at her again.

"Slide down and get on my cock," I demand.

She pulls her pussy from my face and goes up on her knees. Her soft fingers grip my cock and she positions it at her sweet opening.

"Fuck me, baby. Fuck me the way you need to be fuck."

She whimpers and sinks down onto my cock, and the world fades to black around me.

Her hot cunt squeezes so tight in this position, I have to bite the inside of my cheek to hold on. She moves her hips, and lifts up and down, massaging my dick with each stroke.

"That is so good," I groan. "We should fuck like this every day."

"Yes...every day," she says breathlessly, and leans forward to press her lips to my chest. I move my hips, power into her, and she gasps.

"I want all my cum in you. Tell me you want that too."

"I want it all," she says as she peppers me with kisses.

As much as I like her lips on me, I say, "Sit up and touch your tits for me, Nina."

She does as ordered and squeezes her beautiful breasts.

Her nipples are hard as she takes them between her fingers and gives them a squeeze.

"You are so beautiful," I say, and her eyes dim with desire. I lift my hips, drive into her, and her mouth opens. "Touch your clit," I say.

She takes one hand from her breasts and puts it between her legs, and her hot cum pours over me the second she connects with the sensitive bundle of nerves. Her cum sears me, drips down my cock and onto my balls. Fuuuuuck, that is good.

My body spasms. "I'm there," I say, and jettison my cum into her, filling her with every last drop. She collapses on top of me, and when she shifts, my cock eases out of her, still rock fucking hard.

Her mouth finds mine for a lazy, soft kiss. One that tells me she's sleepy and drained.

"How about a few hours' sleep and we do this again? Only I get to tie you up."

She chuckles against my throat. "While I like the sound of that, your concussion, remember?"

"When I'm better, I'm tying the fuck out of you and having my way with you, all goddamn night," I warn.

She goes still against me, too still, and I nudge her. What the fuck did I say?

"Nina?"

"Yeah."

"Untie me." She reaches up and releases the bindings, then slides into bed beside me. "You okay?" I ask.

"Just sleepy," she says, but I get that it's more than that.

I just told her I wanted to continue this after I recuperated. But the fact of the matter is, when she gets the information she needs, and I'm better, she's out of here. We've already established that.

With a knot tightening my gut, I reach for her. "Come here. Let's get some rest."

I hold her in my arms, her breath warm on my chest as she drifts off. I close my eyes, exhausted, but they fly open when she suddenly sits up, equal amounts of horror and shock on her face.

I nod as I look at her, because I figured sooner or later—and from the look on her face, I can see it's sooner—she'd come to her senses and realize I'm not the kind of guy she should be playing games with. I am so beneath her standards.

"Cole," she gasps

"Yeah," I say, and make a move to get up

She grips my arm to stop me. "Where are you going?"

"Uhh..." In the dim light, I take in the unease on her face. "I thought you wanted me to leave."

Her face is scrunched up, perplexed. "Why would I want you to leave?"

"I don't know." Cripes, what am I supposed to say? You're a nice girl, and smart enough to eventually catch on to that I'm not good enough? "What's wrong, then?"

"We didn't use a condom." Her eyes go wide.

That shocked realization sends cold shivers through me. "Dammit, Nina. I'm sorry. I'm so fucking sorry. I've never in my life forgotten a condom. I was so caught up in the moment—"

"Me too."

I push my hair back and ask, "Are you...on the pill?"

She gives a slow shake of her head, and I scrub my face. "Fuck, man. I can't be a father, Nina." I have zero idea on how to raise a child. I'd make him all kinds of fucked up. A wife and family are all the things I can never have.

I guess that's why I've yet to take her to my man cave on the lower level of my house. What I have in there represents a life that's not meant to be mine.

I briefly pinch my eyes shut, and the sudden image of Nina, pregnant with my child, fills my head. My heart stalls at the visual, but then I quickly shut it down. That life is not for me.

"Cole," she says and touches my arm. "I know where I am in my cycle, and getting pregnant isn't what I'm really worried about."

"Ah, shit, yeah." Of course she'd be worried about her health, as she should be. Fuck, she knows my reputation. "I'm clean. I promise you that. I've never gotten carried away like that before. I use protection all the time."

"Not *all* the time."

I scoff. "Apparently not."

"I'm clean, too."

"I know."

"How do you know?"

"Nina, I know this isn't the kind of thing you do all the time."

She lies back down and averts her eyes. I shift and cup her chin until she's looking at me. "Why are you embarrassed?"

"I don't know why I said that. It's not like I want you to think I'm a puck bunny."

"I know you're not. You're a nice girl, Nina."

"The kind of girl your decorator designed this house for." As soon as the words leave her mouth, she blinks rapidly, and her mouth opens and closes like she's working through an entire pack of gum. "I mean...I'm not saying..."

"Say what you want, Nina." I press my lips to hers. "None of it matters because we don't even like each other, remember?"

Nope, we don't even like each other one bit.

Yeah, I am so fucked.

11

NINA

As Cole jumps from the sofa and does a fist pump, my heart races, I'm so happy for him and his team. They made it to the playoffs, and he's over-the-moon happy. I just pray he gets the all clear so he can rejoin his team. I drop my notepad and stretch out on the sofa.

"That was one hell of a close game," I say.

"Yeah, it was. But our man Luke came through." Cole sinks back into the cushions and briefly closes his eyes

"You okay? Headaches back? You did get a little worked up in the end there."

"No, it's been almost a week without one. I'm hoping tomorrow Doc will give me the all clear to get back on the ice. Maybe we can hit the rink after my appointment." He opens his eyes and turns his head to see me. "I need to be in the playoffs, Nina. It's the most important thing in the world to me," he says, a shadow of worry on his face.

"I know. You will be. I'm sure of it." I look him over, feel stress vibrating through his body. We've been relaxing all week, swimming and cooking together, but maybe he needs a change of scenery. This house is huge, yes, and I haven't even explored it all, but I think he needs to get outside these walls. "How about after your appointment tomorrow, we go to that new Italian café for lunch?"

I put my hand on his thigh, and he closes his over mine. A small quiver goes through me. I'm still shocked at how fast we came to this place, where we're completely comfortable with each other, and we both know that it's a given that I'll be driving him to his appointment.

He gives my hand a little squeeze, humor in his eyes. "Tired of cooking for me already?"

"No, I just thought it would be nice to go somewhere, get out of the house for a bit."

He eyes me, and I try not to shift, try not to show any kind of discomfort, but this is Cole, who can seem to read my every mood.

"Is lunch after the appointment a stalling tactic because you don't want to get on the ice with me?"

Maybe a little.

"No," I say quickly. He doesn't need to know the fall destroyed my confidence and getting back on the ice scares the hell out of me. "I just thought—"

"We had a deal, Nina." His voice is firm but there's tenderness in his eyes as they meet mine. "Are you breaking it?"

I shake my head and turn this around, making it about him and not me. "I just don't want you doing anything too early and risking your chances of getting back to the game. Let's just wait and see what the doctor says."

He glances at my notepad and pulls me to him. I settle against him, feel his strong heartbeat beneath my hand. "Any breakthroughs on story ideas?"

"No, not yet."

"So, what's going on, anyway?" He shifts positions, lying on the sofa and pulling me between his legs. With my back pressed to his chest, I settle in, completely comfortable. He runs his fingers through my hair and I relax into his touch. "Why are you blocked?

"Blocked, huh? I like how you worked a hockey term in there."

"The things I do for you," he teases.

"Truthfully, I don't know what's going on. I can't seem to come up with any good ideas lately." I exhale slowly and wonder if he really wants to be talking about this. Other than Jess, no one wants to hear me go on about my books or my characters.

"How can I help?"

"You *are* helping with all the sex and hockey lesson."

"Seriously, Nina. I might not be able to give you any ideas, but you can use me as a sounding board."

"Are you serious?"

"Hell yeah, I am."

My heart wobbles a bit, touched by his gesture.

"Do you know what a trope is?"

"Not really."

I grab the remote and flick the channels until a chick flick comes on. "This is my favorite Ryan Reynolds movie," I say.

"Never seen it."

I lower the volume and stare at the screen. "You don't watch romantic comedy?"

"Do I need to remind you about my man card again?"

I laugh. "But you read romance books?"

"Only yours."

"Okay, tropes. You know in my book, *Tempt Me Twice*, the hero is a construction worker and the heroine is a rich socialite? They come from different sides of the tracks. That's a trope."

"I get it."

"*Cinderella*, that's a rags-to-riches story."

He nods. "Makes sense."

We both briefly turn toward the TV, in time to see Ryan Reynolds spill his coffee all over himself as he hurries to bring his witch boss her drink.

"Hey, maybe you could use fake marriage, like they do in this movie. That's a trope, right? Maybe one of the hockey players has to get married for whatever reason."

I sit up and stare at him. "Really, Cole?"

"What, that will work, won't it?"

"You're a freaking liar." I point to the TV. "You said you've never seen this, yet you know exactly what the trope is."

A sexy grin curls his mouth. "Good guess."

"Big. Fat. Liar," I say, and he drags me to him.

He runs his thumb over my bottom lip, lust pushing back the humor in his eyes. "This smart mouth," he says, and presses his lips to mine. I melt into him, and his kisses are soft, slow, as his hands slide down to cup my ass. "This ass," he murmurs. His erection swells against my leg, and I move restlessly.

He groans. "Want to take this upstairs? Work on those other moves for your book?"

"I thought you'd never ask."

With heat flushing my skin, despite the air conditioning on blast, we climb from the sofa and head toward the stairs—but a loud noise at his front door startles us, and we both turn.

My heart jumps into my throat when I see a pretty blonde, obviously dyed, burst into Cole's place like she owns it. A wide smile splits her lips when her gaze latches onto Cole, and I slink backward, shrink into myself at the unexpected invasion.

"Surprise!" she says, and throws her arms up in the air as she rushes to him.

"What are you doing here?" Cole asks. He picks the girl

up, even though he shouldn't be exerting himself, and spins her as he gives her a big hug. Honest to God, I've never seen him light up like this before.

A knot forms in my stomach, a new kind of tightness crawls into my dry throat. Who the hell is this girl, and why are they so happy to see each other? He said he didn't have a girlfriend, but from the way they're hugging, looking one another over, I'm beginning to question everything.

Uncomfortable with their open display of affection, I glance around, look for the quickest exit.

"I thought I'd surprise you," the girl says, and rustles Cole's dark hair. She's tall, like him, totally dwarfs me, and I take another step backward.

"You surprised the shit out of me." Cole tugs her ponytail and drops a kiss onto her forehead. "You're the last person I expected to see come barreling through my door. How did you—"

She holds her key up, and then drops it into her purse. "You gave me a key, remember?"

Oh, God, he gave her a key. I really need to get out of here.

She frowns, sadness in her brown eyes. "I would have come sooner...damn work. I had a big case going before the courts. But I got here as fast as I could. I figured you'd be getting cabin fever by now and could use the company. Plus, I wanted to be here to take care of you."

"I'm so glad you're here."

"I hear a congrats is in order. Listened to the game in the car on the way over here. Luke did awesome."

"Thanks. The whole team did."

Cole blinks, like he suddenly remembers I'm there, and he turns to see me backing up toward the stairs. "Nina," he says. "This is—"

Before he can introduce the girl, a guy comes in carrying a

big suitcase. The pretty blonde turns and grabs his hands. "I hope you don't mind, Cole, but I brought Jack with me."

As Jack stands there, gazing at Cole like he's larger than life—clearly he's a fan—Cole goes oddly quiet for a moment, shoulders squared, body tense.

I take him in, my mind racing a million miles an hour. I've seen that look on him before. Once at the grocery store, after the crowd dispersed, and again when I asked him why he didn't hire someone to cook and clean for him. I mull it over as the muscles in his jaw ripple—and that's when it hits me.

Maybe it's not so much about being famous, and more about having a hard time with people in his space.

"Cut it out, Jack." The girl whacks Jack in the gut, hard. "Yeah, he's big-shot hockey player, but here, in this house, he's just my brother, so quit gawking."

Of course! This is Cole's twin sister.

I should have realized it the second she came barreling in. Why didn't I? Oh, because Cole's a player and has probably given out many keys.

Then again, in all the time I've been here, not one girl has stopped by.

Cole relaxes and holds his hand out. "Nice to meet you, Jack."

"Same," Jack says. He takes Cole's hand, and as they stand next to one another, I can't help but compare. Jack is tall, good-looking and well built, but he's no Cole. He looks a bit uncomfortable when he says, "I hope you don't mind us just showing up like this."

"I'll take Tabby anytime I can get her." He frowns at his sister and breaks the handshake, his fingers curling at his sides. "I just didn't know she had a boyfriend," he adds through clenched teeth.

His sister waves a dismissive hand. "Jesus, Cole, don't go getting all barbaric big brother on me. I'm all grown up now."

Tabby exchanges a look with me. "Am I right or am I right? You, of all people, know what I'm talking about."

I do?

"Yeah, yeah, whatever." Cole captures my hand, drags me to his side. "Tabby, do you remember Nina?"

Tabby arches one brow. "Of course. How could I ever forget Nina Callaghan?"

"You were a couple grades above me in high school. I'd seen you around, but we never officially met," I say, and hold my hand out to her, noting how her features and hair had changed over the years. "I wasn't sure you knew who I was."

She stares at my hand for a moment, and I shift awkwardly from foot to foot. Um, is she not going to exchange a handshake? Is she upset to find me here with her brother?

She shoves my hand away and brings me in for a hug.

"I course I know who you are. Your brother was Luke. Everyone knew who you were." After a big hug, she glares at her brother. "Look at that Cole, I didn't go all barbaric just because *you* have a girlfriend."

"I'm not his girlfriend," I say quickly. "He's just helping me with a problem."

Tabby laughs. "Yeah, I bet he is," she says with a wink.

"It's true, I am helping her, and yes, we're sleeping together," Cole says, deadpan, and my gaze darts to his to find him looking at me, gauging my reaction, his body tense, his muscles frozen in place.

I blink at his words, at how he laid it all out on the line like that. But why would he do that? This was supposed to be a secret. Then again, he has a bond with his sister, and the two probably keep no secrets. I just hope she doesn't think I'm some puck bunny who sleeps with all the players.

"No shit, captain obvious," Tabby says, and when she loops her arm through mine, it's my turn to freeze. She gives me a tug to set me in motion. "Come on, Nina." I relax as she drags me across the wide expanse of the room, and as I follow along, I feel an instant connection with Cole's twin. "Let's go raid the fridge, I'm starving."

She practically skips to the kitchen, leaving her boyfriend and my...friend...to talk.

My friend?

Yeah, Cole and I have become friends over the last week. A little laugh catches in my throat. I guess I've worked out a lot of the anger through sex.

She reaches for the fridge, and casts a glance my way. "So, you and my brother, huh?"

"It's just a temporary thing." For some reason, I feel the need to explain. "You see, I'm writing a hockey romance..." Her eyes go wide and my words fall off.

"You write romance, now?" I nod. "Ohmigod, that is so cool!"

"You're a lawyer. *That's* cool."

She frowns. "It's not so cool. Hey listen, I wanted to tell you I was sorry about your accident."

Her words catch me by surprise, and my head rears back "How did you know about that?"

"Cole told me." She frowns. "He called me after it happened. He was a mess."

My heart trips up. *My injury was so important to him, he called his sister? He was a mess?* "Really?"

"Yeah. I really am sorry. He said you were an amazing skater. He told me you were his Pretty BallerNina. Cute name."

Why do I suddenly not hate it anymore?

"You know, if it weren't for you and Luke growing up...." As her words trail, her body stiffens, and I can't help but think how similar she and Cole are in their mannerisms and body language. "I'm just happy to see *him* so happy." She plasters on a smile. "So tell me about your books. I want to download them," she says, shifting gears so fast, it catches me by surprise, even though it shouldn't. Cole does the same thing.

But what was she going to say? What if it weren't for me and Luke growing up? What was she getting at?

As she stares at me, waiting for an answer, my brains snaps back. "Cole has them all in paperback." I gesture with a nod. "In the library."

Her jaw drops. "Cole reads your books?"

"Apparently."

She shuts the fridge and looks at me—*really* looks at me. A small smile quirks her lips, like she knows something I don't. She opens her mouth, but shuts it when Cole and Jack saunter into the room.

"What is all this, Cole?" she asks, and pulls the fridge open again and looks over the fresh produce and meats. "Since when did you start cooking?"

"I cook for him," I say, and that little grin of hers returns.

"Thanks for taking care of him, Nina. I got here as soon as I could, and if you want a break from the duties, I'm totally here to help."

"No," I say quickly. "I don't mind. Plus, Cole is helping." I cast a glance at Cole. "He's becoming a pretty good cook."

Tabby looks at her watch. "As much as I'd like to put that to the test, it's too late to start cooking. How about we order a pizza?"

Cole nods in agreement. "Please..." he says, his eyes big, his look boyish as he pleads. "I've been eating healthy all week."

I laugh and grab my phone off the table. "What does everyone want?"

After I get the orders, Cole tosses his arm over his sister's shoulders, and she grabs Jack's hand. "Let's get you settled in your room."

She says something back, but I can't hear it as they exit the kitchen. Whatever it was, it must have been funny, because they're all laughing. My heart wobbles at their closeness as I punch in the number to the local pizza joint. There's a big part of me that wants that kind of close relationship with my family.

Once done, I make my way back to the living room and flop down on the sofa. I flick the TV back on, waiting downstairs so they can all have their privacy upstairs. I half watch the show, and half go over all my notes from the games we've watched together, but every time I hear a laugh from the upstairs bedroom, my heart squeezes. Their closeness is so nice, and makes me long to have that with Luke, my parents.

When they all come back downstairs, Tabby has a bathing suit in her hands, and Jack has swim shorts on and a towel over his shoulder.

"Who's up for a swim?" she asks. "It was a long-ass flight, and I know Jack and I need to stretch out."

"Pizza will be about thirty minutes, so we have time," I say and stand. "I'll grab my suit."

"I'll help," Cole says with a grin.

Tabby rolls her eyes, wry amusement on her face when she says, "We'll meet you out there."

I dart up the stairs with Cole and he has a perma-smile on his face. "You miss her a lot, don't you?"

We both go to his room, since I moved my stuff into it a week ago, and I pull my bathing suit from the drawer, the one-piece he'd given me that first night. I like the way it fits, so I didn't bother bringing my own.

"Yeah, it makes me happy to see her doing so well, considering..."

I'm about to ask what he means, but then understanding dawns. It couldn't have been easy for either of them growing up without a mother. It breaks my heart to think she just left one day without so much as a backward glance. At least that's what Luke had told me. A sound of disgust catches in my throat.

"Cole," I say and put my hand on his back as he pulls on his swim shorts. "I'm so sorry about your mom."

He turns to me, his brow furrowed. "You never had it easy either, Nina."

"Yeah, but I *had* a mom. I know she cared, she just didn't know how to show it."

He cups my chin, and places the softest, sweetest kiss on my mouth. "As much as I want you in my bed—and believe me, I'll have you there before the night is over—let's get outside. I want to spend as much time with my sister as I can." His nostrils flare, and his big fingers flex. "I also need to get to know this Jack better."

I laugh. "I'm pretty sure your sister is a good judge of character and can take care of herself." I undress quickly, and Cole lets loose a tortured moan as I shed my clothes and pull on my suit.

"Yeah, well you're not a big brother, so you don't get it."

That makes me think of Luke. I guess he was protective, but I'd never seen him go into barbaric mode like Cole.

"Aren't you the same age?"

"I was born one minute before her, so that makes me her big brother."

"Whatever you say." I adjust my straps and tie my hair up. "I'm ready."

"Me too," Cole says and glances down. I follow his gaze to find his swim shorts tented. I giggle. "Again with the laughing at inappropriate times. I'm hard, Nina," he growls, his voice dark and tortured as he rakes his fingers through his hair. "How the hell can I join my sister and her boyfriend in the pool like this?"

"You can't. And since this," I pause and put my hand over

his cock, "is because of me," I drop to my knees in front of him, "the least I could do is help you with it." I grin up at him. "From the looks of things, it won't take long." I tug on his shorts to free his cock, and take him into my mouth.

"Sweet fuck," he growls, and twists his fingers through my hair.

I take him deep, swirl my tongue around his swollen crown, and cup his balls. He grows thicker in my mouth, his veins filling with blood, and I know he's there, right there. I moan, wanting to taste him, to savor his flavor for the rest of the night. My body warms with need as I pleasure him, but the night won't end with an orgasm or two from me. Cole is a man of his word and will see to that.

I work my mouth and hand in tandem, and he tugs on my hair, but I'll have none of that. "I'm there," he growls, and I keep my mouth on him when he releases. His cum fills my mouth, and I swallow every last drop, staying between his legs to milk him dry.

When he finally stops spasming, I glance up to see him, and the warmth in his eyes as he gazes back flips my heart inside out.

"That was…"

"Fun?" I say.

"Yeah, fun and—" His voice falls off at the loud splash and squealing sound coming from outside.

"We'd better get out there." He helps me to my feet, and I wait as he adjusts his bathing shorts. I'm about to leave when he puts his mouth to my ear and says, "Tonight, you're all mine."

"I know," I say, a part of me wishing I was his tonight, tomorrow…forever.

Oh, God.

We make our way outside, and as I approach the pool, Cole scoops me up.

"Don't you dare," I say. He gives me a mischievous look. "Cole, put me down. Your concussion, remember?"

He frowns. "Fine, but when I get the all clear, you'd better watch out."

With those words of warning, I jump into the pool, and the cool water feels refreshing against my warm skin.

I surface in the deep end and Tabby swims to me. "Nice suit. Glad to see someone is getting use out of it."

"You mean it's yours?"

"Yeah, Cole bought it, if you can believe it. He likes to have everything stocked for me when I come, but it didn't fit. It wasn't long enough in the body. It looks good on you, though."

Cole bought this for his sister, not some bunny?

"What?" Tabby asks when I go quiet.

"I guess I just thought he bought it for one of his girl-friends."

She angles her head. "How well do you know my brother?"

"I've known him since...forever."

"Yeah, but how well do you know him? Like, who he *really* is?"

Who he really is?

I've known him my whole life, but after spending so much time with him, I'm beginning to believe there's another side of him, one he hides from the world for reasons I don't understand. But glimpses of that Cole sneak out from time to time, even though I get the sense he doesn't want them too.

"I guess not that well."

She gives me a smile. "I'm assuming that's all going to change."

"When we finish—"

"He would never have a suit here for a bunny. He doesn't bring girls to his home, Nina."

"Oh," I say, oddly delighted by that. Far more than I should be.

She slides me a sly grin. "But he invited you."

I spread my arms, and water skims beneath my fingers, creating ripples in the pool. "I sort of invited myself, actually. And I'm guessing he's just doing his best friend a solid by helping out his kid sister."

Don't read more into it, Nina.

"He's not who the world thinks he is," Tabby says, her voice low, a little sad.

"What are you two whispering about?" Cole asks as he surfaces in front of us.

"You," Tabby says and splashes him.

"Hey," he says and lunges for Tabby. He grabs his sister and as he dunks her, he shoots a glance my way, a devilish grin on his handsome face. "Lies, all lies," he says. "You can't believe anything she says."

"Don't worry, I won't."

Tabby comes up sputtering. "Cole, I'm going to kill you!" As Cole swims away, I shake my head to get it on right. No way, no how, can I for one second believe there is a deeper reason that Cole invited me into his home.

12

COLE

With water dripping from my shorts, I hurry inside the house, grab my wallet off the table and meet the delivery guy at the front door. I turn the money over and he hands me three extra-large pizzas. Guess Nina must have thought we were all starving. She wasn't wrong.

"Ooh, food," Tabby says, and lifts a box when I set them on the kitchen counter. "Smells delish."

"I'll get the plates," Nina says, and reaches into the cupboard, looking so natural in my kitchen, it hits like a punch to the gut. I can't take my eyes off her as she stretches, her towel lifting slightly, exposing the soft curve of her backside as she reaches over her head. She sets the plates and four tumblers on the counter. "I'm going to get changed first, I'm freezing. Cole keeps this place like a meat locker."

"When was the last time you were in a meat locker?" Tabby teases, and Nina laughs.

I slide in beside Nina and put my arms around her, warming her body with mine. "Maybe I keep it cold for other reasons."

"Do you think of anything else?" she asks, and gives me a playful whack.

"Hockey, remember?"

"Right," she says with a laugh, and pushes me away.

As she heads toward the stairs, Tabby bites into her pizza, snuggles up to Jack and says. "Well, it's working." Jack runs his hands over her to keep her warm, and when she smiles up at him, it hits me how good they are together. Jack places a kiss on her head, but she begins to shiver.

"Why don't you go get dressed, babe? You're freezing."

"But *food*." She takes another big bite.

"It will be here when you get back." Jack takes the slice from her and bites into it.

She crinkles her nose. "Fine, just don't eat it all while I'm gone."

"I'll make sure to save you a couple slices," Jack says.

"I won't," I say, and she glares at me, the look reminding me so much of Nina that I laugh.

She places a soft kiss on Jack's cheek. "My brother is a big bully, but I know you'll save me a slice. You're way nicer," she teases.

"I'd give you all the pizza, babe," he says.

She sticks her tongue out at me, turns, and Jack stares after her as she hurries up the stairs to get dress.

I take in the way he's looking at Tabby. Not with lust, but with love. My heart tightens. "How long have you two been together?" I ask.

"What?"

I laugh. Christ, he was so caught up in Tabby, he couldn't even hear what I was saying. "You and Tabby, how long have you been together?"

"Over a year."

"How did you meet?"

Like Luke, I'd set up a trust fund for Tabby, hers to use for school, buy a house, whatever she needs. With that, she made a good life for herself, and has a flourishing career. He'd just better not be using her for anything.

Yeah, I'm a protective dick. So what?

"We work together."

"You're a lawyer?"

He nods. "Just made senior partner."

Nice. "So you like Tabby, huh?"

Jack pushes off the counter and straightens to his full height. I stiffen when he goes serious. Christ, I hope he's not going to say no, that he only came here to meet me, because Tabby sure seems to like him a lot. If he breaks her heart, I'll break his jaw.

"She's the kindest, smartest, most compassionate woman I know," he begins. "And I love her, Cole. One of the reasons I wanted to come here is because I wanted to ask permission to marry her." His look is a bit sheepish when he says, "I'm kind of old fashioned like that."

My heart thumps. I don't know the guy well, but he looks at my sister with love in his eyes, and I have to trust that she knows how to make good decisions. I spent my life protecting her from Dad, taking the abuse, all the beatings, so he was too physically exhausted to turn any of his violence my sister's way. "You want to marry her?"

"Yes, I love her."

I swallow the lump in my throat and pull him to me for one of those guy hugs where we pat each other on the back. "You have my permission," I say.

"Thanks, man," he says and hugs me back. "Don't say anything."

"You have my word."

"I want to ask your father, too."

With my arms still around him, I stiffen. Shit.

Just then, Nina comes back in the room.

"I'm starved..." Her voice falls off when she sees the two of us in an embrace. We back away from each other and turn her way. "Um, if you guys need another minute." She gestures with a nod to the stairs. "I can come back later."

"Get over here," I say, and she crosses the room and falls into my arms. I hug her, and she jumps back.

"I just changed and you're getting me all wet."

I grin at her, put my mouth next to her ear and whisper, "Nothing new about that."

Before she can whack me, Tabby comes back and eyes the pizza boxes. "Feed me," she says, and Jack grabs the plates and divvies up the pizza. We all grab a seat at the table and Nina pours us all sodas.

As we eat, I look at my sister. "How long are you staying?"

"Not as long as I'd like. I could only book off a few days." Her eyes light up. "Hey, maybe when you're better and the playoffs are over, you can come visit *me*."

"I'd love that."

From across the table, Nina smiles, a look of longing on her face. It's clear she misses Luke, doesn't see enough of him. With her parents absent in her life, it must be so hard on her, having no one. Well, she has her friend Jess, and she has me.

Well...she has me for a little while longer, anyway.

We fall into small talk as we eat, and when we're done, I stand and stretch. "I need to get out of this suit."

Tabby shoos me away. "Go. You too, Jack. When you come back, I want to play a game."

I groan. "Why do we always have to play a game? Can't we just watch a movie?"

"No, we can't. I want to play a game, so we're playing a game," Tabby says.

"See what I have to put up with," I say to Jack.

He laughs. "What Tabby wants, Tabby gets."

I grunt. "Women," I say, as the two women in my life clear the table and put the dishes in the sink.

"Men," they respond at the same time.

Jack and I dash up the stairs, and I step into my room, the scent of Nina lingering in the air. In the bathroom, her swimsuit hangs from the shower. With any other woman, it would feel like an invasion, but not with Nina. No, with her it feels right, like that's exactly where her swimsuit belongs.

I peel off my shorts and toss them over the rod next to her suit, then tug on a pair of jeans and a t-shirt. I hear Jack—my soon to be brother-in-law—in the hall, and we walk to the kitchen together, only to find it empty.

"Where the hell did they go?" Jack asks, as an uneasy feeling moves through me, because I'm pretty sure I know where they are. There is only one room in this house Nina has never seen, and it's the same room where Tabby keeps all the board games.

Shit.

"I think they're downstairs." I open the door to the lower level, and when I hear their voices, I follow the sound to the one and only room I designed myself. Jack follows me, and when I round the corner and see Tabby sitting crossed-legged on the floor, going through the stack of cards and games, and Nina beside her, looking at my old movie collection, I try for casual and say, "Find anything good?"

Nina turns at the sound of my voice, and my heart jumps at the softness on her face. "These movies," she says. "There're all my favorites."

I shrug. "Yeah, I remember you and Jess watching them over and over."

"How come...did you..." Her words trail off when she sees the framed pictures on the shelving units on either side of the big-screen TV. She drops the movies she has in her hands and examines them. There are a ton of Luke and me, Tabby and me...and just as many of Luke, Nina and me. A smile comes over her face when she picks up the one of the three of us at the Aerosmith concert.

"I never in a million years expected your man cave to look so warm and homey. It's so different from all the other rooms in your house." She goes quiet and runs her finger over the picture. "Who took this?"

I shrug. "Luke gave his phone to someone. I can't remember."

"How come *you* have it?"

Because I asked for it.

"I don't know."

"You hated me, Cole. Why would you ever frame so many pictures of me?"

Oh, maybe because you and your brother represent family, all the things I want but can never have, and I've been fucking crazy about you for as long as I can remember.

Shit.

"Cole?"

I could lie and say my decorator did it, but I already told her this room was mine.

From the floor, Tabby turns to me. I meet her eyes, and she gives me an understanding look. She knows what the Callaghans mean to me, how hard my life was at home.

"How about a game of Cards Against Humanity," she says. "Always a party favorite."

"Yeah, sounds good." I step up to the card table and pull a chair out. Nina sits beside me, her face still perplexed, her eye a bit distance, like she's remembering days gone by.

"Do you have any chips?" Tabby asks as she sits across from me.

As the tension in the room lightens, I laugh and say, "Is food all you ever think about?"

"Not all," she says, and grins as she leans in to Jack and gives him a kiss.

"There are some things a big brother never needs to know."

Tabby laughs, and Nina joins in when I grab her head and run my knuckles over her scalp.

"We have chips," Nina says.

We.

Damn, I like the sound of that.

"And wine?" Tabby asks.

"You know I always keep your favorite white wine here."

"Oh, it was Tabby's wine I drank last week?"

"Yeah, but I have a few more bottles stashed." I look at Jack. "Beer?"

"Sure."

I slide from the chair, and Nina stands. "I'll help you."

"I'll shuffle the cards," Tabby says.

I point at her. "No cheating."

Her jaw drops like I just said something ludicrous. "I do not cheat. Besides, you can't cheat at this game."

"Knowing you, you'll still find a way."

I turn and find Nina smiling at me.

"What?" I ask as we make our way back to the kitchen.

"I really like your sister."

"She likes you, too."

"You think?"

We reach the kitchen and I pull her to me. "What's not to like, Nina?" I say, and close my mouth over hers. I've been dying to kiss her all night.

"What was that for?"

"No reason. Kissing anytime I want, remember? All part of the arrangement."

She gives a curt nod at the reminder, then roots though the cupboards for the chips and a big bowl. I grab the wine, and beers, and Nina helps me with the glasses. We head back downstairs, and Tabby's eyes go wide when she sees the chips.

She rubs her hands together. "Mmm, barbeque, my favorite."

"Same," Nina says.

"I knew there was a reason I liked you," she teases. "And not just because you're here taking care of my brother. I can't imagine any woman wanting to put up with him for any length of time."

"Hey," I say, feigning offense, even though I know she's teasing.

"I like being here with Cole," Nina says. "He's not so bad when he's not calling me names."

"*You're* not so bad when you're not making me paint a damn daisy."

Tabby chokes on a potato chip. "You painted a daisy," she says, laughing.

"Dude, what happened to the man card?" Jack teases.

"Right?" I shoot back.

Tabby glances around. "I want to see this painting."

"Not a chance."

"It's actually pretty good," Nina says. "I think he should frame it and put it in this room."

"I am not framing it." I uncork the wine and fill their glasses, then pick up my cards. "Can we leave my man card alone and play these one's already?" I read over my cards. Jesus, I have some pretty raunchy ones. I grin at Nina as she makes a face. This is going to be fun.

"I'll go first," Nina says. She takes a sip of her wine, picks a card from the stack, then cringes. "I'm not sure I can say this out loud."

"Sure you can, Nina. You can say anything around me, remember?" I add, alluding to all our dirty talk.

Color moves into her cheeks, and she reads the card. I

look at the ones in my hand and, because I know her well, probably more than she ever realized, it's easy for me to pick the one she'll find the funniest.

When my turn comes around, will she know the best card to play for me? Probably not, since I keep my cards close to my heart, so to speak.

Would Nina like that guy if she got a glimpse of him? Even if she did, I'm not good enough for a girl like her—a point I can't ever forget.

By the time we finish our fourth round—Tabby with the highest wins—my gut hurts from laughing. Most of the wine had been drunk and Jack and I are on our second beers. My heart fills as I look around the card table. God, it's so nice to spend time with my family like this. Well, Jack's not family yet, but he soon will be, and Nina...she's the family I always wanted.

Then do something about it. Make her yours.

Fuck.

Nina takes her turn to read the card again, and when it says something about a helicopter and its pilot, my gaze flashes to Tabby to find her looking back, a measure of worry in her eyes.

"What?" Nina says, her cautious glance going between the two of us.

Recuperating quickly, Tabby says, "Oh, nothing. Cole used to talk about being a pilot when we were kids. After Mom left, Dad bought him a chopper..."

Her words fall off and tension fills the air, takes up space.

"A pilot, huh," Nina says. "Here I thought you were born with a hockey stick in your hand," she teases, her words cutting the tension and lightening the mood. Goddammit, I love her for that.

I love her?

Fuck, man, I'm in more trouble than I thought.

She turns to Tabby. "What are you plans for the rest of the weekend?"

"I'm not sure. What are you two up to tomorrow? I want to spend as much time with Cole as I can."

"Cole has his checkup tomorrow morning. I was going to take him, but you can if you want."

"No, you can. After all the traveling, and time change, I'm going to force myself to stay in bed longer to adjust."

"If I get the all clear, Nina and I are going to go for a skate. Come with us."

"That sounds like fun." She turns to Jack. "Feel like skating tomorrow?"

"Only if you want me to make a fool of myself."

Tabby laughs. "Don't worry. I might laugh but that doesn't mean I don't still love you." Jack beams at that. "Plus, these guys will help. Nina used to be a professional skater."

His eyes go wide. "Yeah"

"Key words, used to be. I haven't been on the ice in...forever."

"Since her fall," I say and her gaze flashes to mine. "Tomorrow, we're going to tread lightly together, right Nina."

She nods, and I hear her swallow as she turns back to Tabby. "Any friends still in town that you're looking to catch up with?"

"Yeah, a few. I want to introduce Jack to my best friend, Tawny. We're still close"

"That's nice. Will you see your dad?" she asks.

Without missing a beat, Tabby says, "Oh, for sure."

She shoots me a quick glance and I play along, like I've always played along. We never let anyone know what went on behind closed doors. We always kept our dirty little secrets just that...a secret. I'm guessing she never told Jack too much about her childhood, which is why he wants to ask our father for permission to marry her.

"I was hoping to meet your dad," Jack says.

Tabby gives an easy wave of her hand. "Oh, yeah, we'll make that happen."

"He's been crazy-busy lately, though," I say.

"Is that why he hasn't been around?" Nina asks, her brow furrowed in concern.

"Yeah. He wants to be here, but work, and his health hasn't been so great."

Nina's hand closes over mine. "I'm so sorry to hear that."

Tabby grabs the bottle of wine and holds it up. "We polished it off, Nina."

"Want me to grab another?" I ask, grateful for the change in subject.

Tabby stretches. "I'm kind of tired. I think it's bedtime."

"Agreed," Jack says, and finishes his beer. The two make their way up the stairs, and I turn to find Nina glancing around the room again, taking it all in.

"Nina?" I ask and bring her attention around to me. "Ready for bed?"

"I'm exhausted. How about you?"

I grin at her. "Been ready for hours, and never too exhausted."

She rolls her eyes at me, and I give her ass a slap to set her in motion. She yelps and darts upstairs. The second she enters our room—correction, my room—I shut the door and lock it.

"Tonight was so much fun," she says, the happiness in her tone fucking me over. I want her happy like this all the time. I want to be the guy who makes her happy, the guy who puts a smile on her face.

"You think the night is over?"

She spins to see me, and I crook my finger.

"Come here."

She saunters toward me, exaggerating her wiggle. "You have something on your mind?"

"Maybe I do."

She steps up to me, and I slide my hand around her back, drag her body to mine to show her just how hard I am for her.

"Maybe you should tell me," she says.

"I'd rather show you."

She laughs, and the sound travels through my body. "I'd rather like that."

I close my lips over hers for a soft kiss, and when she opens, my heart misses a bit. It's insane how responsive she is, how much I want her in my arms, my bed...my life. Her hands sweep around my back and I pick her up.

"Don't strain yourself," she whispers through deeply intimate kisses, and my heart squeezes at the way she cares about me. I set her on the bed and stand back to remove my clothes. Once I'm naked, I crawl over her and find her mouth again.

A surge of protectiveness moves through me as she adjusts beneath me. "I'm not hurting you, am I?" I ask.

"No," she says, and pulls my mouth back. We exchange heated kisses, then I go back on my heels to undress her. She sits up and lifts her arms for me, and I tug her T-shirt off over her head and release her bra.

I nudge her until she falls back on my pillow, her curls splaying. I grip her shorts, and she lifts her hips so I can shimmy them down her legs.

"You are the most beautiful woman in the world, Nina."

She swallows. "You don't have to say that."

"I'm telling you the truth, and if you're wondering, no, I've never said that to anyone before."

"Cole," she whispers, and reaches for me. I fall over her, put a finger inside her to find her so hot and wet and ready for me, it shuts down my brain. She widens her legs. "I need you."

I power into her with one fast thrust, and as I sink into her softness, need doesn't even begin to describe what I'm feeling for her.

When I wake and find Cole sleeping soundly beside me, the world around me spins, my emotions on a complete roller coaster ride as I take him in—think about the gentle, protective way he touched me between the sheets. My heart aches with longing as I put my finger on my kiss-swollen lips. In this bed last night, well, what we did felt a lot like lovemaking to a girl who signed on to hate fuck Cocky Cole Cannon—The Playmaker

Although calling him that no longer seems right.

I ease from beneath the covers, about to dash to the bathroom to get myself together, when Cole says, "Where do you think you're going?"

My stomach flutters at the playfulness in his voice. "I thought you were asleep."

"Get over here." He turns and drags me to him for a good-morning kiss, and I snuggle in beside him, not in a hurry to go anywhere, despite the fact that we both slept in. But we were up all hours of the night...making love. At least I think we were.

"We need to get moving." I point to the late hour on the clock. "You have your appointment."

"I know," he says.

As I note the strange hitch in his voice, I go up on my elbow to see him. "Are you worried?"

"Yeah. Hockey." He scrubs his hand through his hair. "Kind of my life, right? If I can't play…"

I put my hand on his face, and give a silent prayer that he gets back on the ice sooner rather than later. "He's going to give you the all clear. I know it."

His smile is forced as he drops a kiss onto my forehead, one that travels all the way to my wobbly heart.

"Playoffs are coming up fast," he says, holding my forehead to his mouth. "The team will be back home practicing before I know it. I need to practice with them to get ready. First game of seven will be here in Seattle, on our home ice." He inches back to see me. "Luke will be home soon. I bet you're happy about that."

"I am. I miss him a lot."

"He misses you, too." When I go silent, a strange look comes over him. "He cares about you a lot, Nina."

I kick the sheets off. I don't want to talk about Luke. The distance between us—physical and emotional—makes me sad. I'm not so sure I believed Cole when he said Luke wanted to take me places when we were kids. Then again, we grew up with distant parents, and maybe he just didn't know how to display affection. Still, he could reach out to me every now and then. I want to be a family, the way Cole and Tabby and their dad are a family.

"We need to move or you're going to be late for your appointment. I'll shower first."

"I'll join you."

"No," I say, and place my hand on his chest so he can't get up. "If you climb in there with me—"

"You don't want my cock in you again?"

A fine shiver of want goes through me. "You know I do."

"Then what's the problem?"

"Your appointment. You just told me how important hockey is to you."

He opens his mouth like he wants to say something, then frowns and closes it. Silence ensues for a second, and then he says, "Okay, go. I'll just stay here with my hard-on and wait for my turn."

He pulls the blankets off and exposes himself to me.

I chuckle. "You are so bad." He takes his cock into his hand. "Cole," I warn. He laughs as he strokes himself. "We had sex three times last night, how can you be—"

"I can't get enough of you, sweet Nina," he says, and I take in his expression, see no humor behind his words. "If I get the all clear, I'm tying you to this bed tonight."

Don't read more into it, girl.

He winks at me. "You want that, don't you?"

I want a lot of things.

"Yeah, I want."

Fire burns in his eyes as I dart to the bathroom. I have a fast shower, and when I finish, I find Cole in the bathroom waiting his turn. He drops a soft kiss onto my mouth, and I go back into the bedroom to dress quickly. Not wanting to disturb Tabby or Jack as they try to sleep in and adjust, I quietly make my way to the kitchen to scramble us some eggs.

A noise at the door catches my attention, and I walk to it to find the mail being slid through a slot. I pick it up and carry it to the kitchen. I toss it onto the table, but one bill jumps out at me. Cole has had medical bills, sure, but this one is from Renal Care. Why the hell would Cole be getting a bill from Renal Care?

My pulse leaps as understanding dawns. Could this be why

his father hasn't been around much? He has kidney failure? And Cole pays the bills for him?

My throat tightens. There really is more to this man than he lets on.

I hurry to the fridge and pull out the eggs. Cole and Tabby must be so worried about him, and with Cole unable to drive, and his dad not well, they've not been able to see each other.

Since they've kept his illness a secret, I'm not about to say a word. It does give me an idea, though. They've both been so nice to me, I want to do something nice for them in return.

As my plan takes shape, one I'm anxious to put into action, I grab my phone and shoot Jess a text. I'm going to need a few hours away from Cole if I'm going to make this work.

"Hey," Cole says when he enters the kitchen. I turn to see him, and my heart stills. How is it possible that he gets better looking every day? That I seem to fall for him a little more with each passing minute?

"Mail came," I say.

"Thanks."

I make toast and scramble eggs as he goes through it. I put our plates on the table. "I'm going to hang out with Jess this afternoon. It's been ages since I've seen her."

He drops the bills and picks up a fork. "You're still going to go to the rink, right?"

"Yeah, she'll meet me there. I also want to give you and your sister some time together."

He leans toward me conspiratorially. "I'm not supposed to say anything, but I know I can trust you."

"What?" I ask, a little thrill going through me that he wants to share a secret.

"Jack is going to ask her to marry him. He asked me for permission last night."

I squeal, then cover my mouth quickly. "That is so exciting, Cole!" I think back to last night, to when Jack said he wanted to meet Tabby's father. I can only guess he wants to ask him for her hand, too. The gesture is so sweet, and that makes me more determined than ever to make my plan work.

We finish our breakfast, and traffic is light as we drive through the city and make our way to the clinic. I give Cole a reassuring kiss before he enters, then I make myself comfortable in the waiting room. I flip through a magazine and think about tonight, how I want to surprise Cole and Tabby.

When the door to the doctor's office finally opens, I jump up. The smile on Cole's face fills me with equal measures of happiness and unease. I'm thrilled the appointment went well, but I do *not* want to get back on the ice.

Then again, with Cole by my side, maybe it won't be so bad. I do wonder, though, why he made this part of the deal. Does he really need me to spot him? Doubtful. What is *really* driving this need?

I'm about to open my mouth to ask how it went when he picks me up and spins me around. I squeal, and he plants a warm kiss on my mouth, one that trickles all the way to my heart and curls around it, cocooning me in warmth.

He sets me down and grabs his phone. "I need to text Luke and Tabby to let them know."

"What about your dad?" I ask.

"Of course," he says, and my already too tight chest squeezes harder, making it difficult to breathe. I love the closeness he has with his family and my brother. If something good or bad happened to me, the first and last person I'd call is Jess. He shoots off texts as we walk back to the car. I dig the keys from my purse and hold them up.

"I bet you want to drive."

"No, go ahead. I've been getting used to you chauffeuring me around." He runs his hand along the top of his car.

"There's not too many people who can handle this girl," he says. "You can use it for as long as you like."

Ridiculously pleased with his compliment, I slide into the driver's side, and he climbs in next to me, a new energy about him.

"Tabby and Jack are going to meet us at the rink. She's bringing my skates. Do you want to stop at your place and grab yours?"

I shake my head. "No, I'll just rent a pair."

Cole watches me carefully, and I back the car out of the tight spot. "What did you do with your skates?"

"Nothing, they're at Mom's, and I don't really feel like driving across town to get them."

He nods and sinks back into his seat, his fingers beating restlessly on his door, his antsy energy needing an escape. His phone pings, and he turns it over. "Luke's on his way home. He should be here by tomorrow night. I think he's going to stay at the house for a few days."

"That will be nice," I say. Unlike Cole, Luke never bought a house. When back home, he just stays with Mom and Dad. It isn't like they interfere in his life. They're never around anyway.

"Yeah," he says, but I hear something uneasy in his voice.

I swallow against the thickness in my throat, because that agitation can only mean one thing. Luke is moving in for a few days, which means it's time for me to move out. He's better now, and my lessons—sex and hockey—are over.

Do I want it to be? No. Do I have a choice? Maybe…

"Cole," I say.

"Yeah?"

"I know we agreed that we'd end things when you got better and back on the ice, but I was thinking…should we extend these lessons until after the playoffs?"

He scrubs his face, his brow furrowed. "Luke—" he begins but I cut him off.

"I'll move out while he's here. Give you two the time and space to catch up. We can reconvene after he leaves. Unless of course you don't think I'd benefit from seeing the season through until the end."

His smile is slow, sexy as hell, and there is a fire in his eyes as he looks me over, like he has a lot of dirty things going through his mind. "I see the benefit."

He jacks the tunes as I drive to the rink. I park, and after we make our way inside, I go to get a pair of rental skates. I finish signing them out, and I turn to find Cole on his phone again. He seems a bit agitated, more restless than usual.

What's going through is mind? I'm not sure, but he's definitely lost in thought. He has to be worried about getting back into the game, being ready for the playoffs after being out for so long.

I hold the skates in my hand and glance out at the ice, at the kids and adults laughing and playing. I can't for one second believe I'm going out there again, that Cole made this part of the deal. I run my finger along the blade, my heart beating a little faster in my chest.

"You okay?" Cole asks, and my head jerks up, surprised to find him standing over me.

"It's been awhile."

"I'll be with you."

I force a smile. "Do you really need me with you out there?"

He looks at me long and hard, and I shift under his scrutiny. It's like the man can see into my soul, knows every insecurity lurking there.

"Yes," he says quietly.

"What if I..."

"Fall?"

"Yeah."

"I'll catch you."

A lump lodges in my throat. We might have grown up hating each other, but in my heart, I know Cole would never let anything happen to me.

"Okay." I sit on the bench and kick off my shoes, and he turns to wave Tabby and Jack over as they enter.

Tabby runs up to her brother and they hug.

"I'm so happy you got the all clear," she says, then glances at me. "I'm sure it's all because Nina has been taking such good care of you."

I smile at Tabby. I can't believe Jack is asking her to marry him. Cole is getting a brother-in-law, and dammit if Tabby wouldn't make the best sister-in-law to me.

Oh, Jesus.

Jack and Tabby go rent their skates as Cole and I lace up. "All set?" he asks.

I nod and climb to my feet. He holds my hand as we step onto the ice and panic moves through me.

"You've got this, Nina," he says. He skates backward and wiggles his finger, the way one would with a beginner.

"I'm not a child," I say, and plant a hand on my hip.

"Oh, I know that," he says. "Not anymore." His gaze is suggestive as it rolls over me.

I push off and skate toward him and he spins to skate with me. We do a couple rounds and then pick up speed. The cool air moves over me, and my hair catches in the breeze as we race around the rink. Cole slows, and his smile is wide.

"Told you, you've got this."

"Just like riding a bike," I say to him, exhilarated. I'd forgotten how good it felt to skate, the freedom and enjoyment. "So do you. I don't think you needed me here at all."

"That's where you're wrong, Pretty BallerNina."

"Cole—"

"Hey, I always meant it as a compliment." He skates backward again, and I go after him. "You just took it the wrong way."

"I'm not so sure about that." I skate past him, and he comes after me. He slides his arms around my stomach and his mouth is near my ear when he says. "It *was* a compliment, and I *did* need you here with me."

"Why?"

"Because you're the one who needed to get back on the ice, Nina. Not me."

I freeze in his arms, and he holds me tighter. "Cole," I say, my voice a bit broken as I break from his hold and turn. "What are you talking about?"

Green eyes full of tenderness meet mine. "You haven't stepped foot in a rink since the accident. It kills me to know you've hung up your skates." He spreads his arms wide. "You always loved it out here, there was this freedom on your face and in your eyes when you skated."

"How—"

"I know you don't do it professionally anymore, but to give it up altogether, because you're afraid—"

"I'm not afraid," I say quickly, defensively, even though he's right. I just don't want anyone to see that in me, although Cole has seen more in me than anyone; seems to know more about me than even I ever knew.

"Nina," he says, and pulls me back in. "It's okay. You don't have to hide anything with me. What you went through was hard. I know you're strong and independent. We all do."

"What do you mean, 'we all do'?"

He opens his mouth, closes it again, and then finally says, "I know how devastated you were. I wanted you back on this ice for you, not for me."

An invisible band squeezes around my heart. Oh, God, I am falling so hard for this man. I fight back the tears pounding behind my eyes. "It...shattered me. My dreams. For a long time, I was...lost, alone."

He hugs me tight and drops a soft kiss onto my forehead. "I know."

"How?"

"I just... Because I..."

I sniff and lift my head, and my heart swells when I meet his concerned eyes. I am in so much trouble here. "Cole?"

"It killed Luke, too, that he couldn't be here for you."

I look down, and he puts his finger under my chin to lift it. A smile touches his mouth. "You have no idea, do you?"

"About what?"

"About how much your brother really cares about you."

I tug my chin away. "Cole..."

A sound catches in his throat. "Over the years, he'd given out dozens of black eyes, Nina. If a guy so much as looked at you, he was done for." Cole laughs at that, but I go still, partly because I'm touched at what I'm hearing, and partly because I'm angry.

"Why would he do that?"

"Because you're his little sister, and big brothers are protective of their little sisters. Just ask Tabby."

Just then, Tabby and Jack skate by, and Cole's eyes fill with love.

"He shouldn't have done that. I can take care of myself."

"I know. We all know. But Luke was better with his fists than his words." He shrugs. "We all show how we care in different ways, right?"

The rink swirls around me. "I thought...all these years..."

"What?"

"Guys didn't like me. I just sort of blended into the background."

He lets out a laugh. "Yeah, right. Believe me, guys noticed you. A *lot* of guys noticed you, but they were too damn chicken shit to stand up to Luke. That guy's crazy, you know."

I stand there dumbfounded. "I can't believe this."

"Believe it. You are the prettiest girl I've ever set eyes on, Nina. There wasn't a guy on our high school team that didn't want to date you. Luke frightened them off."

"I guess none of them thought I was worth the fight."

He tucks a strand of hair behind my ear. "They were idiots. You're worth the fight."

I lift my head, take in the intense green eyes gazing at me. Luke hadn't scared Cole off. He's here with me now, unafraid of a beatdown from his very best friend, telling me I'm worth the fight. My heart races faster, pounds against my chest. Is it possible that there can be more between us?

A burst of happiness races through me, but he goes serious again. "What will happen if you don't get this series written?"

"I don't know."

Troubled eyes look past my shoulder. What is it he's not telling me?

"Your books pay the bills, right?"

"Yeah."

"If you can't pay the bills, will you have to move home?"

My stomach cramps. "That's the last thing I want to do."

"Luke talked about finally getting his own place here in Seattle. Maybe you could move in with him."

"No. I love my brother, but I don't want to be underfoot. I want to do things on my own."

"It's okay to ask for help. I mean…if you wanted to, you could stay at my place as long as you want."

I stand there for a second, think about what he's saying. Tabby straight up and told me he didn't bring women into his home—ever—yet here he is, asking me to stay. Is he feeling the closeness between us, too? Do I dare hope?

"Are you serious?"

"As serious as a concussion."

I laugh, and he opens his mouth to say something else, but he closes it when Jess calls from the boards.

"I'd better get going."

He pulls me to him. "What time will you be home?"

Home.

There's that word again. Oh, how I want that with Cole.

"Around four, but I don't want *you* home until around five. Enjoy the day out with your sister, and soon to be brother-in-law."

"Why can't I come home before five?"

"Because I have a surprise for you."

"I thought you didn't like surprises."

"I don't." I poke him in the chest. "But you do."

"The only surprise I want is you naked and tied to my bed."

"I'm pretty sure we can make that happen."

"Fuck," he says, and adjusts his pants. "Now I'm going to spend the rest of the day with a fucking hard-on."

I laugh, loving this playful side of him. "See you later," I say.

"Yeah, you will. Every inch of me," he says as I skate off, my heart so full I'm sure it's going to burst.

14
COLE

Jack pulls his rental onto my street, and my heart picks up when I see my Mustang in the driveway. I have no idea what surprise Nina has waiting for, and it doesn't really matter. All I care about is getting my arms around her again. I want—no, need—her in a way I've never needed anyone, and that shit scares the living hell out of me.

Did I really ask her to move into my place?

She was shocked at my offer. Hell, so was I. And what was I really putting out there, anyway? Was I simply offering her a place for her to lay her head, or asking her to be mine? I don't know. Maybe knowing Jack is going to ask Tabby to marry him is fucking with me.

When it comes right down to it, Nina doesn't know the real me. She wouldn't like that guy. No one does. But that doesn't mean I don't worry or care about her. I fucking do.

Earlier today, I wanted to mention the trust fund that Luke set up for her, but she's so goddamn independent. I get that she doesn't want to touch it, wants to do things her way. But fuck, he set it up for her for a reason, and there's no need for her to have her bills piling high and deep. I wanted to tell her that, but stopped myself. She'd probably be hurt or embarrassed if I butted into her financial business. Still, I'm not going to sit back and let her lose her condo, or go back to the home she grew up in, because she clearly doesn't want that.

I climb from the backseat, and meet Tabby and Jack at the front of the car. We had a great day skating and hanging out at the park, getting caught up as we drank coffee. The more time I spend with Jack, the more I like him. But Tabby is keeping secrets from him, as much as I keep them from the world. Will that eventually affect their relationship? I don't know, but I sure as hell hope not.

I hurry to the front door, and when I open it, the delicious scent of garlic reaches my nose. My stomach grumbles as Tabby and Jack follow me in.

"What is that?" Tabby asks. "It smells delicious."

Nina comes from the kitchen, wearing an apron. Her hair is pulled back and there's a flush on her cheeks, but there is also a light in her eyes I've never seen before. I've never seen her look more beautiful or more at home.

Home. Jesus, that is exactly what I want with her.

"Hey. Right on time," she says as she glances at the clock.

"Was dinner the big surprise?"

"Lasagna, and only part of it." She crooks her finger. "Come see."

I follow her into the kitchen—and go perfectly still when I see a male figure sitting at the island.

My skin itches, like a thousand angry insects have taken up residency, as my blood thickens in my veins. My heart thumps, pressure building against the back of my eyes as my nerves fire.

"Hey, what—" Tabby begins, crashing into my back when I come to an abrupt stop. She moves around me, and when she sees our father, relaxed in his chair, that familiar smug look on his face, one that says I never would have made it to the NHL if he hadn't toughened me up, she lets out an audible gasp.

I turn toward Nina, everything from anger and pain, to confusion and grief moving at breakneck speed through my veins.

How could she do this to me? How could she invite the one man I despise into my home, my sanctuary?

"Nina..."

Her eyes are wide, excited. "I invited your dad to dinner! I put it together that he wasn't well and couldn't drive, and you couldn't drive, and I knew Tabby and Jack wanted to see him..." She folds her hands in front of her, and her words slow as her gaze goes from me to Tabby, back to me again. "I...ah... wanted to do something nice."

"Nice." I say though clenched teeth. "You think this is nice?"

"Cole?"

"Son," my dad says, and my gaze flies to his. I take in his grey pallor, his self-righteous composure, despite the renal failure.

"Don't fucking call me that."

A sound catches in Nina's throat, and she flinches.

I shake my head. Why the fuck would she invite my father to dinner without running it by me first?

"Come on now, Cole. Aren't you a little too old to be acting like this?" He makes a grunting sound, disgust for my behavior evident in the crook of his lips. "Still so much of your mother in you."

I pinch the bridge of my nose, my emotions in turmoil. I flinch when Tabby puts her hand on me.

"Cole," she says. "I need to get out of here."

"Tabby?" Jack says, as confused as Nina by this turn of

events. And why wouldn't they be? Tabby and I can put on a good show when we want to. But still, Nina had no right to go behind my back and do this.

"Cole, I thought—"

"Don't," I say, the harshness in my tone striking her like the sting of a skipping rope. I take a deep breath and try to calm down. But I'm such a fucking mess. Never in my life had I expected to see the man who beat the hell out of me on a daily basis sitting at my kitchen island, like it's where he belongs. I walked in here ill prepared for that.

I lift my gaze, direct it at Nina. "What were you thinking?"

Tabby tugs at me. "It's not her fault."

"Then whose fault is it?"

"She didn't know, Cole. You know that."

"Tabby," Jack says again, and she turns to him.

She grabs his hand. "We need to get out of here."

Without question, he nods.

"Tabby, don't," I say, and reach for her. I can't handle her walking out that door on me, too. What if, like Mom, she doesn't come back?

As if privy to my thoughts, she says, "We'll come back later."

"Weren't you even going to tell me you were home, girl?" Dad says, and I place my body between my father and sister, to block his view. Old habits die hard, I guess.

"Okay, go. We'll talk later." I take in the confusion on Jack's face. "Take care of her, okay?" He nods, and puts his arm around her shaking body and leads her outside.

My fingers curl into fists at my sides as I turn back around. Nina brought my father here, and now my sister is leaving because of it.

"You shouldn't have done this, Nina. You shouldn't have

fucking done this. You had no right, and totally overstepped boundaries."

"I thought—"

"We're fuck buddies, remember?" I say, and don't care if my father is listening.

She flinches at the reminder, and the hurt in her eyes tears at my heart. But I'm such a goddamn mess right now, my father's presence throwing me off my game, that I don't seem to have any control over my stupid fucking mouth.

"You need to leave," I say, fully aware that anything else I say is going to hurt her. Okay, maybe Tabby was right. Maybe she didn't know, but she never should have brought anyone into my home without my permission. She knows me well enough to know that, right?

Then again, how could she?

Don't let anyone in, don't get hurt. Isn't that the motto I've been living by?

"I just got here, boy."

I glance at my father. "You need to leave, too." I slowly turn my head back to Nina, and my voice is deceptively calm when I say, "But I wasn't talking to him."

Nina goes stiff and backs up until she hits the counter. "Cole. I'm sorry."

"Sorry?" I say. "Do you have any idea what you're sorry for?"

"I..." She glances at my asshole father. "We'd better go."

Dad stands, stretches his legs out like he has all the time in the world, and shoots me a glance. "You'd be nothing without me, boy. You should be thanking me."

I suck in a breath and hold it. I want to hit something, but I keep my shit together. I've been down this road with him too many times, and I am in no shape to rehash the same fight over and over. I need to reserve my strength for the rink.

"I need to get my stuff," Nina says, her voice as shaky as her body. She casts a quick glance at my father. "I'll meet you at the car."

Dad saunters down the hall. "Nice place you got here, boy," he says before leaving my house.

Nina pulls the lasagna and garlic bread from the oven. "This is ready. Just give it a few minutes to cool and settle before you eat it. I don't want you to burn yourself."

Jesus Christ, I just punched the air from her gut and she's worried about me burning myself. Could I be any more of an asshole?

When she turns to find me standing there, my body practically vibrating, she gasps. "Cole, I don't know what I did."

"You had no right to bring that man into my house. This is *my* house, Nina. My escape. I don't let just anyone in here."

"But...your father?"

"My father? Do you want to know what kind of father he was?" With anger urging me on, I tug off my shirt, let her look over my scars. "Where do you think these came from?"

"Hockey," she says hesitantly.

A choking noise garbles in my throat. "No, these are from the skipping rope he made me train with for hours a day. I was a fucking *kid*, Nina. He beat the shit out of me on a daily basis. Mom left, apparently I wasn't enough to keep her around, and I had no one to protect me. But I fucking protected Tabby from the abuse. I took it all so none of his anger was left for her."

"Cole..." she croaks out, tears in her eyes.

I need to stop, I need to walk away right now, but far too many years' worth of pent-up anger claws at me, drags me under until like a tsunami. As I fight to breathe, to find safety within myself, I say, "Sometimes he'd wake me up in the middle of the night and beat me. Just for the fucking hell of it."

"I...didn't know. I thought he was there for you. He even got you that helicopter when your mom left. I just—"

I laugh at that. A deep, horror-filled belly laugh that scares Nina, judging by the way she's hugging herself. "I had one fucking toy. My mom gave it to me before she left, and he smashed the fuck out of it with his fists, shattering all my dreams with every pound. All my focus had to be on hockey."

"Luke said he was at all your games. I thought he was supportive."

"Oh yeah, he was. He watched everything, and if I made a mistake, I paid for it later. I *hated* going home, Nina. Hated what was there for me."

"Is that why you spent so much time at our house?" I drag my hand through my hair, and she continues with, "And at the skate park."

My head jerks back. "How do you know about the skate park?"

"I used to watch you practice." Her small shoulders curl in as she hugs herself tighter. "You didn't know I was there. I always admired your dedication."

"Yeah, I was dedicated, but I spent hours away because I knew what waited for me when I got home."

She glances at the stack of bills on the table. "All this, and you still pay his bills."

I give a humorless laugh. "Yeah, I'm that fucked up, Nina." I shake my head. "You know who else is fucked up?"

"Me?" she asks hesitantly.

"Yeah, you. You come here to ask for help because you need to write a story. Fine, I get it, you need the money. I saw your bills."

Her eyes go wide, and her shrugged shoulders straighten in a defiant manner. "You did?"

"Yeah, when I went with you to your place. I saw them.

What's fucked up is you'd rather lose your home than use the trust fund Luke set up for you. Why is that, Nina?"

"What are you talking about? Mom and Dad set that up, a way to make up for the years they neglected us. But I didn't want their *money*, I wanted their presence in my life, which is why I refused to touch it!"

"No, Nina. Luke set that up for you."

"But I always thought—"

"You thought wrong."

"I...I had no idea," she says, and reaches for me. "I had no idea about your childhood either, Cole. If I had of I would have done—"

"You've done enough," I say and back up, away from her outstretched arm.

15

NINA

I pace inside my condo, my heart so heavy and empty, I have no idea what to do with myself. My throat hurts from fighting off an ugly cry as I open my curtains and glance out at Cole's car still in front of my place. I needed a fast getaway, so when he told me to take it, I didn't hesitate.

I never meant to hurt Cole or Tabby. When I went to his father's house and brought him over to Cole's for dinner, my intentions had been the exact opposite. His father never let on anything was wrong between them all, and in his head, I don't think he can understand why Cole and Tabby have nothing to do with him. But Cole was right. I did overstep boundaries. I thought we had more between us, but the reminder that we were simply fuck buddies was a good one.

When it comes right down to it, I guess I never knew Cole at all.

I stare at the phone in my hand, wanting to call Jess, but I can't. Those things Cole said to me were private, and even though he probably hates me for what I did, I'd never want to betray him by sharing his deepest, darkest secrets, ones that obviously still haunt him.

Tears prick my eyes and I press my palms to my face, but there's nothing I can do to dispel the image of him standing like a cornered animal, his body tense, in fight-or-flight mode. Water pours from my eyes. Damn. Damn. Damn.

My phone pings, and I nearly drop it as I fumble to check to see if it's Cole. Disappointment settles heavy in my chest as I read the text from Jess, wanting to know how dinner went.

I toss my phone onto my sofa and head to the kitchen. I grab a tub of ice cream from the freezer, a spoon from the drawer, and plunk back down on my sofa, my unpacked bag still sitting near my door. My phone continues to buzz, and I continue to ignore it as I flick the TV on to watch a rerun of *Friends*.

As Joey cracks a joke, my doorbell chimes. Great. I should have answered Jess. Now she's at my door, and I'm a hot mess. I don't want to explain this to her. I don't want to explain it to anyone. I just want to eat ice cream and curl into a ball.

I might be hurting right now, but my heart hurts more for Cole, for the years of abuse he endured and hid from the world—still does. I wasn't sure what his sister meant when she'd said, *if it wasn't for your f*amily. But I do now. Our house was his escape, the one place he felt safe, and I brought all his painful memories back tonight.

Christ, I could be the poster girl for fucked-up good intentions.

When the chiming continues—apparently, Jess isn't planning on leaving anytime soon—I jab my spoon into my ice cream and wipe my hand across my tear-stained cheek.

I unlock my door, pull it open, and I'm about to ask her for a rain check on a gab session—when I find a very solemn Cole standing there, looking so lost and alone, my already broken heart shatters a little more.

"I..." I try to talk, to find my words, but they stick in my ever-tightening throat.

"Hey," he says, looking like he'd just been through the rinse cycle then hung out to dry.

My lungs constrict, and I can barely breathe. I work to pull myself together and say, "Cole, I...I...didn't know. I'm sorry."

"I know. I'm sorry, too." He shrugs like he's making light of getting hurt, but there is so much pain in his eyes. "I'm an expert asshole, remember?"

I'm about to tell him he's the nicest, kindest guy I know, and that I'm so freaking sorry, when he holds a hand out.

"Come with me."

"Where?"

He gives me a small smile, but it's tight, like every muscle in his body. He's so damaged it's a wonder he can actually function in society. "It's a surprise."

"I don't—"

"Like surprises, I know."

I stand there for a second longer, take in the deep sadness on his face. It guts me, and all I want to do is pull him to me, hug him, tell him how sorry I am, that everything will be okay. But I don't think he wants that from me, and I'm not so sure he'll *ever* be okay. He exposed a side of himself he never wanted me, or anyone, to see, and that couldn't have been easy for him.

He glances over his shoulder and rakes a hand though his hair. "I understand if you don't want—"

"I do," I say quickly. He'd lashed out at me in anger, because he was hurt, and he's here trying to apologize. I get that. "Where are we going?"

His shoulders relax slightly. "Can you just trust me on this?"

I nod, and he reaches out and brushes his thumb over my

damp cheek. His mouth turns down, and he swallows. "Grab a sweater, and wear your sneakers."

I note that he's in jeans, sneakers and a hoodie, so I run to my room and dress the same. Night will soon be here, and despite the heat wave, our nights are still cool.

He guides me to his other vehicle, a Jeep, and we mainly sit in silence as he drives out of town. I glance around, but have no idea what he's up to or where he's taking me.

My eyes widen and my heart speeds up when he takes the exit to Auburn Municipal Airport.

"What's going on?" I ask, my gaze going from his smirking face to all the hangars as we pass.

"What part of 'surprise' don't you understand?"

"Are we going on a plane?"

"Not a plane."

"Then what are we doing at the airport?"

"You'll see."

He parks, grabs a backpack from the back, and captures my hand. When I hesitate, he gives a little tug to set me in motion, and I follow him. A few minutes later we're standing behind the counter of Helicopter Rentals and Charters.

"No way," I say, then worry trickles through me. "Wait, you're not going to make me jump out of a plane, are you?"

He laughs. "No."

"Ah, push me out?"

"Jesus, Nina. Of course not."

"Whew," I say. "I know you're mad at me—"

"Mad at myself."

I go quiet at that, and he turns back to the man at the counter. "I called earlier."

I stand back as they exchange information, and as Cole drops a credit card on the counter, I walk to the window to see the helicopter and pilot outside.

"All set," Cole says, coming up behind me.

His hands slide around my body, hook over my stomach, and he puts his mouth close to my ear. His breath is warm against my skin as we just stand there, no talking, just being together like this.

I close my hands over his, and we stand there a moment longer, holding on to one another like it might be the last time we do. An uneasy feeling moves through me, giving me the sense that this is it between us.

But I don't want this to be the end of us. I made a mistake, though had I known, had Cole opened up to me, told me the truth, it never would have happened. But he doesn't really open up. I've only caught glimpses of the real Cole when his guard was down, and he tries very hard to never let that happen, and never in public.

"It's getting late, we'd better hurry," he finally says, breaking the moment.

"Is there is someplace we have to be?" I ask, assuming we're just going on a tour.

"Yeah."

His hand closes around mine—big, warm and strong—and I glance up at him, take in the tightness of his jaw. I follow him out, meet the pilot, Greg, and climb into the seat behind him. Cole sits next to me and, after we buckle up, we're equipped with headphones and a mouthpiece so we can all speak to each other. Cole's hand captures mine again, and he gives a little squeeze.

"Nervous?"

"I've never been on a helicopter before."

"Me neither, actually."

I nod. Too bad, considering he'd always wanted to be a helicopter pilot, but I keep that to myself. I'm sure it was hard for him to dredge up old, painful memories. No need to remind him of it again.

The chopper takes to the air and Cole pulls a blanket,

bottle of wine and two glasses from his pack. He wraps us up, and pours us each a glass. I glance out the window as we sip, and a bubble of excitement wells up inside me when Mt. Rainier comes into view.

Cole leans into me. "It's not ideal, but I know you can't hike it anymore, so I thought this was the next best thing."

On the horizon, streaks of blue and purple bruise the sky as the sun begins to set, and my heart swells. I can't believe Cole set this up. Tears prick my eyes, and I try to turn my head so he doesn't see them.

"Hey," he whispers, and touches my chin. He turns me to face him and brushes the tears away. "I thought you'd like this."

"I love it."

His brow furrows as his gaze roams my face. "Then why the tears?"

"I can't believe you remember me telling you this."

"I remember everything." He puts his arm around me, and I settle against him as the helicopter hovers over the mountain, letting us soak in the sunset. "I wanted to land right there and have my way with you" Cole says teasingly. "But we can't. This bird has to be back before it's pitch black."

"When you drive me home, maybe you can have your way with me then," I say, so touched by this gesture, I'm a little raw inside.

His grin widens. "Yeah?"

I take a sip of my wine and pretend I'm mulling it over, but there is nothing in the world I want more than Cole in my bed tonight.

We spend the next fifteen minutes watching the sunset, and it takes me back to my childhood when I hiked the mountain with my brother and the guy I hated—but secretly crushed on. But that crush has grown into so much more, and deep in my gut, I fear that our time together has come to an end, even though we decided to continue this affair until the playoffs were over.

Cole holds me tighter as the helicopter takes us back to the airport, and we're both a little quiet as we make our way to his car.

"How is Tabby?" I ask as he drives me back to my place.

"She's okay. She came back to the house after you left. We had a long talk."

"Did Jack propose yet?"

"Not yet, I guess he's waiting for the right moment. You know, sort of the same way you do it in your books."

I grin. "I don't think Tabby tortures him the way I tortured my heroes, though. Thank God."

Cole laughs. "Do you like him? Do you think they'll be good together?"

"I do."

"You once said no man is that good. You know, like in your books."

"I know," I say, my heart heavy for all the things I want with Cole. "Maybe I was wrong about that."

"Yeah?"

He takes a turn and we exit the highway. I lean into him, missing his touch. Five minutes later, he pulls up in front of my place and without so much as a word, we both slide from the vehicle and meet on the walkway. I fish my key from my purse and he puts his hand on the small of my back as he leads me inside. The door clicks shut behind us and a shiver skips down my spine when he sets the lock.

He turns me, presses me against the door and his mouth finds mine. His kisses are warm, hard, like he's been dying to taste me all night, and a thrill races through me. I kiss him back with all the love inside me, and once again, tears prick my eyes.

"I need to be inside you," he says, and picks me up. "Where is your bedroom?"

"Second door on the right," I say, and wrap my arms around his shoulders as he moves down my hall.

Once inside my room, he gives a quick glance around and sets me on the end of the bed. He goes down on his knees and I widen my legs so he can crawl in between them. I rake my hands through his hair, and he presses kisses to my eyes, cheeks, and lips. He tastes like sweet wine as he slides his tongue into my mouth for a deeper exploration.

I tug at his shirt and he goes still for a second. "I want to see you," I say.

He hesitates, like he's unsure. Now that I know what the scars are from, does he think I'm going to look at him differently?

How can I not?

"Naked, now," I demand playfully, not wanting him to get caught up in the tension.

He goes back on his heels, grips his shirt and tugs it off. I touch his body, then cup his face and bring his mouth back to mine. He grips the hem of my sweater and I break the kiss and lift my arms so he can remove it.

He tosses it away, and my bra follows. "You are so gorgeous," he says as he gently, lightly strokes the underside of my breasts. His poignant touch goes right through me, curls around my heart and holds tight.

I bring his mouth to mine. "Mmm," I whisper as we kiss, and the sound seems to do something to him. He nudges me until I fall back onto the bed. His smile is slow as his gaze moves over my body.

He unbuttons his pants, but before he kicks them off, he pulls out a condom. "We probably shouldn't take any more chances," he says, a reminder that he doesn't want a family.

Striving to push down all the things I feel for him, I watch as he tosses the condom onto the bed beside me and kicks off his pants. I stare at his gorgeous, battered body as he reaches for the button on my jean. The hiss of my zippers fills the quiet of the room as he releases it, and I lift my hips to make the removal of my pants a little easier for him.

Once we're both naked, I slip under the sheets and position myself in the middle. He climbs over me, kisses a path down my body, then centers his mouth between my legs to prepare me for him. But honest to God, while this might have started as hate fucking, nothing and no one could have prepared me for Cole.

I move against his tongue then he sheathes himself, and slides into me. I hug him to me as he powers home, taking us both to the precipice, where we struggle to hang on.

I don't care what anyone says...what we're doing is love-making, and one way or another, Cole needs to understand that. He says he doesn't want a wife, or a family, but everything in the way he touches me, cares for me, tells an entirely different story.

Tomorrow, when we wake up, I'm going to lay it all on the line, tell him how I feel.

I might be setting myself up for heartache, but how can I just walk away from this, from him?

COLE

I am such an asshole. Such a complete and utter fucked-up douche bag that I'd kick my own ass if it were humanly possible.

I shift on the mattress, and brush Nina's hair from her face as she sleeps quietly beside me. I never should have told her those thing about me. Never meant to shoot off my big mouth, but in the heat of the moment, anger got the better of me and I let loose on her. She didn't deserve that from me, and I'll never forgive myself.

I take a moment to mull that over, go over the turn of events since I showed up at her door. Has she truly forgiven me for being a dick to her, or did she go with me tonight out of pity? I saw the sadness in her eyes, the deep-seated sympathy, and that's the last thing I want to see from her, or anyone. Which is why I fucking keep my painful past to myself, locked deep in the recesses of my brain where it belongs.

After Tabby returned home, we had a long talk, and I didn't need to hear it from her to know how much I'd hurt Nina. I never meant to, just like she never meant to hurt me.

She was only trying to do something nice. She had no idea what we went through as kids.

But now that she does, it's beyond clear that things have changed between us. She looks at me differently. Oh, she can try to hide it all she wants, but it's there, in the depth of her eyes.

People are attracted to The Playmaker, the showboat on the ice, the guy with a different bunny on his arm after every game. The guy I learned to hide wasn't enough to keep my own mother around, and when it comes right down to it, Nina deserves better. Hell, I've read her books, know her expectations. I'm not good enough for her. Not worthy of her love. She needs someone who is.

She makes a soft, sleepy sound, and I inch from beneath the covers. I fix the blankets around her, and take one last look at the girl I love...the girl I've spent my entire fucking life loving. Christ, I want her so much. I never should have started something with her that I couldn't finish. Not with Nina, my sweet ballerina.

She needs someone who isn't a hot fucking mess, someone who doesn't pretends to be an expert asshole so no one sees the real guy beneath. But she glimpsed that guy tonight, and I can't handle her walking away in the end, too.

Besides, she told me in the beginning she didn't believe in happily ever after, and I told her the same. This thing started because she needed something from me—I'm used to people wanting something from me—and I can't hang around and run the risk of her wanting more. Not that I'm certain she will. She agreed to a commitment for the duration of her lessons, and didn't ask for anything more.

Don't let anyone in, don't get hurt.

I always pretend to be someone else, and in the end, if she hangs around longer, and we got involved deeper, Nina won't like what she sees. I need to save her the pain of that betrayal by leaving first and ending this now. I'm sure she's gotten all she needed for her book—hockey and sex lessons—and even though my fucking heart is breaking, it gives me a measure of comfort to know I've been able to help her. She'll get on track with her book. Of that I'm sure.

I back away and grab my clothes from the floor. I steal one last look at the sleeping beauty sprawled out on her bed. The beatings from my father were nothing compared to the debilitating pain of walking away from Nina.

I love her. I fucking love her with everything in me, but she's seen and heard too much, and I can't, just *can't* have her hating that guy she got a glimpse of today. She's better off not knowing who I really am, and finding someone better.

NINA

I glance at my phone, my messages to Cole having gone unanswered for three days.

Three freaking days!

When we flew over Mt. Rainier, I had a horrible feeling it was the last for us, but then he came to my bed and made love to me, which led me to believe we were going to continue this affair until the end of playoffs. But then he snuck out under the cover of darkness. He left without so much as a note, a goodbye, or even a, 'it's been fun hate-fucking you but now we're done.'

"You okay?" Jess asks from my sofa. She's barely left my side for days, and while I love her for it, I need space to figure this out, figure out where I go from here. I've learned so much about Cole, so much about my brother Luke...and myself. It's hard to take it all in, make sense out of things.

"Yeah," I say, and look at my phone when it pings. My heart leaps.

Jess jumps from her seat. "Is it Cole?" she asks, a scowl on her face. It's pretty much taken everything in me to stop her from hunting him down and removing one of his testicles. But I had to remind her that I knew what I was getting into when I seduced him that night.

But did I really know? Did I know I'd fall head over heels in love with him? Maybe there was a small part of me that did, considering I've loved him since I was a young girl.

"It's Luke." She relaxes a bit, and I text him back. "He wants to see me," I say, and I'm thrilled that he's reaching out to me.

"Want me to drive you?"

"Yeah, okay," I say. Cole's car is still out front but I don't want to drive it. Then again, maybe I should drop it off at his place, let him know I got the message loud and clear. We. Are. Done.

I grab my purse from the counter and follow Jess out the door. Twenty minutes later, she drops me off at Mom and Dad's place and tells me to text her when I'm ready to go home.

Home.

God, I suddenly hate that word.

I head up the driveway to my childhood home, and my throat tightens a little for all the things I want, but never thought I could have. A home, a family...Cole.

Luke opens the door before I get there, and my mind travels back to Cole again, and the way he used to wait for me. I love that feeling. Love someone looking forward to seeing me. Being with me.

"Luke," I say when I see him. I take in his messed-up hair, longer now than when he went on the road. He's dressed in a pair of jean and a long-sleeve T-shirt. Always causal, always laid back, but I know him well enough to know he's deeper than that. Growing up without Mom and Dad present in our lives had been as hard on him as it had been on me.

"Get over here," he says, and wraps his arms around me. I breathe in his familiar smell of soap and fabric softener.

I hug him—hard, tight, never wanting to let go. "I'm so proud of you, Luke. I've been watching your games."

"You've got to be kidding me?"

"Nope."

"Little Neaner Neaner, who hates hockey, suddenly has an interest in it. What's up with that?"

"Maybe hockey isn't so stupid. And you know I hate when you call me that," I say against his shoulder as his warmth curls around me, cocoons me.

"Hey, come on. It's a term of endearment. Only special girls get special names."

Pretty BallerNina.

Emotions well up inside me and unable to stop them, tears fall, and when I give a big hiccupping sound, Luke stiffens.

I don't cry around my brother. I never have. But I'm so raw inside, so cut up and confused and hurt, there is nothing I can do to keep the tears from spilling. God, I hate myself right now. Hate that I let myself get in deep with Cole.

Luke gently pulls me into the house and shuts the door. It softly clicks in place behind me. The house is quiet this time of day, with Mom and Dad both at work. Luke holds my shoulders and inches back. His blue eyes take me in and there's real concern on his face.

"What's wrong?" he asks.

"I...I missed you," I say, and while that's true, I missed him like crazy, there is more going on inside of me.

"Hey, I'm here now." He glances past my shoulder, uncomfortable with my display of affection and not knowing how to handle it. "Want to grab a bite to eat?"

I note the way he's changing the subject, unable to deal

with my emotions. Then again, maybe that's just his way, and maybe that doesn't mean he doesn't care.

I nod, and he grabs a tissue to wipe my face. "I'll make something here," I say.

"No, we'll go out." He makes a fist and nudges my chin, and it brings a smile to my face. "The least I can do is treat my sister to a meal, right?"

I nod and I sniff back the tears and wipe my cheeks as we step outside. We climb into his car and a few minutes later, he pulls up in front of one of my favorite restaurants. Not that I eat here often. I can't afford it.

The hostess seats us, places our menus on the table and, as she tells us the specials, I look at my tough-as-nails brother, take in his scars, ones that were made on the ice, not from a skipping rope.

My stomach tightens, the noise inside the cafe fading to a dull roar as I think of the pain Cole endured. I wish I hadn't been so mean to him back in the day. Then again, he did tease me all the time. But still, I'm so glad our house was a sanctuary for him.

The hostess leaves and Luke stretches. "It's good to be home."

"Did you beat up guys who looked at me?" I ask, and his head rears back with the question.

"Ah, what?"

"Did you beat up guys who looked at me?" I pick up my napkin and wrap it around my fingers.

He glances around, like he's being punked or something. "Where is this coming from, Nina?"

"I just want to know." The waitress comes with our water, and we both glance over the menus quickly. We put in our order and when she leaves, I ask, "Did you?"

His nostrils flare and his fingers curl. "You're my little sister, of course I did."

People show love in different ways.

As Cole's words ping around inside my brain, a laugh wells up inside me. Inappropriate considering the circumstances? For sure.

"You know, all these years I never thought guys liked me, only to find out you were scaring them off."

His jaw clenches. "How *did* you find out?"

Damn, he's really pissed that I know he was protecting me from the shadows. Cole protected me, too. He was the one I called when Kenny drove me to the middle of nowhere and demanded I put out. He's the one who wanted to go after the bartender who abused me and made me feel like a whore.

I shake my head. "Doesn't matter." I reach across the table and put my hand over his. "How come you didn't tell me the trust fund was from you?"

Angry fire lights his eyes. "Jesus, Nina, who have you been talking to?"

"I always thought Mom and Dad set it up after my concussion. They never alluded to the fact that it was you. How come you never told me?"

"Doesn't matter," he says, throwing my words back at me. "But it's yours, and I want you to use it for anything you need."

Okay, I'll give him that. He has his own reasons, and he's not about to share. "You've always been watching out for me, haven't you?"

"Where is this all coming from?" he asks, instead of answering my question, and in that instant, I realize my brother and I have very different ways of showing love.

"I miss you so much, Luke. When you're away...I just really miss being close. You're my family. I think that's why I hate hockey so much." Cole was right about that. In fact, he seemed to know a lot about me, more than I ever realized.

I hear his throat work as he swallows. "Nina, I miss you

too. I hate being on the road all the time, but it's my job. I wish you could come. Wish we could hang out more."

"Really? You mean that?" My mind races with all the hockey stories I could tell if I actually went on the road and shadowed Luke. I mean, what's really keeping me here in Seattle? I love Jess, but we'd never lose touch, and I'd be home at the end of every season.

Then again, seeing Cole on a daily basis just might kill me.

"Of course I do."

My throat tightens. I had no idea how much Luke really cared about me. He's just unable to display affection the way I'd like to receive it—Mom and Dad couldn't either, but I knew deep down they cared.

"One more question. When we were kids, did you like me tagging along on your hikes, your concerts, and everything else?"

He goes quiet for a long time, his brow furrowed like he's fighting an internal battle. "Yeah, Nina. I did. I'm your brother, and growing up, we only had each other, right? Still do."

So Cole was right about everything.

"You have Cole, and he has you." I nod, and tears burn behind my eyes. "I want us to be closer, like he is with his sister."

He slowly eases back into his seat. "What does Cole have to do with all this?"

"He's been helping me. My editor asked me to write a hockey series, and since he was home with a concussion, he's been giving me lessons." I decided not to tell him about the sex lessons. There are some things a brother never needs to know.

The muscle along his jaw ripples. "He never mentioned it."

"Oh, I thought he texted you about it."

"No," he says, looking like he's about to hunt Cole down and kill him. Surely, he wouldn't punch his best friend?

You're worth the fight.

"Is there something you want to tell me, Nina?"

"No. Well, maybe just that I can take care of myself, you don't need to go around intimidating people. I'm a grown woman, in case you didn't know."

"Doesn't matter. Any guy who wants to date you has to go through me first."

"Luke..." I begin, but then Cole's words once again ping around inside my brain.

People show love in different ways.

I blink once, twice, as understanding dawns in small increments. I gasp and stiffen in my seat. Oh. My. God. Tabby asked me if I really knew Cole, and at the time, my answer was no. But is that true? When Cole wasn't in The Playmaker mode, I saw many sides to him—kindness, compassion, a man who paid his father's medical bills even after all the abuse. He didn't want me to see that side of him. Didn't want anyone to.

Why?

He's not who the world thinks he is.

My mind races, sorts things through as I go over everything, from our very first trip to the grocery store to the last night we'd made love. Did he leave because he doesn't think I'd like the guy kept hidden by The Playmaker?

"Oh, my God," I whisper under my breath, thinking about all the things Cole has done for me, the way he's been showing me he cares.

"What?" Luke asks.

I glance at my brother. Cole is far more damaged than I ever realized. I never asked for more, told him I didn't believe in happily ever after, and that no man was as good as the ones

I wrote in my books. But he needs to understand that I know who he really is deep inside, and it's that sweet, kind boy beneath the mask that I lost my heart to...many years ago.

"I need you to do something for me."

18

COLE

What the hell is Nina doing here?

It's the first game of the playoffs, and she's the last person I expected to be watching, especially after the way I walked out on her, refused to return her texts. Then again, maybe she's glad it's over, that she doesn't have to hang out with the likes of me any longer.

As the announcer speaks, and we all hit the ice, Luke flies past me on his skates. My thoughts shift to my best friend, who's been acting weird around me all day. He can't know about Nina and me, and maybe her being here is about Luke. Nina and her best friend are seated behind our bench, so he must have secured those spots for them. Still, he's not usually so quiet around me. He had lunch with Nina yesterday. Maybe they had an argument or something.

And maybe I need to stop thinking the whole damn world revolves around me.

Either way, it's my first day back in the game, and I need to keep my focus. From the corner of my eye, I catch sight of Burns. The fucker is eyeing me and grinning, like he's going to take me out again. Fuck that. Jonah, the team's enforcer, is going to be all over his ass tonight.

The ref blows his whistle and I skate to center ice for the face off. My stomach is coiled tight, my nerves on fire, read to play, ready to defeat. I position up, face my opponent and wait for the whistle.

A second later, the puck is poised on the end of my stick, and as I take it down center ice and pass if off to Sundin, I can't help but glance into the crowd. Is Nina taking notes? Watching Sundin, The Stick Handler, do his thing. I follow him down the ice but feel Burns on my heels. I skate around the net and he comes at me. I shift, and he hits the boards, and coming from behind me, Jonah hits him hard.

Burns goes down.

"Stay down, fucker," I say, and skate off and pat Jonah on the back. I love my fucking team. Unable to help myself, I glance at Nina again, take in her big eyes. She gives me two thumbs-up, and I laugh as my heart crashes against my chest. I wish I could talk to her, tease her about wanting to take Burns out in an alleyway.

What the fuck am I doing?

It's over between us, and I need to get my head in the game. Hockey is the most important thing in the world to me. It's my life.

With that thought in mind, I strive to keep my focus. The game continues, and the next thing I know, we're in the third period and the fucking clock is ticking down.

I glance at Luke, and he nods. We need this win. *I* need this win, to show my team I'm back in top shape and can get the job done.

Conscious of how little time we have left, I keep my eye on the Illinois Icemen's captain as he heads toward our zone. He makes a pass, I intercept, throw off his play, and then change direction. The hometown crowd goes wild, and all I can think of is Nina, and if she's enjoying the game. I pass to Luke, who passes to Sundin, and we all race down the ice until I'm in the house. I eye the goalie, read him, and take up position. Sundin passes to me, I pass back. The odd-man rush throws the goalie out of position and Sundin takes the shot and scores.

As the end-of-the-game horn sounds, I race to my team-mate and give him a big hug, and all our teammates join in. As I hug Luke, I steal a glance at Nina, to see her jumping up and down.

When I look back at Luke, he has murder in his eyes.

What the fuck?

I push away, skate around the rink, in total Playmaker mode. Girls are shouting, holding signs up that say they want to have my baby, but the truth is, I'm played out, so fucking tired of the act. I'm completely and utterly exhausted by it, but it's the only thing that gets me through the day, until I can go home to the sanctuary of my own place.

A string of bunnies are waiting for us as we file off the ice. Once girl pushes against me, and in an instinctive move that I've done a hundred times, I wrap my arm around her. She whispers in my ear, telling me all the ways she wants to play with The Playmaker, and I laugh.

I angle my head—and when I see Nina a few feet away, watching the exchange, a world of hurt on her face, my heart falls into my stomach. Over her shoulder, I see Jess, who looks like she wants to castrate me.

How many times am I going to gut her before she realizes she's better off without me?

The bunny gives me a wet kiss on the mouth and says, "Don't keep me waiting."

Inside the locker room, the guys are laughing and fucking

around. Luke is ignoring me, and I want to ask what's going on when he walks past me.

"Hey, meet you at Shades later," I shout to him. Shades is our usual drinking spot after a game.

"Yeah," he says, and keeps going, like he has a shit ton on his mind. What the fuck? We should be celebrating our win.

"Luke," I call after him, and he glances at me over his shoulder. "You okay?"

He stares at his bare feet, then frowns as he returns my gaze. "Yeah, see you at Shades."

I grab my gear from my locker and make my way to the showers behind him. They guys are all carrying on, and lots of pats on the back are given out.

"Hey, Cannon," says our goalie, Matthews. "You hooking up with Claire tonight?"

"Looks that way," I say, and from the corner of my eye, I catch the way Luke stiffens.

He can't fucking know about Nina and me, right? Surely to fuck Nina never would have told her brother about our arrangement. She has to know he'd kick my ass, and I'd have to stand there and take it, because I crossed a line. Luke is my best friend in the whole world, my savior. I'd be lost without him, and I never should have jeopardized our friendship.

But fuck, this is Nina we're talking about. I get that she's hands off, but I've fucking loved her since I was a kid.

Christ, this situation is so fucked up.

Luke leaves the shower first, and by the time I make it back to the locker room, he's long gone. I dress, stuff my gear into my bag, and make my way to the hall. Claire and a dozen or so other girls, all looking for hook ups, are there waiting. She rushes up to me, throws her body against mine.

Any other time, I would have enjoyed the warm body pressed to me, but tonight, well, I just want to go home...to Nina.

Fuck, man, maybe I should take Claire up on her offer, fuck her all night in some stupid effort to expel Nina from my brain. But forgetting her, the fun we had, isn't about to happen now, or anytime soon.

"Hey, rain check," I say to Claire, even though I have no intention of ever cashing it in. She pouts and is about to say something, when Harding comes out the door behind me. She looks past my shoulder and the next thing I know, she's in my teammate's arms.

I shake my head and walk out of the stadium. The cool night air falls over me, and I glance around looking for Luke, for Nina.

Cut it out, dude. She's better off without you.

I find my Jeep, toss my hockey bag into the back, and peel out of the parking lot. I think about going home, but the place feels empty. Tabby and Jack were long gone and Luke only stayed two nights. As I think about my sister, a smile touches my mouth. I'm thrilled that things worked out between her and Jack, and she came clean about our childhood. He accepted all sides of Tabby, and for that, I'm grateful.

Would Nina accept all sides of me?

Shit, I can't think about that. I'm a fucked-up mess, and she deserves better.

I round the corner and as I head toward home, my mind revisits the way Jack went down on one knee to propose. He did it in front of me, Tabby's only family—at least the only one who cares—and I'm grateful that I got to be a part of the moment. He put it all out there on the line, wore his heart on his sleeves, and that really showed both Tabby and me just how much he loves her.

I drive by my house and the lights are all off. Fuck, man, I don't want to go in there alone, everything reminding me of

Nina. Christ, I broke all the rules with her. I let her into my house, my head, and my heart.

I spin the Jeep around and head toward Shades. Not only do I need a drink, I need to figure out what's going on with Luke. I can't lose him from my life.

I squeeze my car between two trucks and power it down. Music filters into the street as I make my way inside. The place is packed, bodies swaying together on the dance floor, and I search the crowd for my best friend. I cut around the dance floor but get stopped by a few girls looking to play with The Playmaker. I politely decline, my only focus on finding my best friend.

I catch a glimpse of him at the bar, and plunk down on the stool next to him. "Great game."

"What are you doing here?"

"Told you I'd meet you for a drink."

He checks his watch. "You done with Claire already?"

I exhale and brush my hair back. "Yeah, well, that didn't work out."

He eyes me, and I nudge him with my shoulder. "What the fuck is going on with you, anyway?"

He goes stiff, his gaze going from curious to murderous, and my heart nearly seizes.

"I think I should be the one asking *you* that question."

"Nothing's going on with me."

"Why you fucking lying to me?"

Jesus fuck, he knows. He has to know.

As the room grows hot, I straighten on my stool. "I'm... you're my best friend, Luke. I'd never want to do anything to hurt you."

"Why did Nina ask me to give you this?" He reaches into his pocket. "I've been thinking about it all day. Trying to figure it out."

I tug at the collar on my T-shirt. "Give me what?"

He pulls something from his pocket, slams it on the counter—and my seized heart nearly jumps out of my goddamn chest.

"What's this all about?" Luke asks.

I pick up the little toy helicopter, my big fingers shaking as I fumble with the plastic model. I examine it, think back to the day dear old Dad destroyed my toy, my childhood...my dreams. I grab the small crushed envelope taped to it, open it up and see she also bought me flying lessons.

I suck in a fast breath and hold it. Never in a million years could Nina know what this means to me. My throat tightens to the point of pain, and I nearly fucking sob.

Jesus, fuck.

I shift on my seat, almost fall the fuck off as the world around me spins. But why would she do this? She has no money to pay her bills, and yet she went and did this for me? Ever since I hit it big in the NHL, women have wanted something from me, and while Nina came to me wanting lessons, the truth is, she gave me more than she ever took.

I turn the toy over in my hand, and then squeeze it in my fist as my pulse jackhammers. Tears pound against the back of my eyes, drum in my ears, and my throat feels like someone had just taken a cheese grater to it.

"Something you want to tell me, Cole?"

"I..." I try to speak, get the words out, but what am I supposed to say? This is my best friend, and I went behind his back and slept with his sister. What kind of a guy does that? Not a very good one. Which again, reminds me Nina deserves so much better than the likes of me

"What?" Luke asks, his voice hard, demanding.

"I love her, Luke," I say fast, breathless.

What the hell am I doing?

I have no idea, but now that the truth is out, I can't help but say it again. "I fucking love her."

He goes quiet, too quiet, and I sit there, uncomfortable as he glares at me.

"She came to me asking for hockey lessons, and, well..."

"Well what?" he asks through clenched teeth.

"Things happened. *We* happened."

He takes a long pull from his beer bottle and when it hits the counter with a thud, my heart jumps.

"So there are a million bunnies after your dick and you go and sleep with my sister."

"Yeah." I tense, every muscle in my body tight as I admit, "But she's the only girl I've ever loved, and I don't fucking want to be with anyone but her."

He glares at me for a long time, and then his hard features soften. "I know."

My head rears back. "You do?"

"Yeah. I do."

"How long have you known?"

A laugh catches in his throat. "Oh, since we were teens, and you used to take refuge at our house." He glances at me, sorrow ghosting his blue eyes before he tears his gaze away, like he can't bear to look at me. Like he's responsible for the years of abuse.

"I should have said something, Cole. I should have told my parents."

I give a hard shake of my head. "No. I didn't want that. I didn't want anyone to know. He wasn't hurting Tabby, and I couldn't risk being taken away, put in a foster home, away from you and Nina. I needed you guys. You were my family, my life. Still are."

"I know, but still—"

"No, Luke. You did what I wanted you to do. I'd take a beating every day from that asshole if it meant being with you and Nina." I put my hand on his shoulder. "Don't do this."

He nods, because he knows that's not what I need from him. "So, my sister..."

"Don't worry. I've backed off. I know I'm not the guy for her." I scoff. "Not that she knows who I really am, anyway."

He finishes the beer in his bottle and gestures the bartender for two more. "I think she knows more than you realize, and instead of running the other way, she bought you this. Kinda says a lot, don't you think?"

I open my palm, stare at the helicopter. I might be an expert asshole, but I'm smart enough to understand what it represents. Nina knows the real me, and she likes that guy.

My heart races with the love I feel for her. How could I have been such an asshole? Here I thought she wouldn't like the guy beneath the jersey—the guy who wasn't even good enough for his own mother.

"It wasn't your fault, Cole," Luke says quietly, like he's privy to my innermost thoughts.

My gaze jerks to his. "What?"

"Your mother. It wasn't your fault. You were an innocent child, and she left for her own reasons. I know you're the oldest by a few minutes, and that you feel responsible for everything that happened because of it, but this had nothing to do with you."

"I was Tabby's big brother. I should have been able to make Mom stay, at least for her."

"No, Cole. This isn't yours to own, and more likely than not, her leaving had everything to do with your father."

"How does a mother just walk away like that, like we meant nothing to her?"

"I don't know, but believe me, this is on her, not you. You're worth loving Cole." Luke puts his hand on my shoulder, and my heart pinches. "I fucking love you, bro."

"I love you, too," I say around a tight throat. I'd be lost

without him, without Nina. I'd never do anything to hurt either one of them.

You hurt Nina.

"Jesus, what have I done?" I look at my best friend. "I totally fucked up."

"Yeah, you did."

I pinch the bridge of my nose and realize what's going through his head. I fucked up when it came to our friendship.

Christ, not only did I make a mess of things with Nina and me. I fucked up my relationship with Luke. I can't lose him. I just can't. "I'm sorry, Luke. I tried not to touch her. I really did. I never wanted to do anything to jeopardize our friendship."

Luke stands, and I slide from my stood. We stand eye to eye, and he puts his hands around my head and brings my forehead to his. "You fucked up, Cole, but not with me."

"What?" Jesus, that's the last thing I expected Luke to say.

"You shouldn't have pushed Nina away. You fucking hurt her."

"I'm such an asshole."

"Yeah, you are." He gives a long, slow exhale. "I've been beating guys off her for years. Do you have any idea why?"

"Because you're her big brother, and that's what big brothers do."

"Yeah, that...and I was waiting for you to grow the fuck up and be the man she needs you to be."

"Luke, I'm...I'm not sure I'm good enough for her." But I want to be. She makes me a better man, which makes me want to realign my priorities and be everything she needs.

"I know you had it hard, Cole. Believe me, I fucking know everything, and I'm telling you this—you are the only guy I'd *ever* want my sister with. You're the only guy I'd ever *allow* her to be with." He pokes me in the chest, and his love for me, his belief in me, helps me let go of past hurts, old insecurities—everything that had me hiding behind The Playmaker. "Underneath this 'asshole' shit, you are the best man I know. That's the man she fell in love with. Guaran—fucking—teed."

I breathe deep, and let it out slowly, expelling the pain of my past. I look at my friend, ready to face the future as a new man. "You...you think she loves me?" Could I be so goddamn lucky?

"Jesus Christ, how fucking dense are you? Of course she loves you. *You*." He pokes me again. "Not the fucking Playmaker." He gestures to the helicopter. "That says it all."

After I left her bed, she still didn't leave me. She believed in me, showed up to my game, bought me a gift that speaks volumes, even after I was such a cruel bastard. The fact that she came to the game, sat in the stands and rooted me on, is proof that she cares about me, the real me. The guy I never let anyone see...but her and Luke.

"I can't believe this." I swallow hard. "You really think she loves me, the *real* me?"

"Yeah, I do...but still, you went behind my back and slept with my sister, and well, I'm going to have to punch you in the face for that."

I laugh, thinking he's joking, but then his fist connects with my eye.

"Fuck," I say, and stumble onto my stool. "What the hell, Luke?"

A hush comes over the crowd, and he hovers over me as people gather. "You going to go for it?"

I stand and square my shoulders. "Yeah, I'm fucking going for it."

"You're not going to back down like a pussy because I hit you?"

"Fuck no." I might not deserve her after the stunt I pulled at the rink. But my fuck, from here on out, I'm going to do everything in my power to be the man she needs me to be.

"So she's worth fighting for?"

"Yeah. I'd do anything for her. I need her so much, it hurts."

"Then what are you fucking doing standing here with me?"

19

NINA

I spent the last two days swallowing past the gripping tightness clogging my throat, unable to sleep, eat... breathe. Could I have been so wrong about Cole? That underneath it all, he's *not* a good man. I can't believe that. I just can't. My heart won't let me.

Then why did he go off with a bunny as I stood there watching?

"Come on, you have to eat," Jess says as she slides a slice of pizza onto a plate and hands it to me.

I finish the wine in my glass and gratefully accept the food, even though I haven't had an appetite since the night of the hockey game. I've been staying with Jess for the last two days, trying to get my head on straight before I go back to my place, to the bed Cole and I shared before he walked out of my life. But I have to go back soon and get my head back in the game. I have books to write. Bills to pay.

A laugh catches in my throat. Isn't that how this all started with Cole?

Started and ended.

My editor emailed me yesterday, looking for a synopsis, and I have to figure out a plot before I lose this gig. But when it comes right down to it, I'm not sure I can sit in front of my laptop and write without thinking of Cole, and everything we've been through.

As a bone-deep weariness settles into my body, my phone pings. I exchange a look with Jess, and she reaches for it first. "It's Luke." She hands me the phone and I read his message out loud.

"You coming to the game tonight?"

I stare at the phone. How can I not be there for my brother? Heck, we talked about me going on the road with him. Not only will it be great for our relationship, it would certainly help me come up with hockey stories.

"You going?" Jess asks.

Before I can answer her, Luke messages again. *You need to come. Tell me you'll be there. I'll get you and Jess seats behind the bench.*

"He wants me to come. He says I *need* to, and that he has seats for both of us."

"That's weird. He's never *needed* you to come before."

I shrug. "We're working on our relationship."

Jess nods. "Okay, I'll go with you, but so help me, if Cole so much as looks at you, I'm going down on that ice and slamming his face into the boards."

I shake my head. "You can't do that."

"Oh, I can. I just shouldn't."

"Jess—"

"No guy is going to hurt my best friend and get away with it."

I exhale heavily and rest my head against the sofa. "I knew what I was getting into when I started this, Jess. We were hate fucking, nothing more." Too bad my heart saw it differently. Thought we had something real.

Your heart is right.

She waves a dismissive hand. "I don't care. He turned on

his Playmaker charm. How could a girl not fall for that? This is all his fault."

"That's the thing though. Yes, he can be charming when he's in Playmaker mode, but he's also a cocky, arrogant bastard in that mode, too. Sure, the crowd loves it. But you know what, that's not the guy I fell for."

She gives me an odd look. "Why are you defending him?"

I can't tell her too much without giving away Cole's secrets. He's a private guy, and I respect that. Yes, he's a showboat on the ice, but that's an act to prevent the world from seeing who he really is. He doesn't think anyone would like that guy. But I do. I love that guy.

"Because you don't really know who he is."

"Then who is he?"

"He's so sweet," I say, and hug a pillow to my chest. "He's funny, caring, an all-around nice guy. He doesn't let many people in but when he does, he'd do anything for them."

Like give Kenny a black eye. Make me get back on the ice.

"Nina, I know you're in love with him, but he's clearly not in love with you, or he wouldn't have left with that girl. Maybe you're mistaken about who he really is."

"I'm not," I say adamantly. "When Cole is just being Cole, he's the most amazing man in the world. That's the guy I fell in love with."

I take in the concerned look on my friend's face, and I can't blame her for being worried. She was right by my side when Cole pulled that little stunt with the bunny—and then met my gaze to be sure I saw the entire exchange. Why the hell did he do that?

"I'm not wrong about him, Jess."

"Then maybe you need to figure out why he did what he did."

"Something is off about him leaving with that girl."

"Why? He's done it a million times before."

"I know you're right, but we were at a place..." No way could Cole touch me, kiss me the way he did—make love to me—if there wasn't more between us. So if there *is* more, if he's feeling everything I'm feeling, then why is he running? Especially after I bought him that gift—showed him I knew and liked the guy he really was. That he didn't need to pretend around me.

I go over everything in my head again. Was he afraid that guy was too damaged to be liked...loved? That he couldn't even keep his mother around, so why would anyone else stay? Cole hurt me on purpose, pushed me away for a reason, of that I'm sure.

"I think I know," I say past the knot in my throat.

"Want to enlighten me?"

My stomach coils tight, my heart aching for the young boy who lost his mother, had no one to protect him. "He's leaving me before I can leave him."

"And if you're wrong?"

"If I'm right..."

Her eyes lock on mine. "Is he worth fighting for?"

My heart jumps in my chest. "Absolutely."

"Then you need to talk to him, smack some sense into his head. Give him another concussion if you have to."

Hope and excitement welling up inside me, I laugh, and jump from the sofa. I'm in the same frayed jean shorts and tank top that I wore that first day Cole and I watched hockey together. "Should I change?"

"No, you look hot."

"But I thought you said I looked like hell in these."

"Yeah, I know." Her grin is evil when she adds, "There isn't a guy in a hundred-mile radius that isn't going to notice you, Nina."

"If only my brother would stop beating them up."

"What?"

"All these years I thought guys didn't like me, overlooked me, only to find out they were afraid of Luke and the beating he'd give them if they so much as looked at me the wrong way."

"Ohmigod, that brother of yours. Maybe I need to knock *him* into the boards." She has a strange look on her face as she jumps off the sofa, and I'm left with the impression that knocking my brother into the boards holds all kinds of sexual innuendo, but that can't be right, because those two have never really liked each other. She goes to the kitchen and grabs a bottle of champagne. "Come on, let's get ready for the game."

"Champagne?"

"Yeah, I always drink champagne after my team wins."

"I didn't know that."

She puts the bottle into her big purse. "That's because you never come with me."

"I was at the first playoff game."

"You were in no mood for champagne then," she says and usher me outside.

An hour later, Jess and I are settling into our seats and game two of seven is about to begin. The lights dim and the players all come onto the ice. I zero in on Cole, and note the way he's checking the stands.

Is he looking for me?

My heart gives a little leap at that thought and before I know it, the game is underway. Beside me, Jess is enthralled, and cursing up a storm at the opposing team. Good God, how are we friends? By the time the second period is over, and my team— Wait, when did I start thinking of the Settle Storms as my team? No idea, but my team is up by a score of one, thanks to a fantastic play made by Cole. And of course, like he once said, he couldn't have done it alone. He has a team behind him.

"I need to go to the bathroom," I say to Jess, as I wiggle uncomfortably in my chair.

"You can't." She grabs my hand tight and hold me in my seat.

"But I have to go."

"I don't want you to leave your seat."

I crinkle my nose. "Why not?"

"Just...third period is about to start."

"But I have to go."

"Wait until the end," she pleads, and I stare at her. Why is she acting so weird?

Cole comes back onto the ice, his helmet in his hand—that's when I get a really good look at him, see his black eye. "Ohmigod," I say to Jess. "What the hell?"

Behind us, I hear two girls talking about The Playmaker. "Did you hear?" one of the girls says to the other.

"Oh, I heard."

I turn around and glance at the blonde and brunette as they gossip. "What did you hear?" I ask.

They stare at me for a moment, like they're trying to figure out who I am, but then the brunette says, "That Cannon turned Claire down the other night, and then he got into a fight with Luke. That's how he got that black eye."

My heart nearly seizes.

He turned Claire down?

"Yeah, he led her on in front of us all, then he ditched her. What a jerk," she says.

"Typical Playmaker," the blonde says, like she's not bothered by his behavior at all, and would take her turn with him if given the opportunity.

I glance at Jess, who's watching me, wide-eyed. "I...uh... think your theory is right."

I suck in a breath to get my heart racing again. "I need to talk to him."

"I know, but it will have to wait. They're about to start."

Desperate to go to the bathroom, and needing a minute to myself, I stand. "I'll be right back."

Jess looks at me, her eyes pleading. "Hurry."

Good Lord, what's gotten in to her?

I head down the hall toward the bathrooms, and a measure of unease trickles through my veins. Luke gave Cole a black eye. I guess he must have figured out what was going on between the two of us. Not too hard, considering the gift I asked my brother to give his best friend, one that showed I knew who Cole was beneath the jersey, and there was only one way I could know that—by stripping him bare.

Would Cole back off like all the other guys?

As I mull that over, I hear the crowd go crazy behind me. I turn—and find Cole rushing toward me, stick still in hand.

I gasp as he closes the distance between us and hovers over me. "Cole, what the hell?" I say, my voice breathless, panicked. I look over his shoulders, see his teammates and the ref on the ice, thrown off by his departure. They're not the only ones.

"Don't leave," he says.

What is going on with him?

My heart thumps in my ears as I point to the little girls' room. "I was going to the bathroom."

His breath gusts out of him, his body less tense.

"What are you doing, Cole? You're going to get kicked out of the game, and hockey is the most important thing in the world to you."

He stands there a second longer, shifting from one foot to the other, like he's not sure what to say.

"Cole?"

"Just promise me you won't leave." His mouth dips into a frown. "I won't blame you if you do, I'm an expert asshole, and I don't deserve for you to stay."

"I'll stay." I point behind him, my nerves firing, worried sick about him blowing this game. "Now *go*. No matter what's going on between us, I'd never want to do anything to come between you and your game."

"I know, and that's why I lo—"

"Cannon, for fuck's sake, get back here!" Luke yells, and Cole's head jerks around.

"I have to go, but don't go anywhere." He dashes back to the ice.

I stand there, a complete mess as he disappears. What was he going to say to me?

Every nerve in my body leaping, I hurry to the bathroom and afterward make my way back to my seat. The game is underway as I slide in beside Jess, my mind racing a million miles an hour. Jess grabs my hand and I turn to her.

"What the hell did he say?"

The two girls are whispering about me over my shoulder but I ignore them. "He thought I was leaving. He told me not to go." She nods, and I don't miss the little smile on her face. "What?" I ask.

"Nothing," she says, and looks back at the ice. "Let's watch."

I can't focus on the game, not after my run in with Cole in the hall. I numbly watch the plays, the clock tick down, Cole make the winning shot. The crowd goes crazy but when he seeks me out, my heart crashes.

I love him so much.

The opposing team leaves the ice while the Shooters skate around, sticks in the air, celebrating their victory. When the cheers finally die down, Cole skates up to one of the local news stations filming the game, and takes the cordless mic as Luke skates toward me. Luke stays on the ice, a grin on his face, as Cole holds his hands up to quiet everyone.

"What the hell?" I whisper.

The place grows so quiet you could hear a pin drop.

He puts the mic to his mouth. "Nina," he says, then exhales slowly, like he's letting out a long-held breath, one that's held years of pain, secrets and demons. Jess grips my hand and holds me tight. "As you know, I'm an expert asshole, also known as The Playmaker."

The crowd goes crazy, and he grins at them, but then something happens. His expression changes, from that of The Playmaker to that of Cole just being Cole—the man I love. My heart crashes harder against my chest as his shield falls away.

"You're the girl I never thought I could have, thought I never deserved. The girl I've wanted since I was a teenager. I'm sorry I was such a dick. You deserve better than that from me."

"Oh my God," Jess says, and starts jumping up and down beside me. "He's doing it!"

"I love you, Nina. I've loved you for as long as I can remember," he says, his arms wide open, everything about him honest and vulnerable. "I always believed hockey was the most important thing in the world to me, but man, I was wrong."

"Cole," I whisper under my breath as my brother leans against the boards and grins up at me. OMG, he knew Cole was going to do this. He was in on it. Tears prick my eyes and I try to hold them back.

"If you give me a chance," he begins, his voice breaking, "I promise to be the man you need. I know you said no guy was as good as the ones you write about, but I want to try. Will you give me a chance, my Pretty BallerNina?"

"Cole," I say again, my heart beating too fast as Jess gives me a little nudge to set me in motion. I make a move toward the ice, and my brother skates over and helps me on. Another play comes onto the ice, and hands something to Cole before skates up to me. "You're better than any man I could ever write about, Cole," I say.

He touches my chin, his warm gaze moving over my face as I lift my eyes to him. "You don't hate me?"

I take a long, steadying breath. "You hurt me, Cole."

The sadness on his face guts me. "I know, and I'll never forgive myself for that."

"Luckily, I can...and you should know, I never stopped believing in you." I poke him in the chest. "*You*, Cole. Not The Playmaker."

He puts the mic back to his mouth. "Did you hear that, everyone? My girl believes in *me*." He jabs his thumb into his chest. The crowd goes crazy, and I glance around, having momentarily forgotten we were in the rink. His expression is no longer guarded as he looks at me. "You came to me asking for hockey lessons, and I had a few conditions."

My body warms as I recall those conditions. "I remember."

"One was that we were monogamous, no one else while we were together."

"I agreed to that."

"But I made a stupid rookie mistake."

My heart jumps. What's going on? He told me he loved me. What mistake did he make?

"One of those conditions should have been that I get to give you hockey lessons until we're one hundred years old."

My heart stalls. "What do you mean?"

He drops to one knee in front of me and his features soften.

"Cole..." I say, choking on his name.

He holds his hand out, revealing what his teammate had just handed to him. A ring box. "I want it all with you, Nina." He opens the box, and showcases the most beautiful ring I'd ever set eyes on. "A house, a family, kids...a home. I want to grow old together."

I stare at the man I'm in love with, the most private person I know. He doesn't let the world see the real him, yet here he is, exposing his true self to the world, for me.

As my heart swells, I instantly realize two things: happily ever after does exist for me, and the plot for my hot hockey romance is going to be a very personal one.

"Say yes," he says.

I drop to my knees, and he pulls me to him. "One condition," I say.

"Oh, now *you* have a condition, do you?" He flashes a grin toward the crowd and they go crazy once more.

I lean in to him, put my hand over the mic, and whisper, "You continue to help me spice up my books. This hockey series is going to be hot, and you *did* mention something about tying me up. I believe you're going to need to follow through with that."

"What did she say?" someone in the crowd yells.

Cole clears his throat. "Sorry, folks, Nina's brother is here and there are some things he should never hear." He points to his eyes. "One black eye from my best friend is enough. Crazy Callaghan has a mean right hook." The crowd laughs. "But Nina is worth the fight."

The crowd laughs harder as Luke skates over. Cole slides the ring onto my finger, then pulls me up with him. The two men hug, and Jess comes onto the ice with the bottle of champagne.

I stare at her. "Ohmigod, you knew."

She gives me a grin. "Yeah, Luke called me."

"But you wanted to castrate Cole."

Cole makes a face and puts his hand over his crotch.

"Yeah, I did. He hurt you, and if he didn't do right by you tonight, he'd be walking out of here with one nut." I laugh as

Jess hugs me. "I needed to make sure he was the one you were willing to fight for, Nina."

"He is."

"Good." Jess uncorks the champagne, and it sprays all over us.

"You're all wet," Cole says, and brushes his thumb over my face.

"Isn't that the story of our life?" I whisper, and he grins, knowing exactly what I mean.

"The story of our life is just beginning, Nina. And you know what? Real love stories never have endings."

I blink up at him. "Now *that* I'm going to have to use in a book."

His grin is wicked, full of sexual promises. "You know I'm always here to help you out with your stories."

I kiss him with all the love I have in me. "I love you, Cole."

"I love you too, Nina." He glances at my brother. "Get in here, Luke." Cole pulls him in for a hug, and my heart fills as I get sandwiched between my brother, and the man I'm going to marry...my little family...all together again.

EPILOGUE

One year later

I shift in my chair and tears stream down my eyes as I type 'The End.' I sniff, push back in my plush seat, and glance around Cole's library. Well, I guess technically it's my library, too, since I moved in here with him after we got engaged. We spent all of last summer here at the house, redecorating and making it our own. I even framed our daisy paintings and hung them side by side in the front foyer. Cole wasn't too thrilled at first, but I think he's grown to love them.

When hockey season hit, I went on the road with Cole and my brother. After watching an entire season, I have a million story ideas, and just finished the second book in my series, *The Body Checker*.

A movement at the door gains my attention and my heart flutters when I see my husband.

Husband.

I don't think I'll ever get used to that. Cole wanted to get married right away, and I agreed. We didn't have a big wedding. Well, it wasn't supposed to be a big one, with a ton of guests, since neither of us wanted that. But that didn't stop almost every member of his hockey team from showing up. I didn't mind, because the most important thing was having our family with us—and to Cole, he considers his team his family.

The ceremony was held on the lawn of our home, with a celebration out back at the pool. Tabby and Jack flew in, Jess was here, and even my parents came for it. It was perfect.

Cole lost his dad before the ceremony. It was a sad time for him and Tabby, despite everything they'd gone through. But they've both come a long way, healed so much.

"Hey, what's wrong?" Cole asks quietly as he crosses the room and sits on the edge of the desk.

"I just wrote the end."

He wipes my tears away. "Sounds like it's going to be a great one. I can't wait to read it."

I close my laptop and lift my mouth to his for a kiss just as the doorbell rings. Excited, I jump from my chair, and Cole captures my hand as we make our way to the door. It's the long weekend of May, and Cole and I are having our family over for a barbeque. Having all my family under one roof gives me so much joy, and I've been looking forward to it for weeks.

Cole pulls the door open and the warm afternoon sun shines in.

"Tabby!" I say and throw my arms around her, pulling her inside. I hug my sister-in-law, but not too tightly, seeing as she has a baby bump.

"Why didn't you use your key?" Cole asks.

She looks at him like he's dense. "Uh, you're married now. I'm not going to just barge in and catch you doing…things."

"Things?" Cole asks, laughing.

"Yeah, I read Nina's books, you know. There are some things a sister never *needs* to know."

We both chuckle, and Cole pulls me to him. He slides his arm around my back, and I bask in his heat as Tabby looks around the house. "Where's the food?" she asks.

"Some things never change," Cole says, and runs his knuckles over her head.

"It was a long flight and you promised food. Now feed me."

Cole and Jack hug as he carries in the bags, and I loop my arm through Tabby's. "Cole cooked for us."

"Oh, God." She rubs her belly. "Sorry, little one."

I wink at my husband. "You'd be surprised at how good he is in the kitchen."

"All thanks to you," he says.

"And my first hockey book was a best seller, all thanks to you," I respond, as he leans in and places a soft kiss on my mouth.

"Jesus, get a room already," Tabby says as the doorbell goes off again.

I open it to find Jess and Luke standing there, both looking a bit awkward, if not uncomfortable, as they shift restlessly on the stoop. I hug my friend and look out into the street to see only one car. I crinkle my nose as my gaze goes from Jess to Luke. "Did you two come together?"

"Uh, yeah," Jess says, and pushes past me, like she can't meet my gaze.

WTH?

Why would those two be traveling together? Back in the day, Jess and my brother got along about as well as two cats in a duffle bag. They were always sparring, much like Cole and I.

Wait a minute...!

AFTERWORD

Thank You!

Thank you so much for reading The Playmaker, book one in my Players on Ice series. I hope you enjoyed the story as much as I loved writing it. Up next is The Body Checker. Be sure to read on for an excerpt of Confessions of a Bad Boy Professor.

Interested in leaving a review? Please do! Reviews help readers connect with books that work for them. I appreciate all reviews, whether positive or negative.

Happy Reading,
Cathryn

VIOLET

What the hell am I doing?

Justin steps back from me, his hands going to the buttons on his shirt. I don't need for him to remove it to know he's got a freaking killer body. He's all lean muscle and broad shoulders, so different than the boys my age.

"I don't think this is all that fair," he says, his grin sexy, mischievous.

"No?" I take in his the hard planes of his face, the light dusting of a beard. How will that feel against my skin? He is by far the hottest guy I've ever seen, and he's no college boy. My eyes drop to his big hands. No, he's no college boy at all, fumbling around with my body and having no idea how to please me. A guy like Justin can please just from his words alone.

"You had a big head start." He cocks his head. "By rights, I think you should remove your clothes too."

"Really, you think?"

"Yeah, I do."

I toy with the button on my blouse. This game is

completely out of character for me. But Jesus, I'm twenty-one, practically a virgin. I've only been with one guy and I don't classify that horrible experience as having sex. No, what we did was sloppy and unsatisfying. In three days I go off to college. I'm older to be starting, I know, but I've had to work and save and scrimp before I could afford it. I certainly couldn't count on my folks to help. They're too busy fighting and drinking to care about their only daughter. But I saved, determined to make something of myself, and just once I want to let go, do something just for me before I buckle down to study for the next four years.

"*Yeah, I do*, isn't convincing me that I should strip," I say, and wonder who *this* Violet is. I guess it's sort of freeing to know I'll be leaving here on a bus tomorrow, and can say and do whatever I want with this guy that I'll never see again.

Justin's dark eyes dim, looking at me with a hunger I've never known before. "Okay, how about this. If you take your clothes off with me, I promise you a birthday you won't forget."

Confident. I like that in a man. "When you put it that way."

I pop the first button as he sheds his shirt to expose the hottest body I've ever set eyes on. My mouth waters, and my hands itch to touch him. This is all so new to me and I should feel embarrassed and awkward, but I don't. We have an instant connection, and there is something about him that has me feeling needy, desired. I want to go wild, do something crazy before I hop on a bus and turn my back on Virginia for good.

His big fingers go to the button on his jeans and he pops it. I suck in a breath as his zipper hisses in the quiet of the night. I steal a quick glance around. We're alone but it does occur to me that we could get caught. So what? I'm leaving this place and don't ever plan to return.

I slip from my shirt and his gaze latches onto my breasts as I reach behind my back, putting my hands over the clasp. I pause.

He sheds his pants and his cock presses hard against his shorts. It's quite the turn on that this older guy is so hot for me. Most guys don't pay me too much attention. Then again, I keep my head down, work two jobs, and don't give off any signals.

I free my breasts and his quick intake of air fuels the need inside me.

"You are so beautiful, Violet."

Does he say that to all the girls? I don't know, and I don't care. The way he's currently looking at me screams want, and tonight I just want to be wanted.

"Your turn," I say, and point at his shorts.

He tugs them down, and his big, magnificent cock springs free. Now it's my turn to suck in a quick breath. He takes his shaft into his hands and rubs. My body moistens, never having been so turned on in my entire life.

"Your turn," he says, his voice deeper than moments before. I wiggle my hips, and he groans as I shimmy out of my skirt. "Keep going."

As I admire the perfect male specimen before me, hotter and more cut than any boy I know, I tug the elastic on my panties and bend forward to remove them. Once we're both completely naked, he steps up to me, runs the back of his knuckles down my arm. I shiver.

"Cold."

"No. Hot."

He smiles. "I'll say." His hands slides around my body, and cups my ass. "Happy twenty-first birthday, beautiful." He pulls his hand back and gives me a firm slap.

I gasp at the spanking, and run into the water, which feels so cold against my heated skin.

"Twenty spankings to go, Violet, and you're not getting off that easy."

"I never said I wanted to get off easy," I say.

"Fuck, girl. You shouldn't say things like that to me." He follows me in, splashing behind me. I swim, but he catches up to me pretty quickly, his strong arms and legs cutting through the water easily.

"Why not?" I ask.

"Because giving it to you hard is all I've been able to think about, and I'm not sure you're ready for that from me."

My entire body quakes as I snake my arms around his neck, and push against his body. It's amazing how hot he feels despite the cold water. His hard cock slides between my legs and I clamp them together. He groans against my ear, his breath caressing the outer shell and eliciting a shiver from me.

"Hard," I whisper against his skin. "That's what I want for my birthday."

He cups the back of my head and his lips find mine again, only this time the kiss is firm, deeper, more demanding. Good. I'm not looking for a gentleman tonight. I kiss him back, tasting the scotch on his tongue, and lightly drag along his skin with my nails as I explore his muscles.

He hisses, and backs up until we're ankle in the water. He sits, and settles me on top of him. His lips curl around one of my nipples and I arch against his mouth, wanting, needing for him to devour me. I hold his head, rake my nails through his hair, and hand myself over, his to do with as he pleases.

He licks my nipples, sucks until hollows form in his cheeks, then bites down until pain mingles with pleasure.

"Yes," I whisper, my words fluttering away in the breeze.

Catching me by surprise, he flips me over, and falls over me. I sink into the sandy bottom as water laps at my body. But I can't think about that right now, not when Justin is settling himself between my legs, and dragging his hand down my body, running it over my breasts, my stomach, and stopping when he reaches the apex between my legs.

"It might be your birthday," he says, his voice hoarse, "But fuck, if I'm the guy getting the cake and eating it, too."

I spread my legs for him. "Eat away," I say, and he groans as he repositions himself and buries his face between my thighs. That first sweet touch of his tongue to my clit has my hips coming off the ground.

"Justin..." I whimper, never having felt anything so erotic against my body. The one guy I'd been with wanted his cock in my mouth, but didn't return the favor. Not that I'd want him fumbling around down there anyway.

But Justin, he's doing anything but fumbling. His expert tongue swirls over my clit, lashing at me with erotic precision, taking me higher and higher, until I feel like I'm free falling without a net.

He softens his tongue, and goes lower, until he's probing my opening. Desperate to see him, I go up on my elbows, and he inserts a finger.

"Jesus, Violet, are you really this innocent?" I nod, and he briefly closes his eyes like he's battling with himself.

"I want this, Justin. I want you."

"My cock is going to destroy you."

"I know."

"You want that? Tell me you fucking want that, or I'm stopping right now."

I love the gentleman side of him, but tonight I want the savage he's holding back, keeping under tight wraps. I knew from the second I met him he was a man who took without asking, a man who would own his lover's body completely. Perhaps that was what attracted him to me in the first place. I've spent my whole life governing my actions, working, studying, eager to get out of this place. I'm tired of making all the choices, and just want to let go, give the control to someone else. Justin is all power, dominant strength tethered in some cage, but I want to free him, unleash the part he's afraid to show me because he thinks I'm some delicate flower.

Tonight I don't want to be that delicate flower. I want to be taken, owned, used and abused by this man's hard cock until I can't breathe or think. All I want is to feel. I at least deserve that on my twenty-first birthday, right?

"I want that," I say, having a hard time finding the words as he keeps fingering me. "I want your cock in my tight pussy. I want you to hold me down and give it to me hard." As soon as the words spill from my mouth, a change comes over him. His nostrils flare, the savage in him tearing through the cage and catching me in its crosshairs, like a predator stalking its prey.

He pushes another thick finger inside me, stretching me in preparation for his big cock. I cry out, feeling so gloriously full. He dips his head again, and eats at me, a man starved for nourishment. I lift my hips, push against him and he places his hand over my stomach to hold me in place.

"Don't move," he commands in a voice that sends a thrill racing through me. I go still, obediently following his orders, and he says, "Good girl."

He drags his hot tongue over my clit, and crooks a finger inside me, brushing over the hot bundle of nerves I discovered years ago when I first began masturbating. But his skilled touch is so much better than mine. It takes me higher than I've ever been before.

"I want your cum," he murmurs. "I want every fucking drop of it in my mouth. I want it to pour out of you, and land on my tongue. Don't even think about holding back."

I quake under his dirty words, and he forcefully inserts

another finger, widening me, pushing me beyond my limits, but I love every second of it.

"Please..." I beg, my body burning up, heating the water around us. I'm so wet his fingers are soaked, sliding in and out easily.

"When I'm done eating you, I want to put my cock in the sweet mouth of yours. Want to see how much of me you can take."

Yes!

"You're going to let me destroy that pretty mouth too, Violet," he says, a statement not a question. Fire licks through my veins as I visualize him shoving his cock down my throat. Choking me, just a little. God, I want that. It's crazy just how much I do. I have no idea what's come over me, or how this man was able to strip away the layers and turn me inside out so fast, but I don't care. I just want...

My body heats up, blood pooling between my legs, and when he sucks on my clit, I let go, the entire world closing in on me as an orgasm wracks my body. I quake, violently, my hot flow of release dripping into his waiting mouth.

"Fuck, you are so sweet." He laps at me, and dips to catch the dribbles on my thighs. I have never been so wet before, never come so hard. I throb, clenching around his thick fingers, an instant addiction, and I want more.

I'm still shaking, my body lost in the aftershock, as he sits me up. He strokes his cock, and I reach for it, taking his long hard length between my small hands. So big. He's definitely going to destroy me, but I want to feel.

He climbs to his feet, and grips my hair. "Open your mouth," he growls. I open. "Wider."

I relax my jaw and expand my lips, but he's still going to stretch me. He feeds me his crown, and I lick the pre-cum dripping from his slit. I moan in appreciation and at the tangy, manly taste of him, and he tightens his hold on my hair, like he's ready to reach his breaking point. It's crazy to think a quiet, bookish girl like me can make this hot alpha male so stiff.

My lips burn as he enters, a hot melee of sensations rocketing through me. I take him deeper, and work to relax my throat, ever determined to swallow all of him, even though it's impossible.

He rocks his hips, and fucks my mouth. I'd smile at his hot, heated curses if I didn't have his cock in my mouth.

I change angles to open my throat, and plunge forward until he's halfway down my throat. "Fuck, Violet," he curses. "You're killing me."

He eases back, and I cup his balls and suck on his crown, pushing my tongue into his slit. He swells, and his veins fill with blood. "Stop," he orders, and pulls from my mouth. I look up and find him shaking, and to know I've done this to him, is the hottest thing I've ever experienced.

He races his hands through his hair, tugging like he's in total agony. Maybe he is. I know I am. "I need to fuck you."

I widen my legs. "I'm yours to fuck."

He curses again, and glances at the shore, where our clothes are. "Don't. Fucking. Move."

He hurries to his bag, grabs a condom and sheathes himself. When he comes back and finds me stroking my clit, he drops to his knees and watches. He presses his palm to his temple, and takes quick, short breaths. "Your innocence is killing me."

"Should I not be doing this?" I ask. I never touched myself in front of the one guy I had sex with, and really I had no idea it would this kind of effect on Justin.

He shakes his head. "I'm going to fuck you until you can't walk," he says.

I reach lower and widen my lips, opening my pussy up to him.

"Sweet fuck," he grumbles as he falls over me. His mouth finds mine for a hard kiss as his cock breaches my small opening. I wrap my leg around him, and brace myself for the pain and pleasure he's about to give me.

"Take a deep breath," he says. I do as he asks and once I fill my lungs, he powers his hips forward, ruining me for another other man as he drives deep into my tight hole.

"Oh, my God," I cry out and scratch at his back as he seats himself high.

He pauses, giving me a minute to catch my breath. "You still with me?" he asks, inching back until our eyes meet. He smooths my hair from my face, his animal temporarily leashed as he checks in with me.

My heart wobbles. "Yes," I say and move my hips.

He slides out, and drives in again, creating friction and need inside me. "You feel so good. My cock is throbbing." He pulls out, and I tighten my legs over his ass, and draw him in to me. He groans and sinks back in. When he pulls almost all the way out again I go up on my elbows.

"You want to see? You want to see the way you take my big cock?" he asks.

"Yes." He shifts his body slightly, and I grow hotter, wetter as I watch his beautiful, engorged cock sink in and pull out of my sex. That, by far, is the hottest thing I've ever seen.

"You have the tightest, hottest, prettiest pussy I've ever seen." I open my mouth to respond but my words dissolve when he changes the speed, driving into me with a fierceness that steals the air from my lungs. Moisture breaks out on his hard body, and I struggle to take in air as he reaches a fevered, punishable pace. His groin crashes against my clit with each thrust, and once again I'm reaching the precipice, standing there arms spread, not a care in the world as I topple over. A rumble sounds in Justin's throat, and it vibrates through me until I'm clenching around his gorgeous cock.

"Jesus," he bites out. "Your cum is so hot, I'm not going to be able to last."

"Don't try. Just come for me," I say, wishing we didn't have to use a condom. I want his cum, every last drop of it inside me, but that wouldn't be wise. Maybe next time. Wait, there isn't going to be a next time. That thought flies out of my brain when he throws his head back and shoots into the condom.

My heart crashes against my chest as he falls over me, pinning me with his heavy body. I ease my legs our from around him, and lay there, sated, exhausted, never, ever having felt so gloriously contented in my entire life.

"Violet," He murmurs against my throat. "What the hell?" He lifts his head, and I touch his face. "That was un-fucking-believable."

I smile. "Yeah, it was."

"I...never...Jesus...I... just..."

I laugh, never having reduces a man to one-syllable words before. I lift my head, and press my lips to his. He cups my head and kisses me back. When he breaks, it we're both left shaken. He rolls, and I gasp a little as he slips out of me. Cum drips down my thighs, tickling my flesh. I should get up and wash off, but my legs aren't working.

He discards his condom, then looks at my quivering body, his eyes full of tenderness. "Let me warm you up." He helps me up, spreads out our clothes and lays me over top of them. With unhurried movements, he falls in beside me, his eyes and hands roaming my body, touching like he wants more. I absorb the warmth in his touch, and while one part of me can't believe I just had sex with this stranger, there is another part of me that can. I wanted this. I wanted him. One night. Tomorrow life goes back to normal.

I stare at the stars overhead, the sliver of the moon, and sleep pulls at me.

"I didn't forget about those twenty spankings," he murmurs, his voice drowsy.

I chuckle, and snuggle against his chest, his strong heartbeat lulling me to sleep. It's funny how close I feel to this stranger, how comfortable I am with him. He puts his arm over me, dragging me closer. I stay like that a moment longer, even though it's getting late and I need to get going. In no time at all, Justin falls asleep, and I take one last look at his beautiful body. Should I wake him, leave a note? No, better to just leave things the way they are. He lives here and I'll be on a bus in a few hours, ready to begin a new life. I gather my clothes and climb into them. Once dressed, I carefully cover him with his clothes and cast him one last glance.

"Happy birthday to me," I whisper.

ABOUT CATHRYN

New York Times and *USA today* Bestselling author, Cathryn is a wife, mom, sister, daughter, and friend. She loves dogs, sunny weather, anything chocolate (she never says no to a brownie) pizza and red wine. She has two teenagers who keep her busy with their never ending activities, and a husband who is convinced he can turn her into a mixed martial arts fan. Cathryn can never find balance in her life, is always trying to find time to go to the gym, can never keep up with emails, Facebook or Twitter and tries to write page-turning books that her readers will love.

Connect with Cathryn:
Newsletter
https://app.mailerlite.com/webforms/landing/c1f8n1
Twitter: https://twitter.com/writercatfox
Facebook:
https://www.facebook.com/AuthorCathrynFox?ref=hl
Blog: http://cathrynfox.com/blog/

Goodreads:
https://www.goodreads.com/author/show/91799.Cathryn_Fox
Pinterest http://www.pinterest.com/catkalen/

ALSO BY CATHRYN FOX

Hands On

Hands On

Body Contact

Full Exposure

Dossier

Private Reserve

House Rules

Boys of Beachville

Good at Being Bad

Igniting the Bad Boy

Bad Girl Therapy

Stone Cliff Series:

Crashing Down

Wasted Summer

Love Lessons

Wrapped Up

Eternal Pleasure Series

Instinctive

Impulsive

Indulgent

Sun Stroked Series

Seaside Seduction

Deep Desire

Private Pleasure

Captured and Claimed Series:

Yours to Take

Yours to Teach

Yours to Keep

Firefighter Heat Series

Fever

Siren

Flash Fire

Playing For Keeps Series

Slow Ride

Wild Ride

Sweet Ride

Breaking the Rules:

Hold Me Down Hard

Pin Me Up Proper

Tie Me Down Tight

Take Me Down Tender

Stand Alone Title:

Hands on with the CEO

Torn Between Two Brothers

Holiday Spirit

Unleashed

Knocking on Demon's Door

Web of Desire

Made in the USA
Middletown, DE
16 March 2018